With beautiful lines such as "heart[...]
scenes, exciting fight images and c[...]
much as Stephen Harper does, Kyn[...]
first edition of a trilogy, is a must [...]

— Jorge Vallejos, Redwire Magazine (Aug. 2006)

There is action and adventure aplenty in this epic tale of conflict between
Humans and other-worldly Kyn, but there is something deeper as well. Like
the magic that imbues his imagined world of spirit-trees and talking beasts,
a true sense of wonder and enchantment wells up through Daniel Heath
Justice's words. This is a realm that fantasy fans can immerse themselves in,
and return to again and again and again; a realm that feels at once fresh
and new, yet old as the oldest myth.

— Alison Baird, author of The Hidden World

Daniel Heath Justice's trilogy The Way of Thorn and Thunder—offers the
best in fantasy fiction.

— Daisy Hernandez for Colorlines,

Come on a journey of ancient worlds, mysterious creatures, warriors and
primeval tales told through remarkable images and fantasy-driven dialogue.
Think of it as Lord of the Rings set in the culture and wisdom of Aboriginal
society in North America....Published by Kegedonce Press, this fantasy epic
could have been written by J.R.R. Tolkien—if he was Indian.

— Spirit Magazine, Autumn 2005

I just finished teaching Kynship in a 21st-Century Native literatures course.
The text is a powerful allegory that reads and teaches well. I can't wait to
read book two!

— Literature Instructor (Manhattan, KS)

DREYD

The Way of Thorn & Thunder

BOOK 3

Book Three

Daniel Heath Justice

Kegedonce Press
Cape Croker Reserve
R.R.5 Wiarton, Ontario
Canada N0H 2T0

Dreyd

Copyright © Daniel Heath Justice, 2007. All rights reserved.
Cover & Inside Design: Heidy Lawrance   WeMakeBooks.ca
Cover Art & Inside Illustrations: Steve Sanderson
Original maps & sketches: Daniel Heath Justice
Author Photo: Kent Dunn, 2007

Editor: Kateri Akiwenzie-Damm

Library and Archives Canada Cataloguing in Publication

Justice, Daniel Heath, 1975-

Dreyd / Daniel Heath Justice.
(The way of thorn and thunder ; bk. 3)
Editor: Kateri Akiwenzie-Damm.
ISBN 978-0-9731396-5-5

    I. Akiwenzie-Damm, Kateri, 1965- II. Title. III. Series:
Justice, Daniel Heath, 1975- Way of thorn and thunder ; bk. 3.
PS8619.U84D74 2007   C813'.6   C2007-904537-5

THE CANADA COUNCIL | LE CONSEIL DES ARTS
FOR THE ARTS | DU CANADA
SINCE 1957 | DEPUIS 1957

ONTARIO ARTS COUNCIL
CONSEIL DES ARTS DE L'ONTARIO

Kegedonce Press gratefully acknowledges the support of the Canada Council for the
Arts and the generous support of the Ontario Arts Council.

Kegedonce Press
Cape Croker Reserve,
R.R. #5 Wiarton, Ontario, Canada N0H 2T0
Website: www.kegedonce.com

Kegedonce Press is a member of the Literary Press Group

Distributed by LitDistco
Tel.: 1.800.591.6250 Fax: 1.800.591.6251

Member of Cancopy

Printed in Canada on Enviro 100 Edition Natural (55lb.)

Acknowledgments

There are so many people to thank as this particular journey winds down, but there are more tales to come and more opportunities to share my gratitude for the many people who continue to inspire me through life and story:

Kateri Akiwenzie-Damm and Renee Abram of Kegedonce Press have been unwavering in their support for these last three years. Whatever beauty exists in these books is due to their continuing vision. Richard Van Camp continues to be a mentor, a friend, and a thoughtful critic. Jorge Vallejos is a first-rate reviewer and a young writer who's going to rock the world! The folks at First Nations House, the Aboriginal Studies Program, and the English Department at the University of Toronto are not just my friends—they're my family, too. The staff members at the Toronto Women's Bookstore have made each book launch a fun and memorable experience, and I'm deeply honoured that they've been so supportive. Thanks to Craig Womack, whose thoughts about the Creek tie-snake inspired the Anomalous, Geary Hobson, for reminding me of what it means to keep a fire, and Jeremy Patrick, for letting me borrow Jhaeman. Appreciation, too, goes to S.F. Said, Lydia Allain, Kelly McFadden, and Steve Sanderson for their readerly enthusiasm, and to Drew Hayden Taylor, Lynda Williams, and Alison Baird for their kind words on the first two books.

My new family, the fine and fabulous Dunn clan: Murielle, Keith, Carol, Troy, and Eric. New friends: Tracy and Craig, Patricia, Terry and Justin, Nikki, Lisa, and Heather. Thanks to all of you for sharing with me the boundless love you have for Kent—it's a blessing beyond words.

My Texas family: Domino, James, Ewan, and Mrs. Perez. My Michigan family: Malea, Michael, Kim, Qwo-Li, and Angela. My Nebraska kinfolk: Barb, Grant, Missy and the kids, and Fran. The Toronto bunch: Sara, Bob, and Michael. And blood kin and good friends scattered here and there: Dan, Nancy, Jeff, Michael, and Sean; Patricia, George Paul, Kate, and Mary; Lori and the Hughes clan; Tom and Gwen; Joanna Findlay; Steve Radney MacFarland and Sky Youngblood; Jeff Simpson; Ken and Molly, Rob and Nicki, Shawn and Tracy, and Janie; Ginny Carney, Lisa Tatonetti, Lisa Brooks, Christopher Teuton, Robert Warrior, and Jace Weaver

To Michelle St. John, for being a sister in spirit, an enthusiastic reader, and an ever-generous friend, and for never being too busy for a leisurely chat over breakfast or scones and high tea! You are one of my blessings.

Sophie Mayer: you're a true wonder woman whose talent continually humbles me, as does the endless generosity of your friendship. The world of these novels would be the poorer without your keen insight. Thanks, too, for letting Pixie have a cameo!

To Kathy and Jim Justice, Mom and Dad, for your boundless faith, your joyful pride, and your ever-giving love. You taught me how to dream, and I've seen those dreams come true ever since.

And to Kent Dunn, for helping me laugh harder than I've ever laughed, for showing me more love than I'd dared to hope for, and for teaching me kindness beyond expectation.

A final note of thanks goes out to all the warrior-women, especially those in my life who show, every day and in ways small and large, the full measure of what it is to be strong. You inspire me to be a better man, and a better human being.

So to all the fierce and fabulous she-warriors in my life and elsewhere—my mother, my sisters, my aunties, my cousins, my mentors, my colleagues, and my friends—thank you.

DEDICATION

To Kent—
for laughter, love,
and our forevergreen life.

CYCLE FIVE

THE REVENANT OAK

The dead bring no comfort when they return, no matter how much you long to see them again in life. The journey to the Spirit World changes them. They still perceive love and pain, fear and joy, but those emotions are like smoke, easy to see but impossible to grasp. The dead forget many things—how else could they endure their half-way existence? But sometimes they remember us, and those are the times when we're in the most danger. If they make the journey back from the Spirit World, they bring poison with them; no matter how much love they had for us in life, that poison eats away at our own love of living, moving us from this world to the next before our time, turning us against ourselves. Life is meant to flourish; death is meant to end all things... for a short while, at least.

When I was just entering my adulthood, in the cold month of deepwood slumber when the snows are high in the forest hollows and the dark nights so often ache with loneliness, my favourite uncle died of the wasting sickness. I prayed fervently at his rock-strewn grave that he'd return, for he was one of few in my family who showed me unhesitant love and regard. Later the following summer, when a friend and sometime lover, Kajia, was killed in a hunting accident, I made the prayer again at the base of her scaffold. One night, some months later, while my spirit wandered in the Dreaming World, they both returned, and they warned me. These prayers are powerful, *they said,* and dangerous. It's a long, difficult journey through the ghostlands to the Waking World, and if I called them across in my prayers, it would change them, and I wouldn't like what they'd become.*

In the given way of things, the dead belong for a short while to the Spirit World, but in time they come back to the Middle Place in the fussy, forgetful flesh of wide-eyed younglings, here to learn again of the terrible beauty of this world. But when our grief drags them back across the ghostlands, the torment of the journey makes them forget what it was to belong to a people. They forget about the balance, and the necessary divide between life and death. All that these tortured souls remember is the need that called them forth, and they seek it out, thoughtlessly destroying the living as they try to ease a thirst that can never be quenched.

So these loved ones came to me in the Dreaming World to tell me to let them go, to unbind them from my love and loss, to love them enough to let them continue on their given path. And I did, reluctantly. Life and love must always continue. It is the way of the Middle Place. Pain is here, true, but so is passion, and we're not meant to stand between worlds in mourning. We're meant to remember; we're most dangerous when we forget ourselves and our histories.

But for the dead it's much different. The dead are dangerous when they remember.

CHAPTER 1

UNFORGOTTEN

"Do you remember me?" the Seeker asked, idly scratching his ragged beard, his rough voice strangely soft in the heavy silence of the pines. He faced the buxom Wielder and her two friends—a dishevelled she-Tetawa with fear-filled eyes and a bloody cheek, and a flush-faced young Man with a Binder's snaring-tome shackled to his wrist—but it was the Strangeling sorceress that drew his fixed attention.

"I remember you, Vergis Thane," Denarra replied. She stood straight and proud, her fingers extended, arms tensed and ready.

She didn't wait long.

When Vergis Thane's thoughts wandered through memory, three images rose up to displace all others.

The first was his younger brother Darveth, a light-haired young Man of exceptional courage who'd long looked to Vergis for guidance, his heart full of awe and adoration for his elder sibling. Darveth had been an awkward youth in body, but no one could doubt the courageous determination in his eyes when he'd reached maturity, or the stubborn jut of his jaw. He had the promising future of a Man of strength and honour.

The second image was of a low wooded valley at the base of a flat-topped butte, the grassy slopes dotted throughout with fat cattle. That herd, branded with the Thane family crest of two fighting goshawks in silhouette, was the brothers' living inheritance, their investment in a promising new life for their mother and sisters, and for the wives and children surely to come. The family had laboured and sacrificed much, and within just a few short years Vergis and Darveth Thane were on their way to becoming Men of substance. Their cattle were strong, their house and outbuildings solid, their family well-fed and increas-

ingly esteemed among the Human settlements in the Certainty Hills.

The third image that wove through his thoughts was the least welcome but most bewitching, a Fey-Woman with golden skin and bright green eyes who'd come to stay briefly in the bustling trading post of Verdant Grange, not far from the Thane homestead. She and two Unhuman companions were destined westward, to the coastal city of Harudin Holt. A fierce spring storm had blocked the higher mountain passes on the Great Way Road, so they'd decided to wait a few weeks until the weather cleared and Goblin steam-wagons in the employ of the Holt's trading guilds could clear a travelling path for the profitable westward traffic.

From the instant he'd seen her, Darveth was in love with the beguiling Denarra Syrene, and although it was obvious to anyone with clear eyes that the Fey-Woman had no enduring interest in the youth, he'd pursued her with dogged determination. Vergis had warned his brother about her, knowing that no good could come of such a union, even if there had been any interest on her part, but his words were useless, and Darveth continued on, undeterred.

It was then that Thane first began to understand the fickle, unfeeling nature of these Fey-touched Unhumans, these Fey-Women who fittingly called themselves the "Sisters of Wandering Virtue." Darveth had the desires of a Man, but he was still a boy in experience, and in Denarra he'd found a captivating object of unrequited love. Her early flirtations faded under his dogged persistence. He gave her armfuls of rare hill-country flowers; she returned them to the earth with a shudder and glare of reproach. He killed a magnificent, six-tined buck and dropped it at her door; she turned away in horror. When a local farmer asked Denarra for a dance at the Spring Planting festival, Darveth challenged him, only to be dismissed with a laugh by the arrogant creature that both Men desired. She'd danced instead with her Unhuman friends and ignored the hungry glances that followed the curve of her shapely hips and the revealing dress, so different from the humble fashions of decent Women. Such was the unthinking cruelty of these three she-Fey, unconcerned as they were with the passions they provoked among weak and lonely Men.

And poor Darveth. Each attempt to win Denarra's heart brought nothing but teasing scorn, yet he refused to surrender. He was determined to have her for his wife. He even started naming their future children when he and Vergis checked the cattle in the early evenings, much to his older brother's growing irritation.

Then one night, after they'd finished their rounds, the brothers returned to the house to learn that the upper passes were clear: Denarra and her friends would be leaving the next morning for Harudin Holt. Darveth went wild. «She can't leave!» he'd shouted at their mother, who advised caution. «She just doesn't know how much I need her.» His voice grew soft. «If I can just make her understand, she'll stay here with me.» Shrugging off his brother's comforting hand, Darveth rushed from the homestead, driving his horse mercilessly toward Verdant Grange. Vergis stayed behind, but dread clutched at his heart, and he followed soon after.

When the older Man arrived at the Grange, the place was in an uproar. Darveth had burst into the Unhumans' rooms, sword in hand, demanding to see Denarra. When her friends tried to intervene, he attacked them and forced his way into her bedchamber, where he found her preparing for the next day's journey. He'd locked the door behind him and tried to talk with her, but she wouldn't listen. They argued, and when she turned away from him again, he swung her around and slapped her, hard, knocking her to the floor. He crawled on top of her, weeping and screaming, and held her down, trying to kiss her. All he'd wanted to do was show her how much he loved her, how much he needed her to return that love. But it had all gone wrong, and he was plunged into cold, aching despair as she spat in his face and clawed at him.

The boy couldn't have known that she was a Fey-touched witch. All he knew was that his dreams were gone, that she'd never loved him or *even thought of him as anything more than an amusing nuisance. His desperation, pride, and strength made him dangerous. But she was Fey, treacherous and heartless, and she had no sympathy for what her beauty had done to him. He meant to show her that he wouldn't be any Woman's fool, whether Human or Unhuman. He was a Man, and she'd learn to respect that.*

When Vergis arrived at the inn, Denarra's desperate friends had ripped the thick oaken door from its hinges. He rushed in to find Darveth lying in a spreading pool of blood, a long hunting knife broken on the floor beside him, smoke rising from his clothes and charred flesh. Denarra stood over the boy, the glow of purple fire fading in her hands, her eyes glazed and face pale with pain from the deep cuts that Darveth had inflicted across her hands and upper arms.

Vergis knocked her friends aside with a roar and attacked the Fey-witch with his own drawn blade, but Denarra wouldn't be caught off-guard a second time. The dullness in her eyes cleared away and she stood firm, a sinuous wooden staff suddenly flowing into existence in her hands. He lunged low, but he was a simple rancher, unprepared for the twisting coil of crackling blue flame that leaped from her staff, burning into his sword and up his arm, sending him spinning to the ground. He threw himself forward again, but this time she stepped aside and caught the edge of his sword with the impossibly hard end of her own staff. The impact threw off the momentum of his attack, and when she drove against their clashed weapons, he lost his footing and again went sprawling. His sword landed at her feet. He grabbed for it, and she stomped on his fingers, sending the ringing blade under the bed with a decisive kick.

Giving only a backward glance to the broken, sobbing Man who clutched the motionless body of her much-jilted suitor, Denarra gathered her belongings and left the ravaged room, followed closely by her friends.

Vergis carried Darveth home, where the boy was buried the next morning. That evening, Vergis took his weapons and travelling gear and left his ashen-faced mother and weeping sisters with the promise that he'd avenge his brother, no matter how long it might take.

It wasn't that he'd fully approved of his brother's actions. If Darveth had lived, Vergis would have beaten him for trying to take a Woman against her will, even if she was a Fey-creature without morals of her own. There was no honour in rape. But neither was there honour in making a Man into a laughingstock, or denying him the love he rightly deserved. Darveth had wooed her, given her gifts, promised her a fruitful life. Any one of a hundred Women throughout the Certainty Hills would have been more than willing to marry the youth for less than that. Darveth would have been a good, faithful husband to her, but she dismissed him, threw him away, and then killed him when her scorn drove him mad. It was this dismissal as much as the murder that Vergis couldn't forgive. It was one thing to kill him; it was another thing entirely to geld him in the eyes of his family and people before spilling his blood. Darveth had done what he needed to keep his pride, and Denarra had denied him even that. When he was buried, he was a boy, not the Man he should have been.

Vergis knew that he was no match for his brother's killers—not then, anyway. He was just a cattle rancher, more familiar with herding cows through the Blue Sage Valley than tracking three Fey-Women to an unknown city far from home. But he was clever, and he was patient, and he relied on these skills to guide him to Harudin Holt, where he robbed, bullied, and butchered his way through the underbelly of that lawless city, slowly strengthening his skills and learning to push the limits of his abilities, until he found what he was looking for.

They'd lingered in the city for months, enjoying the wild culture of a settlement renowned for its excesses, even hiring themselves as adventurous mercenaries to one of the many trading guilds that ruled the city through guile and force. When Thane picked up their trail, the Unhumans had just left on a raid against some of the many pirates who attacked merchant ships off the Reaving Coast Cliffs. By the time they returned, Thane knew where they lived, the names of their employers and friends, and their arrival date, and he'd even been inside their small suite of apartments overlooking the roiling waves that crashed against the jagged coast.

Thane was waiting in their rooms when they finally arrived home laughingly singing a sea-chant, and his attack was swift and merciless. The first Fey-Woman stopped and screamed when she saw him silently emerge from the darkness, just before he cut the blue-haired creature down beneath a rain of swift, savage blows. He'd brought his sword down on another one, a green-haired female who dressed more like a Man than a Woman, and cut off two of her head-stalks before she could raise her sword to defend herself, but Denarra had stopped him before he could finish the task. That hated brown staff—which he knew now to be made of ensorcelled wyrwood—exploded again in flames and pushed him away from his wounded prey.

Thane was stronger now, faster and more skilled with sword and Darveth's re-forged hunting knife, but Denarra was stronger still, more merciless now that she'd lost one of her friends. She and the stalk-wounded warrior fought back, and the blood of all three combatants stained the ornate carpets as the Unhumans drove him out onto the roof where, in a frenzied joint attack, the Fey warrior's wide-bladed sword tore through his cheek and left eye as the Fey witch unleashed a bolt of crackling flame that threw him from the roof and into the surging waves below.

He remembered the pain of that night, the smoking flesh of his belly, the hot desire for vengeance that drove against the freezing coastal water, the stubborn Thane pride that kept him from drowning. He remembered the pale-faced Human healer who found him on the rocky shore and introduced him to the sensible philosophies and goals of the Dreydcaste, who were then still a widely-dismissed but growing sect whose commitment to the purity of mind, body, and nation had few friends among the sensual masses. And he remembered his subsequent initiation into the Dreydcaste and his training as a Seeker, which he pursued to aid in his fulfillment of another vow he'd long ago taken over the grave of his beloved younger brother.

Thane was too much of a pragmatist to pretend that he fully believed in the promises of the Dreyd; the only thing he now believed in was himself. But the Dreydcaste could give him what he wanted, including the freedom to live as he saw fit, with minimal obligations to others. Such an arrangement worked well for both the Man and the institution. Each new bit of training honed his skills, strengthened his flesh, will, and spirit, and made him ever deadlier and more determined. He learned to hunt Unhumans and how to turn aside their foul witchery, all the while knowing that these early lessons would one day serve him well when he once again faced his brother's killer. The weakness of his former life soon faded away, and the name of Vergis Thane came to be known and feared by both Men and Unhumans throughout the Reach. There were more skilful warriors, flashier and more romantic fighters, but there were few blades as certain, and none of their bearers had Thane's patience. What he didn't have in physical strength he more than made up for in unrelenting diligence and cunning.

All these memories haunted his nights and shadowed his days. Two images—brother and home—were lost to him. He'd never been home or even sent word again after they'd buried Darveth; it was likely that his one of his sisters had married and now ran the ranch, for his mother was probably long dead. The wounded Fey warrior who nearly blinded him had largely vanished after that night in Harudin Holt, and although he caught her trail a few times in the years that followed, it had been nearly a decade since he'd seen the last signs of her existence. She'd simply disappeared from the world like morning mist in the sun.

But the other one, the third vision that came to his thoughts in the darkest hours of night—she was a different story altogether. She couldn't seem to keep out of trouble, and she was known in small towns and large cities throughout the Reach, a notorious, unpredictable creature who took an uncanny delight in chaos and devastation. He'd been too busy with his Dreydcaste duties to hunt her down, but he knew that time and patience would one day bring their paths together. If anything was the will of the Dreyd, it was this simple truth: he would one day have justice, for himself, for Darveth, and for the dreams of a peaceful future that the Fey-witch had so cruelly denied.

And he was right. Here she was, after nearly twenty-five years, the treacherous creature who'd murdered his brother and aided in his own disfigurement. While green-haired Jitani was in Thane's mind when he gazed at his shattered face in a looking-glass, it was the shapely witch's face he saw when a whore recoiled at the sight of the fire-forged scars on his belly; it was the witch's eyes that burned into this thoughts when the pains would come, the scar-tissue deep inside that constantly ate away at his innards, a wound that would never fully heal; it was the witch he recalled when a hunted Unhuman begged for mercy to find only cold scorn in response.

Yes, Vergis Thane had given much thought to Denarra Syrene.

Merrimyn stepped in front of Denarra and Quill, his body trembling with fear but lips tight with determination as he faced one of the deadliest Seekers in all the Reach.

Denarra rolled her eyes and gently pushed him to the side. "While I appreciate the thought, darling, I'm no weepy princess in need of a hero with a big codpiece to rescue me. There's not a lot you can do here."

«Listen to her, boy,» Thane growled in Mannish. «I'm not here for you, although I'm sure the Purifiers in Bashonak will be interested to know that they've got a rogue Binder out here. Anyway, that's not my concern. My business is with them.» He pointed to the Strangeling and Tetawa. «Don't interfere and you're likely to stay healthy for a while longer.»

Quill looked around desperately. She remembered the Man quite clearly from his brief visit to her home in the Tetawi settlement of Spindletop, and now she understood why his presence had filled her with such dread. He was a Seeker, one of those Dreydcaste dedicated to hunting down Wielders and all Folk with *wyr*-rooted talents. But it was more than that. There was an icy disdain in his expression, an utter lack of sympathy or kindness. Even the thin, mocking smile on his face was devoid of humour. He wasn't evil so much as *empty*, and for some reason that was so very much worse.

She'd travelled far from her little moundhouse since their first brief meeting. At the time, things had seemed so simple and straightforward: after her beloved Tobhi had left on his own adventure to help preserve the future of their people, Quill had determined that she would go to the capital city of the Reach of Men, find the leader of the Humans, the Reachwarden, and convince him to intervene in the suffering of the Folk. Doing so would, she assumed, quickly put an end to the Human invasion of the Everland by the militia of the politician Lojar Vald, the zealot Dreydmaster of the province of Eromar. She had no idea at the time how naïve the plan truly was. Not only was Chalimor hundreds of miles from the borders of the Everland and far beyond her very limited travelling experience, the lands of Men were largely hostile to all the Folk, the Tetawi little people among them. Even the Everland itself was no longer a safe haven, for it was within the Folk homeland that she'd been set upon by Human slavers made bold by the Dreydmaster's intrusions. If not for the timely intervention by an eccentric performance troupe, led by the bold and flamboyant Denarra Syrene, a mixed-race Strangeling with fiery Wielder powers, Quill had no doubt that she'd have been tortured or worse even before leaving the Everland.

It was Denarra who'd agreed to help the Dolltender travel to Chalimor and make her appeal to the Reachwarden; it was Denarra who'd taken pity on the young fugitive Binder, Merrimyn, in spite of his sorcerous ties to the murderous Dreyd; and it was Denarra who'd once again come to Quill's rescue when she'd been attacked by the shape-shifting Jago Chaak, a cannibalistic Tetawi-creature who'd stalked the little Dolltender for weeks.

Yet the expression on Denarra's face filled Quill with dread, for it was clear that the Strangeling wasn't going to have an easy victory against this enemy, who now stood amidst the litter of shattered pine trees and branches that surrounded Jago's ravaged corpse. If appearances were any measure, Thane wasn't much to look at. Rather plain, even homely by Mannish standards. On the short side, with a weather-stained cloak that reached nearly to the ground, and a worn, wide-brimmed hat that covered most of his face. The Seeker was about twenty yards away, but even from this distance his tightly-muscled body gave testament to a speed and agility that made the distance and growing darkness meaningless.

Escape was futile. Quill could see that certainty both in Thane's shining single eye and the resigned gaze of the Strangeling Wielder who faced him.

Denarra had no intention of fleeing. She'd dealt this Man before, more than once, and she was as familiar with his reputation as he was with her own. Of the many enemies she'd encountered in her long adventuring life, he was the only one who still gave her nightmares. That long-ago night in Harudin Holt still burned in her memory, when he rose out of the darkness and butchered Essiana, an ever-gentle she-Kyn fiddler and dear friend. So much pain and death, and all because Denarra had killed Thane's fawning, pimple-faced brother when the boy tried to rape her after shadowing and harassing her for weeks.

The Strangeling had always expected that she'd face him again, some day. She wasn't exactly certain which of them would walk away this night, but she didn't much like the balance—three to one odds weren't nearly good enough when facing Vergis Thane. For the first time in many years, Denarra Syrene was afraid.

Still, there wasn't any use in embracing that unhappy possibility of fate. If she *was* going to die this night, Thane would be taking a few new scars away with him, or at least invest in another eye patch. She clenched her fists. The air crackled and hummed as Denarra called the *wyr*-spirits to her aid.

Thane nodded. It was no less than he'd expected. Her powers had increased significantly over the years.

But so had his.

Almost at the same instant, Thane and Denarra burst into movement. The Wielder's eyes glazed over as she ran forward with arms extended in a wide arc. The air warped and buckled in front of Thane to become a wall of howling wind that snatched his hat into the air and wrapped his long cloak around his body, pinning his arms to his sides. Without stopping to admire the results of her first Wielding, Denarra began the second. She cupped her hands and twisted them back and forth rapidly, as though smoothing a clay ball. There was a sudden flash, and a small globe of writhing blue fire came to life between her carefully manicured fingernails. As her hands moved faster, the globe grew larger, until it was nearly the size of her own head. With a triumphant grin, Denarra released the wall of wind with a twist of her left hand and hurled the sizzling ball with her right.

The fireball exploded where Thane had been standing, but Denarra's smile vanished as she saw the Seeker roll to the side with blinding speed. His cloak bulged, and the silver gleam of a knife blade sliced cleanly through the thick cloth. He was free now, and moving forward.

Merrimyn's face contorted in rage, and he moved to intercept Thane, but the Seeker had fought Binders before and knew their limitations—the unusually high number of Binders in parasitic administrative duties among the Dreydcaste was testament to their general uselessness beyond great Craftings. Merrimyn's one victory against the young Seeker he'd killed in southern Eromar made him overconfident; against an enemy like Thane, that was a deadly weakness. Thane met the Binder head-on, using his muscled bulk to drive the spindly youth backward a few steps. Merrimyn cried out in fear, then pain, as one of Thane's callused hands jerked the youth's snaring arm up and away from its protective stance over the closed book. The tome fell open. Thane's knife flashed again and he plunged it fully into the pages. Merrimyn shrieked in wordless anguish as scarlet-bright blood exploded from the book and showered the two Men. It wasn't a fatal wound—the entire hand would have to be removed for that—but it was more than enough to incapacitate the Binder for the rest of this fight.

Thane swung toward Denarra, expecting her to be distracted with worry for her fallen friend, but a blistering curtain of purple flame met him instead. She'd learned many years ago, on that dark night in Harudin Holt, that a battle with Vergis Thane required total attention. Whatever part of her heart ached to help her fallen young friend was shadowed by the immediacy of the battle; sympathy would be their undoing. So she held out her arms, and a slender wooden staff shimmered into existence out of the air. She held it tightly and waited, watching the Seeker's movements with the fixed intensity of a she-cougar.

Thane stumbled back from the fire that singed his beard and eyebrows. He was impressed. In their last battle she'd hesitated, and the cost then was nearly her life. In spite of all the laughable stories about her addled adventures, Thane could see the steely resolve of a hardened *wyr*-warrior beneath those gaudy silks and jewels.

An itching tingle at his back warned Thane that the flame had surrounded him. His eye narrowed. The flames were trouble enough, but he could feel the breathable air swiftly disappearing within the shrinking circle. Of the two, the fire was the better chance. Seekers had long learned to carry with them special Craftings that would minimize the impact of common forms of Fey-witchery. Taking a deep breath, Thane pulled what remained of his cloak over his face and whispered the protective words as he threw himself through the flames.

It was the moment Denarra was waiting for. She snarled and swung the flowery head of her staff hard against the Man's skull. The staff erupted in golden light, and Thane bellowed as he hurtled through the air and back toward the tree where his horse was loosely tethered. He smashed into the flanks of the screaming beast, and they fell together in a dusty, smoking tangle of bodies and tree limbs. Denarra leaned heavily on her staff, the weight of her Wielding heavy on her spirit, and turned toward Merrimyn, who lay curled in a pain-wracked, sobbing ball.

The Strangeling staggered suddenly. She looked down to see the charred, feathered shaft of a small dart sticking out of her thigh, tossed at the moment Thane emerged from the fire. The warm tremor that pulsed across her skin gave Denarra a good idea of what coated the end of the dart. Not likely a lethal poison, but it would be enough to end this battle, and not in her favour. She shook her head weakly and looked up. The flames had diminished, and just beyond them stood Thane, his face crisscrossed with cuts and small scratches, his cloak in tatters, one boot nearly gone. But he was smiling, and as she sagged to her knees, Denarra knew that she'd lost.

Watching in horrified fascination as the battle began, Quill felt suddenly distanced from the events taking place in front of her. She wanted to help Denarra and Merrimyn, to drive Thane away, but as much as she tried to be mindful of the struggle at hand, something else pulled at her attention.

Time slowed down. The dolls were coming.

Shakka-shakka-shakka. Shakka-shakka-shakka.

She turned to see the trio walking out of the dark forest, their dried-apple faces bobbing in rhythm with their corn-husk garments. Her eyes bulged. Although she'd long known they were alive, they'd never moved like this before—she'd only ever seen the results of their secretive travels. But now Green Kishka, Mulchworm, and Cornsilk shuffled forward in a line, each step part of a rhythmic dance, moving in a growing circle that edged closer to the Dolltender with each rotation.

Shakka-shakka-shakka. Shakka-shakka-shakka. Shakka-shakka-shakka.

Her eyes grew wider as the air shimmered inside the circle to reveal another night sky, one much different from that of the land of Men. A familiar world opened up to her within the dancing circle, and tears streamed down her face as she saw the Greatmoon of the Everland come into view, its ringed, pearly expanse shining brightly in this strange, faraway land. A wave of homesickness washed over her.

When the dolls reached her, Cornsilk smiled broadly, her polished stone eyes gleaming. *We've got to go, Spider-child. It en't safe here for ye no more*, she said, her rustling voice inside Quill's thoughts.

"I can't go yet. My friends need me."

Green Kishka shook her head. *There en't nothin' we can do for them, cub. But we promised to look after ye, and that's what we're here to do.*

Quill squinted at them in puzzlement. "Vergis Thane is too fast. He'll come after us."

Not where we're goin', he won't, Mulchworm laughed, his wrinkled face pinched tight.

"I don't understand," the Dolltender whispered. "Where *are* we going?"

There en't time to talk now, Spider-child. Cornsilk looked at the skirmish in strangely slowed movement beyond them. *Just know this: we walk the hidden ways of the world, as we did in the Old Times. That's how we served the People, by comin' back in the dried-out bodies of these spirit-dolls, cared for by generations of* firra *and bringin' guidance from the Spirit World when needed.*

Quill knelt beside the dolls. "Why didn't you ever speak to me before?"

We did, they all insisted, *but only in the Dreamin' World. Ye weren't ready to hear us in the Wakin' Time.*

"And what's different now?"

Yer need is different. If we don't leave here now, the line of Dolltenders will be broken, and we'll fail to serve the People as we was meant to do. Come with us, Spider-child. We must go, now.

Tears welled up in Quill's eyes. She'd heard so many stories from her mema and granny about the dolls, about the joyful friendships they'd shared with the little beings during their own days as Dolltender. Those stories had filled her with such longing as a youngling cub. In the years that followed, when she became the keeper of the dolls, the longing often turned to dejection, for although she never doubted their power, she always wondered what was wrong with her, for they were mute in her presence. She'd despaired of ever really knowing the dolls as the *firra* in her family had done for generations. Now she'd come into her own, and she could leave with them. But the price was much too high.

"I can't leave my friends," she said, her voice quavering. "Either you take them too, or the line of Dolltenders ends with me, right here."

A wail broke out from the dolls. *We don't have the strength, Spider-child. There en't enough of us to do the ceremony. We're too few, and they're much too big—they'd draw too much strength from us. We'd need more of our kind to do it.*

A wild look suddenly flared in Quill's eyes. "Then teach me the ceremony."

The dolls stared at her in surprise. *Ye don't know what you're askin'. The teachin's take much more than ye know. If ye failed, ye could kill your friends, all of us, and then there wouldn't be any help. Even if ye do succeed, it will take more from ye than ye know. It demands too much of the livin'. Be sensible!*

"I don't care," the Tetawa said stubbornly. "Those are my friends, and they've saved my life more than once. Let me help you, and let my strength be part of the whole." They looked at each other, and then to her again. "Please do this," she whispered. "I can't leave them behind to die."

Mulchworm sighed heavily. *Just like her granny,* he groaned. *These Spider-clan firra are goin' to give me an early rot.*

He nodded. *Let's go, then. We're runnin' short of time.*

Even with the sleep poison coursing through her body, the Fey-witch could be dangerous, so Thane moved quickly. She'd already proven to be more resourceful than he'd expected, and the damage was significant. His head spun; he could barely think through the red haze of pain from a dozen or more injuries. One hand was swollen and use-less, at least two fingers broken; blood dripped from his nose and mouth. His left shoulder had been dislocated from being thrown against his now crippled horse, which lay screaming on the ground, her back hip shattered. At any other time Thane would have killed the creature and put her swiftly out of pain, but not tonight. The Seeker had far more immediate concerns.

As he'd expected, the poison slowed the witch down, but it didn't make her helpless. The ground broke open beneath his feet, and great tree roots shot up through the soil, a swift, woven tangle of dirt-crusted spikes rising to block his way. Even he could feel the suffering of the trees as the desperate Fey-witch twisted them against their will into a dying defensive wall.

But he was close enough to put his next plan into action. Reaching into his belt-pouch with his good hand, Thane removed a thick hand-ful of dull grey granules, which he tossed over the wall. The witch cried out as thousands of miniscule iron shavings rained down on her exposed flesh, searing her skin like a sudden swarm of stinging wasps. The simplest tools were often the most effective. There would be no more witchery this night, not while the iron blistered her skin and the poison slowed her blood.

He smiled through his battered lips. The Fey-witch was down, and the traitor-Binder with her. It might take him a while, but he'd make it over the tree-root wall and collect his prizes.

Suddenly he stopped and cursed his stupidity. In the heat of battle, he'd forgotten the Brownie.

Thane's good blue eye peered through the cracks in the wall, which writhed with slow suffering like hook-skewered worms. He'd half expected her to have run away in terror, but what he saw instead filled him with amazement. The Brownie and three small, wizened creatures no taller than her knees were walking in a slow circle, shuffling their feet as they moved. Rivulets of sweat pasted her sandy hair to her brown forehead, but her face was radiant. The Man imagined that he could almost hear her singing, but the screams of the crippled horse were too loud to tell for certain.

«What is she doing?» he whispered in puzzlement, then choked on the words as he watched another world open up in the centre of the dancers' path. A tunnel shuddered into being, swirling larger and larger with each expanding circle of the dance as the Brownie and her dolls moved toward her fallen friends.

Thane cursed with wordless frustration. Taking a deep breath, the Seeker grabbed his left shoulder and heaved himself into the wall with the right, heedless of the blinding pain. He pulled back again and drove onward. Fragments of wood and dirt-thick roots flew high, and again he lunged at the wall, feeling it give way a bit more with each attack. The pain sent his head spinning, and a wave of sudden nausea nearly forced him to his knees, but his desperation and persistence were rewarded, for at last the barrier crumbled beneath his frantic assault, and he stumbled into the circle.

The gate was closing. The Brownie, her dolls, and the Binder were gone, but the witch was still in sight. Gritting his teeth, Thane jumped out and grabbed the trailing edge of her dress. Denarra screamed and fell forward, her back legs sliding out of the shrinking passage. She spat and kicked and cursed, and his grasp held true until one of her sharp-heeled boots connected with his inflamed left shoulder. He howled in agony and his fingers released spasmodically. The fabric disappeared from his grasp, and with a soft sigh, the gate slid closed.

Thane lay shaking on the ground. For a moment all he could do was clutch at the broken pine needles and shattered earth as his shoulder pulsed and he vomited his last meagre meal. His vision gradually cleared. When he was finally able to breathe without wincing, he slowly rose to his knees, and at last to his shaky feet.

He was alone. He kicked furiously at the crumbling wall, cursing under his breath with each blow, until the movement sent his shoulder spasming again and he had to stand still to let the rage and dizziness pass. The Fey-witch was gone; her witchery no longer had power, so the ravaged roots slowly returned to the earth. The Seeker pushed his fury down and buried it, but his body still trembled.

Vergis Thane was a patient man, much accustomed to the unexpected and to delays of many kinds. It was one reason he'd survived for so long in an occupation that had killed more Men than he could count. And he knew the Fey-touched witch and her habits. She wouldn't return to her wagon among the travelling actors—she was too badly injured for that. But she was too vain to go for long without her pretty clothes and fancy playthings. He knew where she'd be soon enough. They'd meet again.

And the next meeting would be the last.

CHAPTER 2

HAUNTINGS

A letter from Thanael Tibb-Wooster, Dreydcaste proselytor and delegate to the Everland affiliate of the Friends of the Folk, to the honourable Mardisha Kathek, Friends general secretary (no record of a response sent):

1,008 Year of Ascension
14th Day of Markmeasure
Dear Madame Secretary,

It is with deep sadness and no small frustration that I inform you of the temporary suspension of our outreach efforts to the Unhumans of the Ever-land. The continuing controversy and discord surrounding the passage of the Oath of Western Sanctuary has made our heretofore tireless work untenable, as there is much resentment among the unsanctified, and increasing fear among the edified. Even these difficulties we might be able to overcome if not for the influx of the basest sort of Men into these surrendered lands, callous brutes who seem to delight in proving true all the worst prejudices and expectations of our opponents among the Unhumans. Our teachings of undying hope and humility among the enlightened sons and daughters of Men are every day undone by the thieves and brigands who now claim this soil, and nothing we do will avail against the daily humiliations our ignorant charges endure.

While I have no doubt that the Dreydmaster's purpose and policies are noble, the practical reality of those policies is difficult, especially for the Friends, who have so long laboured to teach by our own lived example. We are now overwhelmed with requests for our assistance, and for each Unhuman we aid, ten others stand waiting. There are now few safe havens in these lands, and the proselytor settlements are islands of relative security, at least for the moment. As much as it pains me to admit it, we have even suspended our Creed instruction for the services provided, as the need is too immediate and our numbers too few. At present we have five score Kiin and half again that number of Brownies housed in a temple built for no more than forty, with thirty unredeemable half-Beasts in the stable yards. I realize that the latter are quite explicitly outside of the purview of my purpose here, but Madame, the Creeds instruct us to be merciful, even to those who have no hope of elevation, and these once-proud creatures have been driven to such an undignified station that even the most rigid adherent to the Supremacy Creed would be moved to tears of pity. And every day more come to us for protection that we simply cannot provide, for not only are our numbers utterly inadequate to the task, we have had our own properties threatened with seizure for our continued service to the unsanctified. How much longer we will be permitted to remain is known only to the blessed Dreyd.

Should we be forced to leave these lands, I have instructed the other Friends in the affiliate to return to Chalimor to share the story of our struggles. I will remain with my charges to further demonstrate the importance of Creed teachings to their own sanctification. We have worked too hard for far too long to surrender in these times of trial. The Unhumans are growing more frightened with each passing day; their faith in their foolish ways of old is greatly weakening. I will walk with them and give them guidance so that they will understand the true purpose of these difficulties. It may well be that these unhappy days will lead us to the victory that has so long evaded our efforts.

In service to the Sanctified,
Your servant,
Friend Thanael

After the Tree fell, the dying began.

Even though less than a month had passed since the destruction of Sheynadwiin, Tobhi's mind could barely contain all the pain and horror of that short time. All he knew was that sleep was always long in coming, and it was unwelcome when it arrived; the nightmares were often just as bad as the terrible things he saw in his waking hours. Indeed, he sometimes preferred not to sleep; there was no escape from the ravenous darkness that now stalked his dreams. At least in the daytime he could bow his head and turn away from the sights that sent his spirit quailing back in numbed despair.

He was tired beyond imagining, and he was afraid in ways he'd never been before. Past fears were brief moments, temporary frights followed by a defiant, rallied heart. The fear of the Darkening Road was something else entirely. It was the unyielding fear of uncertainty, of watching the world die around you and wondering when you'd be next. It seeped its way into his very bones, dogging his weary steps, settling down with him at night. It was a hated constant companion, and it sapped his spirit until the living world took on the grim grey haze of the ghostlands. It was no comfort that their path took them westward, toward the land of the dead.

Tobhi had never known the particular fear of dying. He'd always expected that life would endure, that he would see the next sunrise and sing its praises. Even the toxic madness of the world of Men wasn't enough to destroy his certainty of purpose; that was one reason why he'd travelled to Eromar City without hesitation. He'd faced death a hundred times before, and in all those times it had never once touched his heart. But it was all different now—and he feared that he would never be the same again.

Something inside of the little Leafspeaker had vanished in these days of endless death and marching. At one time he might have called this lost thing hope, or anger, even hatred: these were all things that gave a measure of strength. But he knew now that it was something else, more basic and essential to the deepest part of his understanding of the world and his place within it. Without this lost bit of himself there was nothing left. He'd lost the fire within.

The spark had dimmed with the hundreds who died in those horrible days following the fall of the Eternity Tree, and it faded with each death along the Darkening Road. It had faded so much that he didn't even try to find hope in the storied patterns of the lore-leaves; they'd remained wrapped in their red cloth since the fall of Sheynadwiin. All the Folk felt the Tree's destruction. The severing of the link between the People and the land was a cold iron blade in their spirits and minds. They'd fought on, valiantly, desperately, but their hearts had been broken, and there was too much hatred against them, too much greed and cruelty and unrelenting madness as Men poured into the sacred valley and set upon its *wyr*-touched people like blood-maddened hounds. The Folk died by sword, club, knife, axe, musket-ball, bolt, and arrow. They died defending themselves, fleeing, or hiding. The weakest were the choicest targets—few younglings and elders survived—and too many she-Folk and zhe-Folk met horrors worse than death at the hands of the Men who found them. Iron was everywhere: in the black smoke that boiled into the sky, in the muddied water that brought no relief to parched tongues, in the blood as life slipped away and keening rose in waves of wordless grief.

After the first bloodbath, the city's survivors were herded together in the ruins of the great Gallery of Song, now a blackened, ash-coated skeleton so utterly decimated that not even the ghost of its glory remained. Tobhi tried to find his friend and adopted Kyn sister, Tarsa'deshae, the Redthorn Wielder, to learn if she'd survived, but no one had seen her since the destruction of the Tree. The former ambassador to Eromar, the brooding he-Kyn Daladir Tre'Shein, was also missing. The Gvaerg Wielder, Biggiabba, still lived, as did the he-Kyn leader of the Sevenfold Council, Garyn, and good old Molli Rose, the Tetawa Speaker, although she'd nearly lost a foot in the chaos.

Tobhi's long-time riding mount, the feisty, black-nosed deer Smudge, had spotted him in the first wave of destruction and rushed to be by his side, heedless of the horrors taking place around them. Tobhi's initial relief at seeing his four-footed friend turned to sudden panic when he spotted a grinning Man raise his flintlock and take careful aim. The Tetawa screamed and waved his arms, trying to drive Smudge away, but the stag was too far in panic and ran on, nearly reaching his frantic friend when the musket thundered and a crimson blossom burst on the deer's flank. Smudge flipped over, crumpling to the ground, his legs kicking in confusion and remembered desperation as the life-fire swiftly drained from his brown eyes.

Tobhi's sudden grief turned to blind rage as the killer approached. Lifting his hatchet, Tobhi let loose a howl and attacked, driving the Man backward with blow after powerful blow in spite of the difference in their sizes, until another invader, unseen by the furious Leafspeaker, came behind the snarling Tetawa and smashed him in the temple with a hand club. Tobhi didn't know how he ended up with the other exiles after that, but he vaguely remembered the zhe-Kyn healer Averyn patching him up as well as zhe could, hir face hollowed by grief and filthy with ash and dried blood. There was an ugly red scar on Tobhi's forehead now, but he barely remembered it was there any longer; there were other, more important memories crowding his thoughts these days.

Others had lost more than blood or a friend or two. Sethis Du'lorr, the eldest of the Wyrnach Spider-Folk, was the only known survivor of her family—the other three were butchered in the first sweep of Men through Sheynadwiin. She walked alone, head held high, pupilless red eyes unseeing, speaking to no one, refusing all sustenance, until the day she collapsed at the side of the road and never stood again. The history of her brave, melancholy people—always few—was now lost to the Spirit World, for she was the last of them. Myrkash, the Beast-Chief, fell at the very gates of the city, although over twenty Men were broken under the great elk's hooves and piercing antlers. His skinned skull and rack now hung on the food wagon, an obscene, blood-stained trophy that brought no glory to its leering possessors. Although the Harpy brood-mother Kishkaxi survived the invasion and was able to escape to her far-away aerie, all her great eagle companions fell to iron-tipped arrows, and their feathers now decorated the belts and hatbands of many a Man who drove the Folk down the Darkening Road.

And what of Guaandak, the Gvaerg emperor? Sinovian Aldaar, the great Kyn warrior, and his golden-eyed sister, Jitani? Ixis, the Harpy Wielder? Jynni, Tobhi's own wise and loving auntie? So many of the People were lost now. Were they dead? Wounded? How many orphans had fled into the mountains, only to die lost and alone? Did they escape, or were their bones smouldering in the ashen ruins of Sheynadwiin? So many others were fading away. Each morning was filled with weeping, and every night white, moon-faced owls filled the dark sky. No cry escaped the uncanny birds, no flutter of wings announced their arrival. They covered the forest trees, although the branches didn't bend or break from the weight. When the trees thinned and became windswept prairie, the earth was a blanket of feathered whiteness, and endless dark eyes watched the camp relentlessly.

The Men seemed oblivious to the owls' presence. Occasionally one of the Folk would grow frantic and rush at the owls to drive them into the air, but the birds would always return to their patient vigil, the only movement their bobbing white heads in the shadows. No one ever spoke about the creatures, or of the fact that with each day's march, more owls appeared in the night sky. But all the Folk watched and waited with dread for the day when the denizens of the darkness would outweigh those of day.

Too many were dying these days—there was no time for burial or proper condolence ceremonies; nothing more than a brief blessing was allowed each day before they were on the Road westward again. The sufferings of the younglings were the hardest to watch. Some died quickly, in their sleep or while resting against a weak but comforting shoulder. Others were taken by fever and died in wracking pain and endless crying, some orphaned or abandoned and alone. Those families that remained whole watched helplessly, or raged against the sky and the Men in thick black coats who rode spur-bloodied horses beside the walking exiles. Each day the Sheynadwiin Folk grew fewer, but even now other Folk from throughout the Everland were joining the exodus, driven forward by Men wearing the three-tined star of Eromar. And with them came other stories of pain and torment. Tobhi had no way of knowing whether his family and friends from the southern Everland were in these new groups, or if they'd managed to join the resistance and avoid capture. He wanted to see his parents and the others, to know they were alive and as healthy as life on the Darkening Road would allow, but another part of him wanted them to be far, far away from this misery-filled world, even if it meant that they'd never touch again. There was no hope of anything here but pain, fear, and anguish.

There was one face, though, that often filled his thoughts during these burning stretches of daylight and gave whatever strength came to his step when the inner fire faded and finally vanished under the despair that crushed him down. The presence was brief and fleeting at night, but those glimpses brought the only calm his life had known since the destruction of the great peace-city. Yet he didn't dare hope to see that face again, because he knew now that such hope was doomed to die with so many other precious things on this nightmarish march. He could survive anything but that. He could survive the terrible screams that ripped through the rough camps each night and stole away the slightest shred of much-needed rest. He could survive the rancid meat that twisted his stomach in pain all day long, the gritty, beetle-infested bread that stuck like dirt in his thirsty throat. He could survive the bloody blisters that burst anew each night as he pulled his boots off his swollen feet. He could even survive watching and experiencing the abuse from the Men who drove the Folk westward—the whip across the face, the fist against the bleeding mouth, the boot in the side, the nighttime visitations that too often left their victims crippled or cold with the dawn. All these things Tobhi could endure, but not the thought of Quill sharing in these torments.

Let her be safe, he whispered each morning, gently stroking the red badger sash, now stained with sweat, blood, and grime, that Quill had given him on the last day they were together, his empty eyes raised in solemn acknowledgment of the single sun that blazed down upon the Human lands in this too-hot early autumn. *If I never see her again, please, Granny Turtle, let my beloved be safe.*

They'd passed Eromar City two days before. Tobhi imagined Vald smirking triumphantly as the long procession of the Folk marched slowly across the bridges that flanked the poisoned Orm River on their way to their new "homeland." The Tetawa was too tired and heartbroken to even be able to call up hatred for the Dreydmaster. He didn't look at the city or even try to remember when he had felt so defiant and unbreakable by Tarsa's side as they faced down the Prefect of Eromar in naïve certainty of the righteousness of the Folk's resistance. It was just a memory now. All he could do was put one foot in front of the next, step after step, neither knowing nor caring what would come with the next day. The Darkening Road was the only thing in his thoughts now. It was his past and future. The present was nothing but pain.

There was little conversation on the Road. Most of the Folk had long since fallen into themselves, except those for whom madness was a constant companion. Many exiles had been separated from friends and family, and solitude tended to encourage silence. Some waited until the brief evening encampment to whisper words of hope, comfort, or simple acknowledgment to others, while just as many curled into their threadbare blankets and descended into their own unsteady solitary sanctuaries. On occasion the strain of a mournful song could be heard faintly wandering through the dark shadows of the camp, but it was always lost to the sounds of ever-present misery that chilled the darkness.

The suffering of the Road was so extreme for the Kyn that their earlier stalk-wrappings were no longer enough to keep the pain from overwhelming them. Now they wrapped long swatches of salvaged cloth around their heads to protect their sensory stalks from both emotional and physical agony. It seemed to help a little. It certainly helped to guard against the blazing sun. Without his hat, lost in the scuffle over Smudge, Tobhi's exposed skin burned and peeled until he followed the example of the Kyn around him. His head-wrapping came from the thin striped blanket of a Tetawa elder who'd died earlier in the journey, given to Tobhi during the one brief visit he'd had with Molli Rose. It wounded Tobhi to cut the love-worn cloth, but it was better to use the cloth for the living than leave such precious things behind for the brigands who prowled the edges of the camp each night and looted the bodies of the dead after the mass of exiles went on.

The Men who led the Folk down the Road were little better than the outlaws who followed. If anything, they were worse, as they found sadistic pleasure in tormenting the increasingly fragile Folk with foul water and food, inadequate clothing and firewood, late camps and early risings—each new indignity seemed designed less to kill the Folk outright than to make them wish for a death long denied. Tobhi couldn't understand why the Men didn't just kill them, instead of dragging them hundreds of miles across the Reach. It didn't much matter. The results seemed calculated to end the same, whether accompanied by humiliation or direct brutality.

There were rebellions, to be sure, and the Folk themselves had curbed some of the worst excesses. The militiamen now gave the Gvaergs a wide berth after Biggiabba and some of her she-kith went on a rampage and crushed three soldiers into the dust before being subdued and chained to some of the supply wagons. The old Gvaerg Matron may have been devoid of her *wyr*-fed talents since the fall of the Tree, but her massive muscles and thick, nearly impenetrable hide commanded respect. The Men now generally ceased attacking the she-Kyn and *firra* during the night, but more out of haste than any benevolent change in attitude.

New threats now took the place of these attacks. The Everland had been a place of menace as well as bounty; the Wielders of all the Folk had kept many evils bound in words and rituals, to protect their various peoples and the land from dangers like the malevolent Skeeger shapeshifters and the predatory Stoneskins. Now that the Tree was destroyed, *wyr*-weavings of all kinds were unravelling throughout the old Everland, and these long-hungry creatures were freeing themselves and taking advantage of the chaos. Some remained to ravage their fading homeland, while others followed the exodus, haunting the shadows, waiting for a lonely traveller to wander too far from the firelight, or feasting on the recently dead and dying as they lay far behind in the lonely darkness.

A more mundane, but even more corrosive, threat came from both soldiers and lawless Men in settlements along the road. They'd grown bolder as the Folk had grown weaker, and were now giving fermented sour mash to some of the exiles. In another time this would have offered little trouble. Few Folk had much use for sour mash madness in times of contentment and security. But the appeal of escape—in mind, if not body—was overwhelming for many. Now the she-Folk found entirely new and unexpected dangers, for it wasn't only Men or monsters who stalked the night.

Early one morning, the Leafspeaker awoke to discover that someone had snuck beside him in the night and stolen his boots. Although so worn and tattered that they were hardly sufficient for the journey, they were better than nothing, for to fall behind was surely to die. Tobhi limped through the camp, furious that someone would endanger his life in such a mean and petty way, until he finally spotted the culprit with the boots bound tightly to his thin legs with strips of dirty cloth.

Growling with menace, his teeth gritted tightly in barely-suppressed rage, Tobhi tackled the thief and raised his clenched fist, ready to strike. "Give me my boots, ye thievin' sneak!" he hissed, swinging his quarry around to reveal a young he-Tetawa, face pale with terror, an oozing wound on his jaw. The stink of illness and neglect wafted off the gaunt cub, who looked as though he hadn't eaten or slept in days.

Tobhi stared at the youngling with wide-eyed pity. Then he saw the cub's fear. Self-loathing flooded over the Leafspeaker, choking off his words. Tobhi lowered his fist, fell to his knees, and began to weep. *"What are we becomin'?"* he screamed, smashing his hands against the ground until blood streamed down his arms.

When he looked up again, his boots lay in the dirt beside him. The youngling was gone.

The days and nights flowed together. Dawn was still a long time away, but Tobhi couldn't sleep. It was a cooler morning than most had been lately, yet he could barely feel the change, for his attention was focused on the increasing pain in his right knee. It had started off as a simple twinge that he could ignore in favour of the innumerable other aches that crippled his body; he had no idea that such a small frame could hold so much pain. But the knee grew worse as the days went on, until each step was like a broken stone blade under the flesh. Without adequate time to rest, evening encampments brought him only slight relief, and the rigours of the following day stripped away any hope of healing.

But no matter how bad the pain was, he couldn't stop walking. Those left behind were easy prey for the scavenger Men who lurked beyond the soldiers. There were a few healers left among the Folk in this group, but they were generally overburdened with those far more injured than the little Leafspeaker. He would have to keep going. Death was the only other option, and even after all the horrors he'd witnessed and experienced, it was no real option at all. Not yet, anyway.

"When do you think they'll let us go?" a voice whispered. Tobhi turned to the old he-Kyn who sat up from beneath a thin blanket beside him. The Tetawa had seen the elder many times during the long death march, but they'd never spoken. He hadn't really spoken to anyone in days, maybe longer. He couldn't actually remember the last time he'd had a conversation with another person. For a moment he thought about ignoring the question, but he was lonely, and there was a sudden surge of need, a longing to speak and to be heard, to feel someone respond to his living presence. He needed to know that he was really still alive.

Tobhi's voice was thin and raspy. "I don't know. It don't...it don't seem like they're ever gonna do it."

The he-Kyn nodded sadly. His head was wrapped in a filthy fringed blue cloth from what looked like the remnants of a coat sewn loosely together. The thick wrinkles on his face left his features pinched and tired. "What will we do when it's over? It seems like the Road is all I can remember now. It's all I know anymore."

"Me too," Tobhi whispered, grief rising up, threatening to choke off any other words. They sat together in silence for a while. Finally, the Tetawa turned and said, "My name's Tobhi."

"Braachan, of Apple Branch." The he-Kyn smiled sadly. "I remember you from the Sevenfold Council. You were with the fiery young Wielder during her speech."

The Leafspeaker nodded. "I was. I don't remember seein' ye, though. Where was you sittin'?"

"You probably didn't see me. I was with my brethren behind the screen."

Tobhi's face darkened. "Behind the screen?" he spat. "Then ye're one of them twice-cursed Shields, and I don't have no use for ye or yer treacherous kind. What're ye doin' here with us? E'nt ye s'posed to be collectin' yer blood money from Eromar? Why don't ye be on yer way and leave the rest of us to die in peace."

The old he-Kyn turned away, but his voice held more pain than anger. "Not all Shields are traitors, Tobhi. You haven't the right to blame us all for the offences of a misguided few. We're Folk, too, just like everyone here. We have no love of the Dreydmaster or his minions, and we didn't all desire to leave our homeland behind."

"Mebbe so, but it don't change the fact that none of this would'a happened if not for yer hate for the Old Ways and the Tree. It was yer whole way of lookin' at the world that brought us here, as much as Vald and his earth-killin' poisons."

"My dedication to the Celestial Path doesn't imply a hatred of Greenwalkers, Tobhi. Love of one needn't depend upon destruction of the other." His voice grew softer. "The Celestial Path was never intended to destroy the Deep Green, not by those who really understood it. It was simply another path to understanding. It gives me something that the Green couldn't, just as the Green gives to its followers something unique for them. The Purging of the Wielders should never have happened; it was an abomination, as much to the *true* teachings of the Celestials as to those of the Wielders. It was more about power and fear and short-sightedness than about our Great Mother-Tree Zhaia and Her wisdom. The destruction of the Eternity Tree shouldn't have happened, either. The stars don't shine any brighter when the earth is broken and barren. Too many have forgotten these teachings."

Tobhi looked at the he-Kyn with puzzlement. He'd known very few Shields in his lifetime—they were generally unwelcome among Tetawi, who much preferred to be left alone and to be helped by their various Wielders and Wielder-kin: Beastwalkers, Dolltenders, Cropminders,

Leafspeakers, and others. Those Shields he'd known were far closer to the treasonous Lawmaker Neranda—now Shakar—than to Braachan, who seemed entirely different from those proud, aloof Kyn. Shakar and her kind made no room for other ways of living and believing; it was the One Moon Path of mind purity and body scorn for all, or nothing, and Braachan's words would surely have been nothing short of heresy to their thinking. This he-Kyn didn't make Tobhi particularly comfortable, but there was a peace about him that was missing from those other Shields.

Still, Tobhi found it hard to forget the mass of murderous Shields as they rushed toward the Tree, their white robes stained with the blood of their kith, nor could he easily dismiss the burning violet eyes of one copper-haired Shield as her shining axe came swinging down toward brave old Unahi.

He closed his eyes against the image. It was too much. He'd grown quite fond of the elder Wielder during their brief time together, and it had been a point of brotherly pride to know that he could help care for Tarsa, her niece, when Unahi wasn't around. Now they were both gone, and he had failed.

A single tear trickled down his grimy face. He hurriedly wiped it away and curled into his blanket with his back to the he-Kyn. The stink of the journey washed over him again, as it always did when he let the pain bubble to the surface. *Great Badger, what I wouldn't give for a bath!*

Braachan didn't say anything else, and soon Tobhi heard the he-Kyn's breath rising and falling in a soft, regular rhythm. But it was a long time before the Leafspeaker was able to fall asleep, and the pain that kept him awake had nothing to do with his knee.

Braachan looked worried. "Here, use my walking stick."

"I don't want yer help," Tobhi snapped. After a moment he shook his head. "Sorry. I en't tryin' to be ungrateful; I know ye'r only tryin' to help. But ye'r gonna need that stick more than me. No reason to waste it."

After their initial introduction, Braachan made a point of seeking out the Tetawa, even though Tobhi tried to avoid the Shield's presence. But the he-Kyn seemed harmless, and it was nice to have someone to talk with regularly, even if the conversation consisted mostly of insignificant comments on the weather, the length of the day's march, or the changing landscape.

There was little indeed to say about their surroundings. Western Eromar seemed to be little more than brown grasslands stunted and worn by the merciless winds that tore through the prairie with mad-dening regularity. They encountered few Men other than the militia-men around them and the thugs behind, even though the Road seemed well-travelled. It was a stark and desolate land for those who had spent their lives in deep green forests and high mountain valleys. They felt exposed in the day beneath the wide sky, utterly vulnerable to the one-sun world. The star-choked heavens, far from the belching smokestacks of the Eromar City factories, might have given comfort if not for the owls. Instead, night simply heightened their sense of passing through a strange and hostile land. Being watched and dominated by Men was bad enough; now the earth itself seemed ready to strike at the Folk.

For two days Tobhi had struggled to keep up with the rest, and for two days the pain in his knee had grown worse. The daily heat made things even more difficult, as he felt himself wilting with each step in the blazing heat of the sun. The only time the soldiers let the Folk rest was when the Men couldn't stand the heat any more themselves. They were pushing hard ahead, at any cost, for a purpose that was yet unknown. The dead and exhausted were left where they fell; there was no time for mourning or aid. Tobhi wouldn't be able to keep up the pace, and he knew it. So did Braachan, and for whatever reason, the old he-Kyn seemed almost desperate to help the Leafspeaker endure.

"Please, Tobhi, I insist. Use my walking stick. We can take turns, if you prefer." He held out the well-worn staff of twisted walnut. Sighing deeply, Tobhi took the stick and managed a thin smile of gratitude.

"I lost my hatchet in the battle; it made for a pretty handy stick when I needed it." He peered off into the distance. "I imagine it'll be a while 'til I can get m'self another bit of wood like that, 'specially if we stay much longer in this damn flat country. Don't know who'd want to live here. It en't fit for nobody but wind-addled flatlanders."

Braachan leaned forward and slid his hand under Tobhi's right arm to steady the Tetawa as they walked. "I do hope they don't leave us here. Where would we live? What would we eat? It would almost be kinder to just slaughter us now than to leave us to linger in this place."

Tobhi nibbled on his lower lip. He felt it, too. It wasn't just that this land was so different from the old Everland in spirit; it was fundamentally different in form, too. They could find edible foods in most any place. He'd seen enough antelope and rabbits to know that there was enough for bodily sustenance in the grasslands. It was the other things that worried him, especially medicinals. Each people of the seven Folk had ancient knowledge about the healing plants and herbs that grew in their various lands. But this knowledge was rooted in their relationship with that very soil, and it was specialized in ways that took years to understand. It would normally take generations to learn about the spirits of a place, but the *wyr*-draining influence of the Man-lands made the normal process so much harder. What new sicknesses would they find in this new world? Would they be able to find medicinals similar to those of their old homelands, or would they be helpless? Would they ever be able to speak to the spirits of this strange place? If not, their vulnerability would increase dramatically. Worse still, the strange autumn heat, the rigours of the journey, and the inedible food was weakening even the strongest of the exiles. Winter wasn't that far away. What would happen if the snows came too soon? They were utterly unprepared for winter and its certain cruelty on these wind-blasted lands. Things seemed about as bad as they could get now, but winter's devastation would be beyond imagining.

Tobhi's knee suddenly buckled, and he cried out as he smashed to the ground, the walking stick snapping beneath him. Agony and despair overwhelmed him. It was over. There was no use in continuing. Hope was useless; it would be best to just finish it instead of lingering on to become a desperate wraith in some faraway country, torn from kith and ceremony. At least here he still had his memories of home. If he went on, even those would be swept away in the ever-hungry search for hope. He didn't want it anymore. He just wanted to be left alone.

Callused hands clutched at Tobhi's shoulder, but he remained on the ground, unmoving. He could hear Braachan's voice calling to him, and then the growl of a Man telling the old he-Kyn to keep walking. A boot smashed into the Tetawa's side, and excruciating pain filled his senses, but then he felt the pain slip away, and no kick followed the first. He opened his eyes slightly. Bloody, bandaged feet marched past, tattered boots, thick-soled bare feet, dusty hooves, claws, talons, and pads, hundreds in all shapes and sizes moving forward in a slow, erratic rhythm. He watched them, detached but slightly pleased to be free of the need to continue on. His eyes closed, and he drifted away into darkness.

When Tobhi opened his grit-rimmed eyes, it was still daylight, although the solitary sun moved swiftly toward an orange dusk. Waves of heat still radiated off the rolling grasslands. His only companions were a couple of mean-eyed buzzards who glared at him, as if annoyed at his rudeness for not being dead. He shared their confusion, if not their motivation. For a moment he wondered if he actually might have passed beyond the mortal world, but the burning thirst in his cracked and dusty mouth was evidence enough of life—if the old Tetawi stories were true, as they so often were, the dead certainly wouldn't be thirsty. His hair was tangled and matted with dried blood; he couldn't remember the last time he'd washed it.

Tobhi waited for a long time to move, but when there was no doubt that he wasn't dead, and that the buzzards weren't likely to go away on their own, he painstakingly pulled himself up, and promptly collapsed again. After a few more false starts, he finally made it to his knees and remained there, unsteady but determined. The birds hissed and flapped away in disgust. Looking toward the west, he saw the wide stretch of dusty road and beaten grass that moved far into the horizon, but he didn't see any of the uprooted Folk or the Men who drove them forward. Except for a couple of buzzard-mobbed bodies lying motionless on the rough path in the distance, he was the only Folk in sight.

A sudden chill went up his spine. He might be alone at present, but the Human and monstrous scavengers who followed behind the exiles would be along shortly—the pickings were good these days, and the Men were well armed with iron and other poisons. If not for Vald's soldiers and their unknown reasons for protecting their wards from further attack, these various two-legged parasites would have decimated the Folk long ago. A single crippled Tetawa would pose no problem to them, especially one weakened by thirst, hunger, and heartbreak.

Still, death by oblivion was one thing. Allowing himself to be murdered another entirely. Tobhi looked to the east and groaned. He could see them now, a line of figures in the far distance, moving fast. They would reach him by sunset.

He tried to stand, hoping to hobble into the tall grass and find a hiding place, but the pain in his injured leg was too much, and he collapsed again with a groan. His knee wouldn't possibly hold his weight.

He scanned the ground for options. The grass beside the road was matted down for a long distance, but a couple of wide depressions beneath the broken vegetation caught his attention. An idea suddenly took hold of his thoughts. He might not be able to hide above the ground, but escape might be possible *below* it. He didn't know much about this land, but there was one thing he could recognize, even in this alien place: he knew the look of badger territory. He was, after all, born to the Badger Clan, and the spirit of Buborru the Keeper, wisdom-bearer of the Tetawi Clans, was in the Burrows blood.

Taking a deep breath, Tobhi pulled himself forward on his elbows, ignoring the pain as sharp stones tore into his still-tender flesh. It took longer than he expected to get to the dip in the grass. By the time he reached it the daylight had turned crimson, stretching like a bloody stain across the prairie. The Men would see him soon, and then there would be no opportunity for escape.

He dug into the grass and pulled thick wads free of the hole, spreading dry brown soil across his fingers. It was as he'd hoped—an old badger sett, long abandoned, if the musty scent was any indication. All Tetawi could feel the presence of their Clan-beast and close kith, and there was no such feeling here. For a moment he felt woefully alone, until he realized that, had a badger been in the hole, he might have had to send it fleeing into the very danger he himself was trying to avoid.

Still, he realized with growing desperation, it would be good to have a badger's help, as the hole was too small—he couldn't fit. His wide brown hands dug frantically at the dirt, which crumbled in his fingers and collapsed into the tunnel, filling it further with each movement he made. The heat and drought had damaged the soil and weakened the den walls. Even if it had been large enough, the burrow might well have fallen in as he tried to dig into it.

Such knowledge didn't stop his digging. It was still his best choice, his only real hope. He was much too big for the hole, but if he could just open enough to drag part of his body into it and then pull the broken grass back over his exposed body, the fading light might be enough to hide him. He had to try. Frustration burned his eyes as the dirt flew. His hands moved faster and faster, digging deeper and deeper as soil fell again.

The soft crunch of boots on dry grass nearby brought an end to the

Leafspeaker's efforts. He stopped digging and remained head first in the hole, breathing heavily, tensing for the attack. If he was going to die, he'd do it with some measure of dignity. Badger Clan was proud and defiant—he was too weak to put up much of a fight, but he'd at least draw blood before dying.

His teeth bared, Tobhi spun around with a snarl. At first he couldn't tell what he was looking at, as the blazing light of the prairie sunset burned so brightly on the figure. It wasn't until something dropped beside him that he began to comprehend.

The familiar shape was battered, worn, and slightly more crumpled than it had been the last time he'd seen it, but there was no doubt about it.

It was his hat.

"I think you dropped this a little ways back, little brother," Tarsa said as she knelt down and pulled the Leafspeaker to her. Tobhi trembled in disbelief for a moment, then collapsed in her arms, his body shaking with sobs of joy and relief. She gently rocked him, her fingers stroking his hair, and soothed him like a frightened youngling awakening from a nightmare that had lasted much too long.

He pulled away and looked at her, as though unable to make himself believe that she was really there. "But Tarsa, where've ye been? I thought ye died…."

She smiled. Her face was lined with sadness, but there was something new in her turquoise eyes that Tobhi couldn't quite understand, a strength in her arms that went beyond the tight muscles of a trained Redthorn warrior. "We were separated in the great chamber of the Tree—I couldn't find you. Jitani and Sinovian saved us. We've been following you for weeks."

Tobhi was dizzy. Tarsa was alive. If she still lived, then others lived, too. He looked over her shoulder to see Daladir, Jitani, a small group of hard-eyed Folk, and even a few Humans dressed in Kyn travel garb. The Tetawa turned back to the she-Kyn.

"It happened so fast. I tried to find ye too, but them Men and Shields was everywhere, and then I was bein' pushed out of the city. Last thing I really remember clearly is the Tree fallin'." His voice grew thick. "Tarsa—I saw Unahi die, in the lore-leaves, before we got to the city. I didn't know it'd be her. I didn't know that her death would destroy the Tree."

The Wielder's eyes glowed strangely in the fading light of the setting sun. "The Tree wasn't destroyed, Tobhi."

"What d'ye mean?" he whispered. "It was—we all felt it. It was like the heart was torn right out of me. I en't never hurt like that. The Wielders can't touch the *wyr* no more. It's all gone."

"No, Tobhi. It's not gone. It's just changed, that's all." A cool emerald flame flowed across Tarsa's skin and over the Tetawa's body, and he felt the spirit-deep exhaustion drain from his body in the healing fire that suddenly surged through his veins. There was no more pain, no more fear. He gasped with surprise and delight and watched the flame rise into the air to become a blazing shower of dancing green sparks. The grass rose up around them, and the wind tousled their shining hair. The sparks scattered on the wind to fall on the parched earth, where lush vegetation erupted through the dry soil and spread out in wild, joyful abundance. Tobhi could smell the sweet perfume of rain and flowers in the air. The Wielder's hair rose up like liquid bronze, and her sensory stalks moved in an easy, gentle rhythm, like willow branches adrift on a cooling summer breeze.

"The Tree is fallen, but it still endures." The green glow faded, but Tarsa's eyes still shone with blue fire. "I am the Eternity Tree, Tobhi. And now, so are you."

CHAPTER 3

TRUTH

Thick blue smoke hung like a gossamer curtain in the parlour, so dense that Padwacket could barely see the other side of the room. He smiled, well satisfied with the purchase. Lower Rinj smoke-leaf was hard to find in these days of increasingly erratic trade through Eromar, but it was undeniably worth both the expense and trouble. Eight months of savings, two months of waiting, and a few not-quite-legal favours went into this small purchase. Now, at long last, he had the time and solitude to enjoy one of his preferred vices. He was determined to savour the experience.

The Ubbetuk loosened his cravat and nestled deeper into the red plush sofa. His eyelids grew heavy, and he felt the sweet bite of the smoke on his tongue as he took another deep draw on the brass pipe. It made his head spin a bit, but unlike most Ubbetuk in his position, Padwacket had no deep-seated desire to maintain constant control over his mind and behaviour. Even if such a silly principle had intruded into his character, it would hardly have been an advantage in this particular household. A smoke-addled mind generally minimized the insanity of his current domestic arrangement.

The world seemed to sink into a haze of drifting tingles, and a low moan of pleasure slipped from his grey lips. He reached out with exquisite lethargy for the wine decanter on the sideboard but stopped as a jingling noise in the hallway caught his attention. Someone with a key was coming to the parlour, someone with a firm purpose.

Sudden panic set in. Padwacket leapt up and rushed to a window to clear out some of the smoke, cursing himself for his inattention. Meggie Mar had no love of smoking, and the slightest hint of smoke in the parlour rugs or draperies would unleash her freckled fury. She had an uncanny nose for the stuff, although she sadly didn't discriminate between common ditch-weed and premium stock like Lower Rinj. It hardly mattered that Padwacket was the head valet and ostensibly beyond the authority of the house-matron—all were trembling vassals in Meggie Mar's domestic domain.

He threw open the window and cursed. The unnatural heat of the evening provided no cross-breeze to pull the smoke outside; if anything, it simply added the heavy stink of rotting fish and other pungent sea life to the mix. The door shuddered slightly, and the rattle of keys in the corridor beyond echoed eerily in the claustrophobic room. In desperation, Padwacket grabbed the edge of a heavy red curtain and tried to wave it back and forth to encourage the smoke to move outward. But the curtain was too big, his movements too abrupt, and the Ubbetuk squeaked in terror as the velvet tore away from hanging rod and the entire mass of cloth tumbled down, swallowing his flailing body in its thick folds. He fought for escape until he heard the door open and someone enter the room. He was caught. Resigning himself to his fate, which would no doubt include an hours-long lecture and painful ear-pulling, Padwacket poked his head out of the red fabric, only to see an unexpected figure shaking her head.

"Really, darling, I hardly think that a change of drapes is necessary at this time of night, especially with everything else that's been going on lately. Have you discussed this with Meggie Mar? I'm not entirely sure she'd approve." Denarra walked over to the open window and looked out. "No, I'm quite sure she's not going to be happy about this at all. Well, we'll worry about that in the morning. You'll be sure to tell her, won't you? In the meantime, let's close this window. This ghastly heat is making all of Chalimor smell like a cod-fisher's privy. This is hardly the cultivated atmosphere I promised my guests."

The Strangeling turned and sat in the chair opposite Padwacket's sofa. "I've never known such an autumn. These last few weeks have been absolutely exhausting. Do you have any idea how difficult it is to get a free moment with the Reachwarden? The Man is like a ghost, flitting here and there, always at a different party than the one I'm attending. It's almost like he's trying to avoid me."

Finally free of the clinging curtain, Padwacket stood, smoothed his vest and wiped a layer of fine red lint from his hooked nose. He poured two glasses of amber-coloured wine from the sideboard and handed one to Denarra, who nodded appreciatively.

"Perhaps a direct meeting would be more profitable than the casual encounter. It seems rather unlikely that he would make himself available for an issue of such significance during a mere dinner party." The Ubbetuk drained his own glass.

"I've tried that already," Denarra pouted. "He won't return my letters or answer my queries. His private secretary refused to sign my name to the audience register for the next three months." She glowered as she sipped the wine. "That hateful little bureaucrat has far too much nose hair to be entirely trustworthy."

Padwacket refilled his glass. "Yes, one's true moral character is generally reflected in one's nasal hygiene," he said dryly, his eyes wandering over to the still-smoking pipe on the end table beside his sofa.

"I couldn't agree more," Denarra said, nodding absently. She held the glass up and swirled the liquid around, watching as bubbles drifted through the wine like golden pearls. "Chalimor has changed a lot since I've been gone, hasn't it, Padwacket?"

Yes, he thought to himself as he cast a quick glance at the dozens of small, pitted scars on her upheld arm, a reminder of her recent encounter with Vergis Thane. *And it's not the only thing that is different.* "Changed in what way?"

She turned to him. Makeup concealed most of the iron-wrought wounds to her face, but nothing could hide the hurt in her eyes. "I haven't even been away a year, but the whole place has been transformed. My old friends don't invite me to their dinners and dances anymore; most of them ignore my invitations to visit here. Last week's dinner party was a disaster—only two people came, and they both left before dessert. I've only been to six parties in the month I've been back, and most of the guests had little to say to me, even people I've known for years! Last week, when I went to Ashanna dol'Graever's wedding reception, I was actually relegated to a table half-hidden behind a potted fern, along with a watery-eyed Woman who couldn't speak without her chin-wattle flapping around like a live trout in her throat. I didn't even get an invitation to the wedding—just the reception. I'm rather glad now that I didn't take Ashanna a gift. What's going on here?"

The pain and bewilderment was heavy in her voice, but anger was there, too. She knew what was happening, but she didn't want to be the first to mention it. It had always been that way between them, from the first day the Ubbetuk came to work for his eccentric employer nearly fifteen years past, rescued by her from an ill-planned and extra-legal business venture that nearly went fatally wrong due to inebriation and ill-timed sarcasm. Denarra had saved Padwacket's life and his family's reputation, both of which created a debt that he could never fully repay. Soon, however, friendship succeeded duty, and the Ubbetuk became both a trusted member of the household and a confidant. Denarra expected him to tell her both what she wanted to hear and what she needed to hear, and she trusted him to know the appropriate time for each, even if she didn't always like what he had to say. That was the least he owed her.

But it wouldn't be easy. This wasn't something that her particular charms could fix. Their world, indeed, had changed.

Padwacket coughed once and refilled their goblets. "Men are less trusting of the Folk these days, more willing than ever before to see difference as deficiency. At one time such poison found safe harbour only among the ill-educated or Dreyd-tainted, but it is the houses of learning now that spread these ideas. Alchaemists and philosophers of Men claim to find evidence of intellectual and moral degeneracy in everything about us, from the hue of our flesh to the sizes of our skulls, from the timbre of our voices to the cut of our clothes and devotion to our own ways. The hatreds nestled in Dreyd prophecies have made their way into the Academies, and they feed each other."

Her face was composed, but Padwacket could see that each word wounded the Strangeling's spirit. She was used to rejection and resentment in the wild lands of Men, but Chalimor had been, for some time, a cultivated haven from such ignorance. It was her escape and sanctuary, a place of healing. It was more of a home to her than anywhere else in the Melded world. Now, it seemed, there was no place free of the cruelty of Men.

"Worse still to their minds," Padwacket continued, his heart heavy, "is the idea of any Human bedding an Unhuman. Such unions are seen as tainting virtuous Men, weakening them, stripping away the dignity of their rightful place at the apex of creation. And the products of such unions are to be especially scorned, for they are corruption incarnate."

He stopped. Denarra's green eyes flashed with rage, but she remained seated and drank slowly, purposefully, until her glass was empty. She held it out for a refill and drained that glass, too.

After a long silence, Denarra cleared her throat. "So, the exotic Strangeling lusted after by Men and Women of high station isn't welcome at their parties anymore? The Kyn-blood that used to warm them with desire is now a bit too hot, I suppose? I wonder what so many of these petty society tyrants would say if they knew that their husbands and wives had spent time in my bed, joyously 'tainted' by this Unhuman temptress? And not one of those simpering society sops had the courage to say anything to me. They just thought I'd slink away, tail tucked between my legs like some hide-whipped bitch." She threw her glass across the room, where it smashed against the cold fireplace. "Well, they'll see a bitch soon enough, but this one has sharp teeth!"

A smile crossed her red lips, and she turned back to her valet. "In the meantime, let's have a bit of that pipe. I haven't smoked Lower Rinj in ages, and I have a lot to think about right now; we'll just have to deal with Meggie in the morning." Her eyes darkened. "And then I think it's time to tell Quill what's going on."

They'd arrived in Chalimor during an unseasonably fierce thunderstorm, although whether the storm came with them or was waiting in the harbour was beyond Quill's knowledge, as this was her first gate-walking experience. It was terrifying. She had no clear sense of time or geography. Howling winds tore at them, while rippling currents of white lightning burned through the darkness between worlds, as though they walked in a fiery tunnel through a raging black sea. Worst of all, though, were the milky white faces that faded in and out of sight from the swirling shadow, their eyes deep, dead hollows that ached with endless misery. She and the others were all wounded in body as well as spirit: her own body ached from the battle with the Skeeger and from the gate-walking itself, which had drained her every bit as much as the dolls said it would. Her belly cramped worse than in her moon-time, so much so that the spasms nearly bent her double from the pain. She knew then precisely what the ceremony was demanding of her body, though she didn't want to think about it. It was a blood sacrifice in every sense of the term, and thus far too frightening in its implications.

She'd been scared for more than herself, too, as poor Merrimyn was still unconscious, and Denarra was bleeding and barely able to stand after the battle with Thane. Between the two of them, though, they half-carried, half-dragged the young Man through the otherworldly storm, more certain of their survival even in this alien place than back in the world of Men with Vergis Thane. Quill wasn't even sure if they were going the right way, but when the gate opened all she could think was Chalimor, the home of the Reachwarden and their long-sought destination.

The Dolltender wasn't sure how Denarra had managed it, but a carriage with a well-dressed Ubbetuk attendant stood waiting for them when the gate opened into the stormy streets of the great city. The valet seemed unsurprised to see them as he helped drag Merrimyn into the carriage, although his eyes did widen a bit when he saw the snaring-tome shackled to the young Human's arm.

A brusque Woman with tightly-bound brown hair and a freckle-covered face opened the door of a two story, red-tiled house some-where in the city. It took her little time to bustle the two she-Folk into the house and into steaming baths on the ground floor while she attended to Merrimyn's injuries upstairs. Quill couldn't remember falling asleep, but she awoke the next morning nestled in a soft bed beneath bright quilts in a sunny, oak-panelled room. Her cramping had nearly stopped, though there was still an occasional twinge of dis-comfort to remind her of the strange journey. Her old, travel-worn clothes had disappeared in the night, but fresh replacements lay folded on a small table beside the bed, each garment sized and fitted to her exact dimensions. The Woman, Meggie Mar, arrived a few moments later with the announcement of breakfast. The smell of fresh bread and spiced meat wafted through the door, and the Tetawa was dressed and in the kitchen, almost on Meggie's heels.

Denarra and Merrimyn were still sleeping, but the Woman—of whom Quill had heard a great deal during her evening wagon-chats with the Strangeling before the chaos of the previous day and night—was clearly someone of skill and authority in the house. Meggie Mar wasn't old, but she carried herself with the certainty of a Woman many years her senior. Her crisp blue dress and ironed apron were clean; the smooth calluses on her hands were worn deep and strong like wind-polished wood. She grumbled and snarled at length, in both Mannish and impeccable Folk trade-speech, but her touch was gentle, and Quill noticed kindness and concern in the fuss the Woman made over the maidservant and the Ubbetuk valet. No one went hungry in Meggie's household, nor did they stand idle. When Quill was finished eating, Meggie put her to work right away helping the maidservant

Ellefina on her daily shopping expedition into the mid-city market.

It wasn't until later that Quill understood Meggie's reason for sending her so soon into the city: if this was to be her home for a while, it was important that she familiarize herself with it as quickly as possible. And the giggling young Ellefina was a charming guide, if somewhat addled and rather too flighty for the Tetawa's comfort. They wandered through stalls and into shops, the girl occasionally gossiping with other domestics and flirting with handsome young Men idling on the cobbled street corners, and all the while Quill walked in mingled fascination and terror through the masses of Humans, Folk, and other odd and wondrous creatures who inhabited this strange city. By the time she and Ellefina returned with their arms full of fresh vegetables, a fresh suckling piglet, flowers, and various cooking herbs and pastries, the young *firra* was only just beginning to understand the remarkable character of Chalimor, the Jewel of the Reach.

In her most ambitious daydreams she'd never imagined anything so huge and overwhelming. The sheer scale of the city staggered her. It stretched for miles, from the hewn-granite base of majestic Mount Imor all the way into the calm centre of Chal Bay, where the city was built up on massive limestone reefs that jutted out of the clear blue depths. The greater buildings were in the shadow of the mountain, all white marble, whitewashed stone, and coloured tile; it was here, too, that Denarra's stuccoed brick house stood on a flowery hill that provided a stunning view of the city, which spread out in the shape of a great crescent moon, with the more fashionable districts lining the coast, and those on the lower end of the social scale extending outward into the fish-rich bay. Ships of every conceivable design and style passed through the harbour, from the great scarlet-sailed merchant sloops of the Sarvannadad trade guilds, painted red, gold, and black, that cut proudly through the sapphirine waters, to the swift white Chalimite sculls that slipped past the high-hulled city scows bringing goods from ship to market, to the frail and weather-worn scalloping punts that kept close to the docks and often ended up swamped by the white-capped waves made by the larger vessels—such a common event that dock labourers were disappointed when a day went by without the opportunity of a water rescue.

Humans of all sizes, shapes, and colours swarmed the streets like so many ants, and the noise they made was deafening—all shouting and laughing and calling out to one another. Spices of both exotic and mundane origin were favourite trading good in the city, but anything that could be procured by coin, deed, or bargain could be found somewhere in the city: bold and vibrant dyes drawn from crushed beetles and unpronounceable plants from far-away ports; soft silks, hardy linens, lustrous leathers, and other fabrics drawn from worm, sheep, rabbit, goat, bear, and more unusual creatures; wood and stone in great supply for both building and fine artistry; rare oils, cheeses, honeys, teas, spirits, and Folk-grown tobacco found their way to the city's finest homes. Soothsayers and fortune-tellers had a brisk business in talismans, amulets, Craft-touched bones, sanctified chalices, and other strange magics, much to the vocal dismay of both Rationalist philosophers from the Learnèd Academy and Dreydcaste proselytors who lectured against such superstitions—and each other—in every market square. It was said that in the more dangerous areas of the city even Human or Folk slaves could be purchased; though slavery was ostensibly against the laws of the Reach, indentured servitude was a flourishing legal business, and the line between the two was often quite thin.

Beasts of every temperament and kind were sold as food, pet, or plaything, with little regard to the creatures' own preferences. Fresh beef, mutton, poultry, pork, seafood, and less identifiable meats were readily available, and Ellefina confirmed that many animals offered as pets one day often ended up in the butcher's stall the next. The smells resulting from so many goods and beasts and bodies in such close proximity were also new to the Tetawa. The stench of decaying fish and refuse from the alleyways and docks was bad enough, but when added to the sickeningly sweet perfumes that the wealthier Chalimites used to mask the other smells—it was sometimes all Quill could manage to get through a trip to market without spending the remainder of the day with a pounding headache and rolling stomach.

She had no idea how all these people managed to survive in such a place. The shadow side of the city was as terrible as its beauty was magnificent. Orphans, urchins, and the other desperately poor lived in squalor in the alleys and abandoned buildings of Mariner's Quay, the wharf district, but Quill rarely saw them, for they were driven out of the finer neighbourhoods every night by the city guard to prevent them from offending the sensibilities of the moneyed and powerful. She saw few Folk, either; those who inhabited the city were either celebrated outsiders, like Denarra, house servants, like Padwacket, or struggled to live among the other unfortunates in the more dangerous parts of the city.

It was all quite amazing to Quill, yet troubling, too, like an endless dream with more possibilities than a lifetime of slumber could uncover. Her first few weeks in Chalimor passed in a whirl. She travelled with Ellefina and Meggie through the city, observing most of its respectable areas during the daylight as she was put to work carrying parcels, packages, baskets, and armfuls of vegetables and other goods. She strolled Denarra's private garden, where a pair of bold and beautiful peacocks—previously unknown birds to the Tetawa, but the Strangeling's particular and unsurprising favourites—strutted regally among the dust-grey peahens. With her flamboyant hostess, Quill witnessed something of the glittering night-life of Chalimor, and bedecked in soft-hued silk dresses and some of Denarra's more demure jewelry, she was introduced to many of the people that the Wielder hoped would get them an introduction to the Reachwarden to plead their case.

They'd spent a few nights on starlit terraces, or in shimmering gilded ballrooms filled with the music of soft flutes and harps. One night they saw a play with an elaborate stage designed to resemble the inside of a golden conch shell, far more extravagant than any of the motley shows put on by Denarra's scruffy old performance troupe, Bremen and Crowe's Medicine Show and Repertory of Thespian Delights. The following week they attended a late-night literary salon at the Luminescent Observatory in the People's Academy, where Quill was brought to tears by the Strangeling's lovely friend Pixie, a warrior-poet of Jaaga heritage whose word-weavings lingered in the heart and spirit long after the evening's entertainments were finished. The lightly seasoned food at these parties was, without exception, exquisite, although Quill often preferred the loving weight of Meggie's meals of corn, sweet potatoes, beans, and fresh meat to the florid but impersonal pudding-based cuisine of the High Houses of Chalimor.

At one time she might have felt awkward and rustic among these bewigged Men in velvet coats and high white collars and their tight-faced Women dripping in pearls, gems, and endless folds of bright cloth, but she was pleasantly surprised to find that Denarra's kind supervision helped her navigate this strange world with little discomfort. If anything, she enjoyed the new experiences and grew eager for each night's new revelry. Even the dolls seemed more relaxed in this place, especially after their worlds-crossing efforts. They spent most of their time in sleep, barely noting her presence when she came to feed them their daily ration of tobacco and cedar shavings. It was a period of peace for them all.

But the invitations quickly dried up, and Denarra grew increasingly despondent. Even Quill could see that things weren't going very well.

The Strangeling's tensions grew with her concern over Merrimyn. He lingered for a long time in fever after their arrival, and when he emerged from it, he could remember little of the last few months. The binding of his snaring-tome was cracked and pitted as a result of the battle with Thane; a biting black smoke occasionally trickled out of the book's seam. Merrimyn recalled Denarra and seemed to remember Quill, but of the rest, there were mere glimpses and hints. This discovery threw the sorceress into a deep depression. It was only later, after Denarra came to the moonlit garden from a talk with her valet in the parlour, that Quill discovered the depth of the Strangeling's concern.

"He was our key to Vald's plans, Quill," Denarra said, slipping down onto a vine-wrapped bench on the terrace. "He knew something of Vald's preparations for the Expulsion; he was going to give them to the Reachwarden, to make him understand just how terrible this is for *everyone*, Folk and Human alike." She grimaced. "Merrimyn told me what's happening, at least as far as he knew, but a Man's word is far more valuable these days than that of a half-breed Strangeling."

Quill's throat went dry. She'd come outside to enjoy the peace of the evening, but it was gone now. Now all she felt was a smothering darkness reaching out over them. "What do you mean, Denarra? What's happening?"

The Strangeling smiled sadly. "I didn't want to tell you yet, Quill. I promised to look after you, and I've taken that vow quite seriously. You've been enjoying yourself so much, and after everything you've been through I wanted you to have as much fun as possible before…."

"Before what?"

"The Expulsion isn't just about land, Quill—it never really was. Certainly, that's what's been getting everyone's attention. That's what's driving the endless streams of land-hungry Men rushing from all over the Reach for some choice farmland or mining stakes. That's what the politicians are arguing about; it's what the condescending philanthropists who call themselves 'the Friends of the Folk' are yammering about, too. But it goes much, much deeper than that. Vald seems to be seeking nothing less than the utter destruction of the Folk in this Melded world."

The air suddenly grew chilly, but Quill took no comfort in the cooling change from the humid heat of the earlier evening. Instead, she just looked off into the distance, to the shining lights throughout the city around them. Denarra's terrace looked out over the bay and some of

Chalimor's most famous structures: the great Jurist Temple; the House of States, where the legislators of the Reach Republic endlessly debated government policy; the Hall of Kings, where the Reachwarden worked to unite the contentious territorial and political factions; the grand library and lecture halls of the Academy. It was a lovely sight at all times, but none so much as this cloudless night, as the light of the nearly-full moon bathed the marble structures in a radiant silver glow.

But the beauty gave no warmth. It was as cold as the fickle sea air, stripping her heart's heat and leaving only emptiness behind.

"There's more, isn't there?"

"I'm afraid so, Quill. I'm sorry."

The Tetawa nodded once. "Tell me what's happened. Please, Denarra, don't try to protect me. I'm tired of everyone thinking I'm so fragile that I always need to be coddled and cared for. I'm not a youngling cub anymore. I've shed the blood of my enemies, and I have the scars to show it, so that should have more than earned your respect. We can't be true friends if you won't trust me with the truth."

Denarra's eyes filled with tears. "It's not that I don't trust you, Quill. It's just that I know how hard…."

"Tell me."

The Strangeling sighed and reached out for Quill's hand. It was freezing. "Sheynadwiin was destroyed on the day we arrived in Chalimor. I only found out a couple of weeks ago. Some of the Folk escaped—perhaps your Tobhi was among them."

Quill's face grew pale, but her voice didn't shake. "You said 'some' escaped. What about the others?"

"Some…many died. But most survived. They're being driven westward by the Eromar militia with iron swords and muskets, to the broken land promised in the Oath of Western Sanctuary, a land once known as the Pit Fields of Karkûr."

"I see." Quill pulled her hand away from Denarra's grasp. "Then we've failed. We've danced and drank and lived high while my peo-

ple—*our* people—have been dying on a lonely road far from home."
The Dolltender stood abruptly and turned an accusing glare on her
friend. "You promised to help me, and I trusted you. You lied to me."

"Quill, truly, I thought this would work," the Strangeling cried,
stricken. "I've always been respected among the right circles in the city;
I've always had the ear of the most powerful Men in the Assembly. But
things have changed! They don't want anything to do with me anymore. Their hearts have hardened against the Folk, and I don't know
why."

"I have an idea," Quill snarled. "Maybe they're tired of shallow
social parasites with more love of fine food and fashion than concern
for their own kith dying in a strange land."

Denarra's anguished sob followed Quill as the *firra* spun angrily on
her heel toward the house. She'd said she wanted to know more, but
now she was sorry to have heard it. There was a certain false comfort
in these shadows, in the pretence that the world would go on as it
always had and that nothing was changing. She could keep dreaming
of parties and dances, of perfumed candles and soft music, and nothing would intrude into that hopeful, dreamy peace.

But then she saw Tobhi's broad smile. She could almost smell the
spice of cedar and pine on his vest, feel the silky softness of his long
black hair in her fingers. He'd given up hope of a false dream, and in
doing so fought to make a reality of peace. She could do no less, even
if he was gone. Even if….

Wiping her hand across her eyes, she straightened her shoulders,
pulled her hair away from her face, and turned back to the door. A
sudden commotion inside caught her attention, and she ducked out of
the way as Padwacket rushed outside and threw himself over the edge
of the terrace into the garden below, Meggie Mar close behind him,
her voice raised in an unintelligible stream of curses about smoke and
curtains.

Quill shook her head angrily. Her world was crumbling, and they were worried about the household draperies. Everything she'd known was gone now: her cousins, Medalla and Gishki, her home of Spindletop, all her other dolls…Tobhi. The Everland itself. Who was she if not part of this web of history, friendship, family, and love? She could never return home again, not unless the Reachwarden came to their defence. But for all these weeks her people had been dying, and the Reachwarden had done nothing—indeed, it mattered so little to the Humans of this city that she hadn't heard even the slightest whiff of rumour or gossip. The icy silence of social sanction reigned supreme in Chalimor, and against that she had no defence. Not without Denarra, anyway.

The peacocks cried out in the garden, their shrill voices so very different from the beauty of their proud tail fans, and Quill's knees buckled beneath her. She fell to the cold tiles and watched the birds slip in and out of the garden shadows, their sapphire and emerald plumage shimmering, ghostlike, in the moonlight.

Betthia Vald could barely remember when they'd first met. Her few friends could all reminisce in fine detail about when they'd come to know their husbands—first glances exchanged, first furtive kisses, first declarations of love—but Betthia's memories held few tender moments. It had been a mournful loss when she was younger, but after many years of marriage, the lost memories worked well on balance; she'd also forgotten the first tirade, the first bloodied nose, the first broken arm.

She sat at the dressing table in her spare room, a small fire burning in the grate, and carefully ran a brush through her greying hair. The rooms on this side of Gorthac Hall were cold, even in a strange hot autumn like this. Many things were strange these days, and they weren't likely to get much better.

The tortoise-shell brush had been a childhood gift from her mother, one of the few things that the emotionally distant Woman had ever given freely. Betthia had been only fifteen when she married Lojar Vald and moved from her beloved seaside home in Chalimor to the wind-weathered butte that crouched over Eromar City. Even now, almost forty years later, she sometimes awoke to the smell of salt water on the breeze, and the shrill call of gulls ringing in the air. Even now she wept at the loss.

Her pale green eyes took a survey of the image in the mirror. It had been a long time since she'd been young. Though she doubted she was ever truly beautiful, whatever beauty she'd once possessed had long since been worn away by life in Gorthac Hall. Other Women many years her senior were radiant in comparison.

Betthia's face was thin and drawn, her long nose bent at the bridge from being broken numerous times over the years. Her hair was brittle and growing thinner with every year, even drawing away from her forehead a bit. It was one of many gradual changes she'd noticed and accepted with stoic disinterest, including the slightly yellow pallor creeping into and hardening her flesh. Betthia suspected that the constant pains in her back and the irregular bleeding from below had something to do with these changes in her skin, but the alchaemists and surgeons insisted that it was a natural consequence of age among the aristocracy. They suggested less sun and more face powder. And she obeyed them, growing weaker every year, becoming a living ghost that even her own children could hardly bear to visit. «The doctors and your father insist,» she'd say to them, and the matter would be dropped, for a while, anyway. She'd long ago given up arguing with Men, even though she knew full well that they were killing her.

Betthia had no doubt that she was dying. The possibility secretly thrilled her. She wasn't strong enough to die on her own; if she'd ever had that strength, she would have killed herself the night her father dragged her screaming from her bedroom and into the wedding coach. She knew then that she'd never see the ocean again, and her long, slow soul-death started that night. No, she couldn't kill herself, not that day nor on any one of a thousand days and nights of humiliation, pain, and fear. It was her lot in life. She was a Woman, and there was little hope in the world of Men for such as her.

She pulled the brush through her hair again, repeating the movement with practiced ease. There had been a time when this evening ritual would bring a certain lustre to her hair, a slight, soft beauty of which she'd been uncharacteristically proud. Now, though, her brush came away with more hair than ever before, and those once-thick tresses were growing sparser. It didn't matter. The brushing hour was one of the few unchanging routines in her life these days, a time when she was left to her own thoughts and image in the mirror. It was *her* room, *her* time, and she hoarded it with miserly insistence.

She didn't know when she'd started talking to that image in the mirror, but she was glad to have the company. Strangely, though, she'd never thought to name her mirror-self. It wasn't so much that the figure was a distinctive personality as it was just nice to have someone to talk to again. It was the only company that never demanded anything from Betthia; the mirror-self only gave, never took, and she was always welcome.

«He visited me tonight, like I told you he would.»

«I know,» her mirror-self answered as she brushed her own fragile hair on the other side of the glass. «I saw him come in. He looked…different tonight.»

«Yes, I suppose he did.» She pulled a few loose strands away from her face. They fluttered to the threadbare rug beneath her.

«What did he want?»

Betthia sighed. «He came to say goodbye.»

Her mirror-self stopped brushing and looked at her. «So he's really going through with this? Did you try to stop him?»

She laughed then, a harsh, awkward sound from a mouth unused to such expressions. «I long ago gave up any hope of changing Lojar's mind on anything. Once he's set his thoughts toward something, he follows the swiftest path to its end. He's leaving tonight. There's nothing I can do.»

«I see,» her mirror-self said, then shrugged. «If all goes as planned, he won't be returning, will he?»

«No. Nor will he return if things go poorly.»

«Do you have any idea what will happen?»

Betthia turned her head sideways and stroked the brush downward; the image in the glass did the same. «It's difficult to tell. If the Dreyd prophecies are correct, he should ascend after the power is released. If they're wrong, well, he's prepared for that, too.»

«I see.» The mirror-Betthia lifted her head and turned it the other way.

«He thinks it should happen quickly, if the Seekers have gathered enough fuel for the transformation, and if there are enough Binders for the transfer. He's lost a few of both, but he insists there will be enough in time for his passage through the Veil.»

«It seems like there's a good chance of problems, don't you think?»

Betthia's expression was more a grimace than a smile. «Oh, yes— this won't be easy. It's quite likely that he'll unleash something that he can't control. It happened before, you know.»

«The Melding. But that worked, didn't it?»

«It did, but it was a close thing at the end. There were many Dreyd in those days; they were committed to the task, and they helped each other.»

Her mirror-self smiled too. «Lojar is at a disadvantage there. He doesn't have many friends these days.»

«No.» Betthia's strange smile faded. «But if anyone can succeed in solitude, it's him. He's put this much in motion already, and no single Man has ever accomplished that much before. The High Hall at Bashonak has sent all its Binders to help; they don't realize they'll all be consumed, of course, but I suppose it's all for the good of the Dreyd.»

«If he has the Binders, what's left?»

«Fuel. He thought that the witch-raids would provide enough, but they were weaker than he'd expected, and the iron shackles cut off some of their strength. So his soldiers are bringing a horde of them in a few different groups to the site. He says there are some strong ones in the last nasty bunch. They should give him more than enough fuel now.»

They sat together for a while, brushing their hair in silence. Finally, her mirror-self said, «Will you miss him?»

Betthia stared intently at the mirror. «What?»

«Will you miss him? He's your husband, after all.»

The Woman shrugged. «I don't know. I've never thought that far ahead. I might, I suppose.»

«Do you think he'll miss you?»

A soft sigh slid from Betthia's lips. «Yes, I think he will.»

Her mirror-self looked at her dubiously, but Betthia continued. «He visited me tonight, just after dinner. I didn't expect him to say goodbye, but there he was, tall and dark and grim, as always. Then, before I knew what he was doing, he reached out and touched my cheek, but kindly. He had an odd look on his face, like he'd only just seen me for the first time and…and he was pleased with what he saw. He was gentle. It…was the first time I'd ever seen anything like love in his eyes.»

The face in the mirror seemed to grow soft and misty, as though looking through a fog. «What did he say?»

Betthia placed the brush on the dressing table and stared off into the looking-glass, past her misty twin, into memory. «Nothing. He didn't say anything. He just touched my face and looked at me, then turned around and left, closing the door behind him.»

She looked up, but her mirror-self had grown silent. The fire in the grate had burned itself out, and a deep chill had crept into the room. She stood, stoked the fire, and rang for an attendant to build it up again. Her body trembled violently from the cold, so she reached to the back of her chair for her shawl. Pulling it away, she noticed something wet on the end nearest the seat of the chair. Lifting it into the light, she saw that it was her own blood.

Betthia looked down at the pool of crimson spreading beneath the seat. Her legs sagged slightly, but she shook her head in annoyance. The attendant would come, then the doctors, then the leeches, then her devoted but incessantly mewling children. And she'd survive this yet again, most likely to witness the results of her husband's success.

But then, if she lived that long, she likely wouldn't live much longer—very few would, especially this close to the site of the ritual. Lojar Vald was a Man of no small ambition. He would show himself worthy to rise to the ranks of the Dreyd, and in doing so would unleash a power like nothing the world had known for a thousand years of Men.

And in the second Melding, Lojar Vald would be among the supreme.

Betthia sighed and returned to her dressing table. Her hair was askew again. Picking up the brush, she began the long, delicate process again, hoping to finish by the time the attendant arrived.

After that…well, after that, it wouldn't much matter.

"All right, Denarra, I want to know what's going on. Who in this Melded world *are* you? How do you have a house like this, with all this finery and these house servants?"

Quill stood defiantly before the Strangeling with her arms crossed and lips tightly pursed. She'd had enough of hints and secrets. Her whole life teetered on the edge of a vast abyss, and she was on the edge of losing everything that she cared about and believed in. She had to stand firm, and it would happen now.

"I've been a good friend to you, Denarra, and you've been like a sister to me, but I can't stand by your side if you're going to keep things from me. I've got to know that I can trust you."

"Now, wait a moment," sputtered Padwacket, his big ears quivering angrily. He sat beside the sorceress, holding a cold steak to the swelling knot on his head from Meggie's wooden-heeled shoe. "She's only saved your life a half-dozen times. She's only put herself in mortal danger every time, and given her home and hard-earned—"

Quill held up a hand, silencing him. "I wasn't talking with you, Padwacket—I'm talking to Denarra. It's as simple as this: either you tell me who you are and give me a reason to trust you again, or I'm leaving and doing whatever I can on my own. I need your help, but not at the cost of everything and everyone I love." Thoughts of Tobhi strengthened her resolve. "I want to know. Now."

Padwacket opened his mouth again, but Denarra shook her head wearily. "No, darling, she's right. Thank you for your valiant defence, but she's right. She deserves to know what's going on. Please, leave us alone for a while." The Ubbetuk reluctantly departed, and the Strangeling turned to Quill, who still stood glaring. "I know you're angry, and I don't blame you. But you really must know that I never lied to you, not fully, anyway. There are just some things that I didn't think you needed to know."

"That kind of secret is still a lie. It hides your heart from the people who deserve to know it."

"Very well," Denarra nodded in surrender. "If you must know, I'm not really a legitimate participant in the world of theatre, although my heart certainly pulls in that direction."

Quill raised an eyebrow. "I pretty well figured that out by myself."

The Strangeling sighed. "In fact, I'm really not associated with *any* legitimate organizations. In fact, you might say that my true associations are likely as *illegitimate* as they come."

"And those would be...?"

Meggie poked her head into the room, her brow furrowed in annoyance. "Oh, for goodness sake, Denarra, enough of this childish dance. Just tell her that you're the most notorious smuggler and pleasure-broker in Chalimor and get it over with. And *you*," she turned and hissed with a quick, withering glance back down the hall, "don't think I don't see you sneaking away. As soon as that swelling's gone down, you're to get yourself down to the scrub-tub and *clean those drapes!*"

As Meggie stomped away after Padwacket, Denarra shrugged. "It's true, Quill. My true calling rests in the procurement of pleasurable entertainments and rare items of fine quality, which I provide to an interested clientele at a significant profit to myself and my employees."

"You mean, you're a…you're…?" Quill didn't know quite how to phrase the question. She'd heard of such things before, but only rumours and hints. *Firra* weren't prudish about their bodies, but they reserved such pleasures for those with whom they shared an abiding emotional connection. Joinings for other reasons were alien to Tetawi ways.

"If you like, you can call me a 'bringer of happiness.' I give pleasure, and I receive pleasure. Whether it involves a visit to the home of one of Chalimor's First Families on Rosewood Hill, where I might have a perfectly lovely evening with a lonely merchant, or simply bringing a rare, blood-heating, and legally inaccessible spice to a customer in the Brownbrick District, I give joy to those denied it by convention or circumstance. I don't harm anyone, and I don't allow anyone to harm me. It's that simple."

The Dolltender sat down. "Have you always been a…'bringer of happiness'?"

"No," Denarra replied with a shrug. "Actually, I was once a rather unremarkable student at the Learnèd Academy just up Assembly Height. There was a movement among Humans at the time to rescue poor, downtrodden Folk from our 'barbaric' lives, and I was rather ambitious to see what excitement could be found in the rest of the world, so I ended up here in Chalimor. Thanks to a *very* earnest group of bored society wives and their brow-beaten husbands—they call themselves the 'Friends of the Folk,' though in truth they're anything but—a small group of us, all Kyn-born or Kyn-sired, were brought to the city and paraded around like well-dressed lap dogs, poised and polished to demonstrate how virtuous and self-sacrificing our sponsors were." The bitter edge of resentment slid into her voice. "And I loved every moment of it. As long as I was an obedient pet—adored by the sages, attending lectures at the Academy every day, memorizing the inane Dreyd creeds and mind-numbing lyric poetry that were so fashionable at the time, and avoiding the slightest whiff of scandal, which wasn't always easy—they patted me on the head and made sure that I had all the pretty dresses and perfumes I wanted."

"What happened?"

The Strangeling chuckled. "I didn't take too well to domestication. Actually, it really wasn't my fault. Some of my friends and I were studying in one of the gardens of the Academy when a group of Human students started harassing us, Men of the most unpleasant sort. Jealousy, bigotry, and fear are a bad combination. I Awakened into my powers that day, and as a result, my friends and I walked away from the garden. Two of those brutes didn't."

She stared out the window. "It didn't matter that we didn't start the fight, or that we were only fighting to defend our lives. All that mattered was the fact that we were Kyn, and that we'd attacked Men. We were expelled from the Academy that day, and we found our few belongings in the street when we returned to our sponsors' home. We heard later that some of the Kyn who hadn't been involved in the fracas still remained in the good graces of the Friends of the Folk, but the three of us had been erased as fully as if we'd never existed. So, being of a theatrical bent and hoping to hide the pain and shame of our situation in frivolity, we took the name of the 'Sisters of Wandering Virtue,' and we learned quite quickly what it took to survive in the shadows beneath the marble grandeur of Chalimor. I found that I had unexpected and not entirely unpleasant talents that were very much in demand among the more discerning sons and daughters of the city; my training in social etiquette turned out to be a quite marketable addition to those other talents. In a relatively short time my friends and I gathered enough money to leave the city and head west, toward Harudin Holt." Her expression was unreadable. "After a few years and numerous adventures I returned alone to Chalimor, one friend dead and the other vanished, and aside from the occasional foray into the larger world, I've been here ever since, honing my skills, learning a thing or two about the nature of Humanity, and ensuring that I will never again need fear the leash and collar. I'm no Man's pet, not anymore. I'm free to choose or refuse, and I take pleasure where I find it."

"But why were you with Bremen and Crowe's Medicine Show?"

Denarra smiled. She was pale after the story, but calm. "Darling, a vocation like mine doesn't limit me to one place. I'd been visiting some business associates in Iradîl, to the south of the Allied Wilderlands, where I hoped to pick up some new…accessories that one of my clients was eager to experience. Because of a brief but rather unpleasant misunderstanding with the High Jurist of the city, I was unable to make it to my ship before it was scheduled to leave, so I was forced to find another way home. As there'd been a somewhat similar misunderstanding in Chalimor before I left, I decided that discretion was wiser than haste, so I continued on with the troupe for quite a few months, and that was when we encountered you. Complicated, as I said, but completely true." She gazed earnestly into Quill's face. "I promise—no more secrets, ever again."

They sat in tense silence for a long while. At last, Denarra reached out. "Quill? Are we…?"

The Tetawa stood again. "I don't know. I'm still trying to understand what's happening, and there's still a lot to decide." She walked to the door, but stopped before leaving the room. "Thank you for finally telling me. I'll see you in the morning."

Denarra was still sitting in her chair when Padwacket returned a while later. He pulled a footstool beside her seat, and together they stared through the window at the city shining in the darkness beyond.

CHAPTER 4

LAMENTATION

The Everland is gone. Forests burn in the rising ash, and the People bleed and die under crumbling branches and the choking sky. Birds can't flee this devastation; not even the burrowing creatures find safety in the damp, dark earth. There is no escape. The Everland is gone.

I rush into the raging waters as the Tree cracks apart, the sound like screaming thunder in my ears. I'm blind to the chaos, to the screams of the dying and the wounded. I'm deaf to the fear that surrounds me, to Tobhi's cry as he's swept away into the mass of fleeing Shields who rush in panic from the cavernous great chamber of the Tree. Even the falling stars and trembling earth fail to give me pause. I plunge under the boiling waves and flail for a moment, and then I see the bent shape bobbing in the water and swim desperately forward. I'm sobbing now, barely able to breathe from the aching emptiness in my chest, but I wrap an arm around Unahi's limp body and cling to it. I can't look at her face; her eyes are wide open and empty, staring at the falling sky.

Why am I so devastated? In truth, I barely knew her. But she was kind to me, and the closest thing to a mother than I've ever known. I want more time—to know her, to know who my own mother was, and to know myself. What will happen to me now that she's gone? There's so much I still have to learn. I try to shout, but my voice is lost in the howling wind, and when I pull Unahi's head back away from the water, my hand jerks away from the massive wound in the back of her skull. But I keep chanting the words; I can't do anything else. I can't let her go, not yet.

I turn to swim to the bank, but the waves are too high, and I can't see anything but the blood-red water under an endless black sky. The water seems to thrash in its own death throes. I gasp and choke as I'm drawn under the waves. Unahi begins to slip out of my grasp until rage fills my flailing limbs and I push myself upward to clutch her body. We surface again, together now, and I weep in pain and frustration. There's nothing too see but boiling waves, and I'm growing weaker. The exhaustion hits me hard, and I sink again. Now my own wounds begin to burn in the smoking water. The shore, like the rest of the world, is gone. I am alone.

"Look to your roots." It's Unahi's voice, but only in memory. There's no chance visitation, no last-moment-before-death resolution. Unahi died before striking the water, and it's only her body now that I hold— the spirit has fled away on soft wings in shadow. But even remembered words give strength, and I feel a light tug at my thoughts, the swiftly-fading tingle of familiarity in my blood. The wyr *is calling to me.*

The waves roll over me again, and I know now that I have to make a choice. Death and destruction rage everywhere. I scream beneath the surge, lungs burning, but my strength is seeping away with every passing moment, and the water smashes me with growing fury. I'll only have this one chance. If I wait, I'll die, and with me all my auntie's dreams.

I make the choice, and Unahi's body vanishes into the flood.

The Wielder awoke crying. A cold wind blew across the prairie, and it chilled her. The others slept in twos and threes throughout the camp, except for Tobhi, who lay curled soundly in a thick blanket beside the fire, and Daladir, who stood watch at the flames. The he-Kyn caught her gaze and nodded. He'd heard her. It wasn't unusual; her nights were filled with this dream and others, many far worse, and she often called out in her sleep. Most of the others seemed used to the late-night disturbances by now. Few of them were silent in the darkness, as they'd all witnessed too much horror to find peace in the Dreaming World, but Daladir was always awake to greet her. He never asked about the dreams, and she never offered any explanation for her cries, but she was glad that she didn't have to spend these times between the dreaming and waking worlds alone. She pulled her blanket around her shoulders, trying to regain some of her lost warmth, and sat beside him on the grass.

"Don't you ever sleep?" she whispered, trying to avoid waking Tobhi, who snored softly on the ground beside the he-Kyn.

Ignoring her question, Daladir looked down and smiled. "You don't have to whisper—I tripped over him a while ago and he didn't even move. I think this is the first real sleep he's had since...." His words trailed off, and he turned his gaze to the western horizon.

Dawn was still a long time away, but the nearly full moon gave the prairies a soft blue glow. It was difficult to imagine that these gentle grasslands were the site of so much pain and suffering. But the evidence cut through the land like a silver scar this night, and the Darkening Road would continue for many days to come. Both Kyn turned away from the sight. They would see enough of it come morning.

"You're going to need some rest," Tarsa persisted. "Everyone is more than willing to take watch for a while; you don't need to do it every night."

He shrugged. "I don't mind. It's hard to sleep these days, anyway."

She looked at him. The struggles of the last few months had changed the he-Kyn. There was still a gentleness in his eyes when he looked at her, but his face was harder now, made haggard by more than exhaustion. It was more than the burning sun and wind. They'd all seen so much suffering and pain, and the experiences had made them all different, but Daladir had seen more than the others. After months of Vald's manipulations at Gorthac Hall, the he-Kyn had grown painfully used to the cruelty of Men, so none of this was a surprise. Now there was something brittle about him now. His unyielding strength would shatter under its own force. He might walk to the Road's end and fight the enemies of the Folk every step of the journey, but he was wounded in a way that Tarsa didn't understand.

The thought alarmed her. She was comfortable with him; he didn't look at her with the same awe and fear that everyone but Tobhi and Jitani shared. She wasn't some strange creature out of old stories to these three kind friends. She was just Tarsa, not the unpredictable salvation of the Folk.

She reached out and touched his hand. He was cold. "You don't have to carry this burden alone, Daladir. I can bring you a healing, if you'll let me." The familiar green flames flickered down her arm toward her fingers.

He pulled his hand away. "No." Seeing the sudden flash of pain on her face, he smiled and slid closer to her. "Don't misunderstand. It's not that I don't trust you, because I do. And it's not that I don't want to know what all these others have felt, Tarsa, because I do, desperately. But we don't know how much of this strength you have left, and we don't know how much we're going to need in the days ahead. There are so many others who are going to need your help; I'll be fine. I promise."

Although the lie was transparent to them both, Tarsa let it go, and the green glow faded. The main thing keeping Daladir going these days was pride; she had no intention of denying him that. She took a small stick and absently stirred the coals for a while, then wrapped her blanket around her shoulders and moved back toward the soft, grassy hollow where she'd rested before. Daladir watched the Wielder nestle into a ball for warmth and slowly fall asleep again. He watched over her until dawn.

"What's a body to eat around here?" Tobhi chirped to Jitani as he drew his fingers through his sleep-tangled hair.

"Nothing different than yesterday," growled the golden-eyed she-Kyn, her eyes darting over to Tarsa, who sat with Daladir a short distance from the remains of the campfire. "And nothing different from what you'll eat tomorrow." She handed the Tetawa a crumbling biscuit and a couple strips of dried meat of unknown origin. Tobhi studiously avoided looking at the withered stumps of her wounded sensory stalks.

"Really, Jitani," a tall, dark-skinned Man named Oryn said in the trade-tongue behind her, "you should try to be a bit more pleasant in the morning. Your sour face is giving me a stomachache." He laughed and reached over to grab another chunk of meat, but the she-Kyn dodged his hand and grinned.

"I doubt your burbling belly has anything to do with me, fat one. Maybe you've forgotten again that you're not supposed to eat the hide with the meat." The others laughed as the Man roared in mock anger and chased her around the camp. Tobhi joined the revelry, even while sneaking a glance to Tarsa, who was regarding the western horizon with concern. He briefly considered going to her, but the freedom of the moment was too irresistible. He'd have to face the grim journey soon enough as it was. Right now all he wanted to do was enjoy himself and forget for a little while the terrible times that were still so close.

Oryn stopped, wiping the sweat from his face. "Would you deny a starving Man a bit of sustenance?" he intoned with dramatic flair. Tobhi laughed again. Although not exactly fat, Oryn of Deldmaar was gifted with a seemingly equal share of firm muscle and ample stomach. He also possessed an endless good humour that served him well in the strains of these times.

At first the Tetawa had been shocked to see Men and Women among the warriors, but Daladir assured the Tetawa that these Humans were firm allies. Some had lived peacefully among Folk for years and had joined the others to help rescue their Folk friends and families; others had watched the horrors of the Expulsion and fought in righteous indignation. It was sometimes still hard for Tobhi to look at the Humans and not be filled with bitterness, but at those times he'd think of Tarsa and all that she'd lost since leaving Red Cedar Town. If she could see past her pain and anger, he could do no less.

There were about thirty others in the group, mostly Kyn, with two

Tetawi brothers, a she-Feral with cloven hooves and two horns that curled impressively behind her pointed ears, six Men and two Women, three Ubbetuk, and a handful of the Strangeling Jaaga-Folk, who travelled these grasslands in long caravans of canvas-covered wagons and followed great herds of antelope, bison, and prairie deer in the summer months. The travellers had a few horses and ponies to carry supplies, but not enough for everyone to ride, so they remained on foot and pushed themselves to cover as much ground as possible each day without being spotted by the main company they followed. They'd escaped detection thus far; it would be disastrous to reveal themselves too soon and to risk more deaths among the exiles.

The thought of detection brought another, more disturbing fear to his mind. Tobhi looked up at Jitani. "What about them bandits? En't ye worried that they'll come up after us?"

Jitani's smile sent a chill through his blood. "Not unless they can do it without their heads." The others around them shared a harsh laugh. "They're dead, Tetawa. We took care of them a couple of days back, the day before we found you."

"There were no survivors, Tobhi," Tarsa said as she walked back to the group. "We couldn't risk them raising up an alarm in the settlements behind us. We've got enough to worry about already." The conversation faded at the Wielder's presence, but she didn't seem to notice. If she did, she didn't betray any discomfort. Among the exiles, only Jitani and Daladir seemed unfazed by her arrival. Indeed, Tobhi noticed with awkward surprise, they both had a similar soft warmth in their eyes when they looked at her.

This was certainly unexpected.

His thoughts returned to the perils of their situation as Tarsa went on. "We've been talking with our Jaaga friends and looking at the maps we were able to salvage from Sheynadwiin. It's another two days to the Shard Ford. They'll be stopped for a few days there, because it'll take a while to get so many of our people into the barges and across the gap into Dûrûk and the Pit Fields. We should be able to strike the boats first; the militia won't be expecting trouble now, not after avoiding it for so long. If we can stop them before they get anyone on the barges, we'll avoid being separated, and they'll be without transportation across the Riven Sea. We won't have another opportunity like this."

"How do you suggest we handle things when we get there?" one of the Women asked. Her hair was shorn down to the scalp, and she wore a heavy wool cloak over her body, as though hiding herself from the world beneath its folds. But the clatter of metal beneath the fabric hinted at dangers unseen from outside. Tobhi noticed that the earlier sense of frivolity among the company had vanished, and deadly purpose now took its place.

"Men are creatures of habit. The Jaaga scouts have confirmed this," Daladir said. "Vald's soldiers have followed the same procedure each night: three guards for every twenty prisoners, with replacements coming at midnight. That makes about one hundred and twenty guards on duty at any one time, with just as many in reserve."

One of the Tetawi brothers snorted. "You don't expect the thirty of us to take on eight times our number, do you? You forget, they've got muskets and cold iron—our knives and bows and spears won't do much against those weapons."

"Those weapons are nothing against the arsenal we've got," Jitani said, and she drew a weapon from the sheath at her side. Tobhi's eyes widened: it was a wyrwood sword, crafted from a single strong piece of an ancient tree's heartwood, burned with the shaping powers of the *wyr*. Its edge was as sharp and strong as any piece of metal. Jitani spun the sword in a dangerous arc, and the Tetawa understood immediately that the she-Kyn and her weapon had a long, deadly history together.

Tarsa looked at the top of her own wyrwood staff and the piece of amber glowing there, gold in the light of the early dawn. "Yes, our weapons will match anything the Men of Eromar have, but if we're smart and lucky, we won't have to use them. We can't risk a direct assault yet;

our people are too weak to fight, and the threat to them is too great. Chaos will follow the destruction of the boats, and it's that chaos that will be our greatest ally—that, and the Jaaga-folk, who are tired of Men crossing their lands, disrupting their hunts, and stealing their herds. They'll help us afterward, but the barges will be our responsibility."

"I don't understand," the cloaked Woman said. "What happens after we've destroyed the boats? The Folk are sick and exhausted; they won't be able to help us much."

"Don't you bet on it," said Tobhi, crossing his arms proudly. "They's plenty of fire left in the Folk. Ye just give 'em some good reason for hope, and ye'll see how much help they'll give ye."

Oryn eyed the Leafspeaker critically. "I'm with Eladrys on this. No matter how defiant they are, they're still weak and underfed. The soldiers will be rested and fit, not to mention fully armed, with many on horseback. Without good weapons, the Folk would be in a bad way, even in their best health. As they are, they're not going to be much help to us. We can't just wait for them to get stronger."

"You're right," Daladir interjected. "We can't wait. But we don't have to." He looked at Tarsa. "It's time for the Wielder to share her power with the People."

The wyr pulls me through the thrashing waves. The world isn't falling down around me anymore. I'm joined with the thunder, a daughter of the storm. It rages in my blood like a war-chant lifted high. My voice is the wind, my tears the sea, my flesh the stars and stones. Spirits of this world and those beyond join the song. The words are unfamiliar, but I know them and I know the rhythm, if not the meaning. I've sung them before, when I first Awakened to the wyr, when I lost my youngling name and came into the name that has shaped my life: Tarsa'deshae—She-Breaks-the-Spear. Now the fear is gone. I still don't understand this dangerous gift, but it's no longer a stranger. I belong to the wyr. The Deep Green courses through my veins, and with it the memories, dreams, and voices of a thousand generations.

My grief for Unahi mingles with that of all those who are dying, who have died before. There is life here, but pain, too, and it's almost more than I can bear. But they belong together in the Deep Green, life and death, joy and pain, the earth and the underworld and the sky. Balance in all things. It's a hard lesson, sometimes. Sometimes, it's the only lesson that endures.

Waves crash over my head, and still I fight forward. My body is dying, but the knowledge brings no grief. All I want to do is reach the shattered Tree before my body fades and my spirit joins the exodus of dark-eyed owls. If I can have that moment of connection, at least, I'll be content.

A shape rises up out of the water, and grief rises up with it as the shattered silver skeleton of the Eternity Tree appears through the crimson flood. The branches are bare; the leaves have all been stripped away by the ferocity of the storm. It is split through the middle, as though hands of lightning have torn it wide from crown to roots. But this wound comes from within. The Tree withstood ages of fire, storm, and drought. It weathered the catastrophe of the Melding, and the years of chaos that followed. Even the Purging of the earth-born Wielders by the sky-blinded Shields didn't dim the Tree's brilliance. But blood in the water, the blood of the Folk, shed in the sacred waters of the Eternity Tree by one of their own—the Tree couldn't survive this violation of the ancient covenant between the People and the land. It is this blood of treachery that threatens to drown me.

The wyr pulls at me still, but its strength is fading. The surge of the bloodsong has diminished, and I can hear the screaming storm lift above the spirit-voices in the brutal rush of wind and water. My own weakness is nothing compared to this slow, mournful bleeding away. I can't bear the knowledge of such loss. It's more than death. It is erasure from the very memory of the world.

"Unahi, help me," I whisper through the salty liquid on my lips.

"Mother. Tobhi. Daladir. Jitani. Biggiabba. Garyn. Averyn. Sinovian. Geth. Spirits of skyfire and earth, of all the worlds we call home. Zhaia, Green Mother, help me. Mothers of old, give me strength. I can't do it on my own."

I sink beneath the waves again, and this time I don't surface, but still I keep whispering, even as red water fills my mouth and the Tree fades into darkness. I'm on the edge of oblivion. It is silent.

No, not quite silent. I look down; a shape is swimming up through the red water toward me, his voice raised in familiar song. I remember him well. Wyrwood spikes still pierce his body, and his yellow eyes narrow in exultation as he approaches. The monster Wears-Stones-For-Skin swims with a speed and grace he never possessed in life. As if to prove it, he spins in an upward arc and laughs through the song, teasing me, his voice bubbling up and surrounding me.

He reaches out with a gnarled grey hand and I pull away, but he keeps singing, and the fire rises in my blood. In life he was one of the Eaters of Old, and he's still dangerous in the Spirit World, but not to me, not now. His blood is my own. The song endures from the ancient days through the lives and deaths of those who hear it, and I'm just one more thread in a woven cord that travels through the Deep Green to the first days of the People. It will endure long after my own flesh has joined the rich soil and stars, but only if I survive now. If I'm lost in this place, I'll be lost forever. That's why he's returned. He's come to keep me a part of the wyr-woven pattern. I'm no more special than all those who came before and those who'll come again after me, but each is needed in its time and place for the pattern to endure. And my time is now.

The bloodsong burns in my ears, and I reach out. His touch is surprisingly gentle; the pebbled flesh of his palm is worn smooth and soft. He grins again and sweeps me upward, moving like a heron toward the surface. The water parts and I'm alone and gasping for breath amidst the great roots of the Tree. I look up at the devastation. The silver glow *is fading. Scales of shimmering bark rain down into the water, and the branches quiver in the shrieking winds. Lightning dances through the sky, but I can see without it, for a deep blue-green glow shines from the shattered trunk, and it calls to me.*

I slip back into the water; the wood is slick. Then I remember the knife Jitani gave me. It's still in its sheath at my side. As I start to slip toward the beckoning waves, I draw the knife and stab it into the wood, and it slides easily, locking in, giving me something to hold. I slowly pull myself up, exhaustion finally catching me, and look down through the broken wood of the trunk into endlessness. Dizziness takes me, and I begin to drift away. My hands flail out for balance and take hold of something unexpected, and then I feel a sudden surge of strength as the Heartwood of the Eternity Tree bursts into emerald flame and envelops my body, binding me to the pulsing heart of the Everland. My chanting sash unravels and falls away; it's kept my mind and spirit whole, safe from being overwhelmed by the wyr, but I don't need it any more.

The Tree lives again.

Dark clouds finally moved in to ease the afternoon heat, but Tarsa felt little comfort. The fickle sky was a constant reminder of the strange and sudden shifts in weather that plagued these lands and made their journey increasingly difficult. Two full days of hard travel through biting cold nights and brutally hot days had brought them to this place, and yet, for all their cautious speed, they were too late: the Folk were already starting across the ford in barges. The Wielder stood in shadow on a small wooded rise overlooking the ramshackle settlement of Kateline Crossing, where hundreds of bent figures stood at the water's edge. A rough collection of haphazard shacks and unkempt stables, the Crossing served a single purpose: to provide basic trade goods at excessive prices to travellers preparing to cross Shard Ford into the broken lands of Dûrûk beyond. The Jaaga-people had long chafed under the traders' ruthlessness, watching as the Men of the Crossing grew increasingly fat from the hard-earned pelts that the Jaagas brought in trade. The place wasn't likely to be any more hospitable to the Everland exiles.

Two barges, each loaded with Human militiamen and far too many Folk, moved with ponderous slowness across the unsteady water. Unlike rope-drawn ferries on some of the smaller rivers they'd travelled, these barges were propelled by coal-fired Ubbetuk steam-engines and paddle-wheels that vomited out great clouds of sparks and black smoke. Even from this distance Tarsa could feel the sweep of iron sickness move off the water. It was little wonder that the Folk below huddled on the shore in quiet, unresisting misery; the barges would no doubt be the final journey for the weaker wayfarers.

"Something terrible is driving them on," Jitani hissed, rage and growing fear mingled in her voice.

Tarsa didn't need to respond. They could all feel the desperation that pushed the Men forward through the days and nights, with little more than survival sleep for the past few days, and now pushed them mercilessly forward into storm-savaged waters. Whatever compelled them was worse than the death and misery that surrounded them. More of the Folk were dying each day on the Road now than had died in a full week before. Where Tarsa and her allies once had time to honour the dead as they walked past in pursuit of the other exiles, they could now only move on and try to ignore the hunger-ravished bodies with their sightless eyes and puckering skin scattered everywhere along the Road. A few members of the group had, like Tobhi, been rescued after being abandoned by the Eromar soldiers, but there were no more survivors these days.

Tobhi lifted the brim of his hat and wiped the sweat from his forehead. "What d'ye suggest we do now? There en't much use in stoppin' those boats, since they already got half the Folk on the water. If we move in now, we'll only be trappin' them on the other side."

A crack of thunder rolled across the sky to signal the arrival of a sudden cold rain. It drove the warmth from the body, but at least it hid them from view, and for that Tarsa was thankful; surprise was their only real advantage now. Even so, it wasn't much.

The winds grew wilder with the rain. Most of the others moved back into the trees for cover, but the Wielder remained just on the edge of the thicket and watched as one of the barges moved ponderously away from the dock and into the grey waters. It wasn't as big a boat as she'd expected; indeed, it looked far too small for the number of Folk crammed onto it. Where once the barge had carried hundreds of cows, pigs, sheep, and other livestock across the Riven Sea, it strained now under a different burden.

Tarsa's cloak slipped away in the wind, but her attention was fixed too closely on the sea below to notice. Something was wrong. She couldn't see very well through the heavy rain and blinding lightning, but the boat was moving strangely sideways, the waves dragging one side downward. Another burst of jagged skyfire tore through the growing darkness, and she saw it clearly: the barge was sinking.

One side of the boat tipped dangerously, and although the Folk rushed frantically toward the other edge, their desperation and panic simply caused the ship to shift more precariously into the water. Screams of horror rose up from the Folk gathered at the shore in response to the cries from the boat. Bodies fell into the raging surge, and for a moment it looked like the barge would right itself. It hung on the edge, quivering, as dozens of Folk clung to ropes, wood, and each other to keep from being lost in the ravenous waves, their voices a unified wail. But then a deep, piercing groan split the stormy air, and the barge split apart under the rushing weight of the water. It was gone in mere heartbeats, a few last clouds of black smoke and steam snaking upward through the rain, and with it went the Folk, many still holding tight to one another as they slipped beneath the swell and died.

The Wielder raised her hands to the sky and called out to the *wyr*, to stop the storm and calm the waters, but the sudden deaths of so many Folk rushed over her, and she stumbled back with a primal scream that shook the hill. She could feel them dying even as she reached out, and now that the gate was open, she couldn't shut it. Each death was like a physical blow, and she thrashed wildly under the overwhelming assault.

Through the searing torment she now understood her terrible danger. True, the Heartwood had made her strong. The elements brought little pain, and she could withstand hunger and thirst like no other mortal. She could change the course of rivers, call down storms, and heal the hurt and dying, all without fear of harming the spirits who rushed to her call. But she was terribly vulnerable, now more than ever before.

Except for the few healing sparks of the Heartwood she'd shared with her companions, the essence of the Tree was now woven into her own. She and the Tree were one. And as the Tree connected the spirits of the living and the dead to the remnant shards of the Eld Green from which all the Folk had emerged, so now did she, and her fragile flesh couldn't bear the burden.

She fell back again, clutching at her head. Voices filled her mind. She saw their faces, but they were shifting, changing, and then the world became blood and white feathers as the owls dove toward her through a red-black sky, their dark eyes glowing. Screams of the dying became rasping shrieks in the night. Her blood boiled. The spirits were talking to her, desperate to tell her something, but she couldn't make out the words.

A burning pain spread across her forehead, and the red fog began to lift slightly as she saw her own blood trickle to the waterlogged soil. She was on the ground, her head against a large rock, as the faces of her companions faded in and out of view. They were with her, but they were muddled and indistinct among the owls that still hissed and screamed out to her. She tried to understand, but it was too much, and she shook her head, trying to push them away. "Not yet," she groaned to the voices. "Not yet."

The red curtain dropped again, and soon another face moved into view, different from the others. He was clear and distinct, and the owls flapped silently away from the small darting shapes that surrounded him. Tarsa held out her hand and watched with delight as a large blue dragonfly landed on the edge of her finger, its translucent wings shining like diamonds in the strange light. Soon the air was filled with streaks of gold and ruby and emerald and sapphire, and the Wielder laughed.

"Ev'rybody wants to tell their story, Tarsa. Remember ol' Akjaadit, the first Dragonfly, and her meeting with Strivix the Owl? Sometimes we don't know the story afore we tell it, but it gives us strength anyhow. And sometimes we can't hear nobody's story 'cause we're so wrapped up in our own. Ye got to give their stories some room afore you'll understand 'em. 'Til then, ye got a lot of work to do." The mist-formed image of Tobhi smiled again, and then faded into darkness. But the dragonflies remained to keep the owls away until the world became rain and earth again and the vision disappeared. Tarsa lay huddled in Jitani's strong arms as Daladir wiped mud and dead grass away from her face. A very real Tobhi knelt on the ground beside them, his face dark with worry.

Tarsa breathed in deeply and turned to her friends, her bruised face firm with resolve. "Hurry," she gasped as she reached out for the wyr-wood staff and her travel pack. "This is our chance. We won't have another."

I don't know how long I've been unconscious, but when I open my eyes I see Daladir beside me. His face is covered with soot and dried blood, but it doesn't seem to be his own. The deep shadows under his eyes seem to lift, and he lifts my head to a clay jar and gives me a drink of cold water. The liquid has a bitter bite to it, but it's clean, and it eases my terrible thirst.

I want to talk, to know what's happened, to find out if the destruction of the Tree is real, but it's safe here by his side, and I don't want to hear what my heart tells me is undeniable. Unahi is dead. Sheynadwiin has fallen. Men have taken the Everland.

My eyes wander upward. We're in a cave, but it's not the massive gallery of the Eternity Tree. It's a rough, soot-stained chamber that smells of sweat and unbathed bodies. The air is thick with smoke; it doesn't seem to be coming from this tunnel. The cave is full of Folk huddled together with faces turned toward the entrance.

Daladir's green eyes never leave mine, though, and I'm more grateful than I care to admit. There's comfort in his presence. It's more than just familiarity. The concern on his face speaks to something deeper than simple friendship, and this time it doesn't frighten me. It's all that I want right now.

I finish drinking the water and nestle deeper into his arms. He stiffens for a moment, uncertain, but finally pulls me close and gently strokes the hair away from my face as we lie together and drift to sleep. And although the world we knew is shattered beyond recognition, and although death and pain and terror fill the air as much as the smoke of the burning forests, we sleep peacefully for a while.

High in the air above the Riven Sea, buffeted by vengeful winds and drenched by fierce rains, flew a score of Goblin airships commandeered by Vorgha for the Dreydmaster's final journey. They and their captured crews belonged to Eromar now. Vald was pleased. It was fitting that he arrive at the ritual site in the style and dignity befitting an ascending Dreyd, and even he had to admit that the artistry of the Unhuman Goblins surpassed all others in this regard. His present transport was cunningly shaped like a large scarab, a diplomatic vessel belonging to an enormously fat Goblin matron whose protest against its seizure resulted in chains, imprisonment, and toil in the iron mines of Eromar. When her sons protested, they joined her. There were no further complaints.

The Dreydmaster sat in a deep chair of crushed black velvet in the old matron's observation room and watched the world through a large, cunningly-wrought window that was shaped like an insect's multifaceted eye. He almost regretted not having had such a ship before, but it was too late for such thoughts. He'd have much more remarkable experiences soon enough. For now he was content to listen to the whirring hum of gears and pulsing air bladders rumble through the ship and watch the savage storm from the carpeted splendour of this wood-panelled chamber.

Storms never bothered Vald. Even when he was a child, he had spent hours on his uncle's covered porch and watched with fascination as his dull town became a more interesting world through the haze of falling rain, snow, and hail. He'd always enjoyed the massive spring storms the best, especially those with much lightning, and thunder so loud that the house and smithy rattled from the blast. It always seemed a shame that his uncle never stopped at the forge long enough to enjoy the town's transformation from a grimy little hamlet, with mangy dogs and scabby-kneed children skulking along the streets, into a silver-grey wonderland filled with wondrous strange shapes and unexpected mysteries. But his uncle had no appreciation for a world beyond his nose, and he'd stomp to the porch and box the boy's ears, then drag young Vald back to work among the acrid fumes and sparks of the smithy. But even from the forge the boy could see what he wanted his world to be, and it helped him through the nastiness of the world he was in.

He'd watched hundreds of storms from the tower of Gorthac Hall. After joining the Dreydcaste and advancing up the ranks of the Reavers, he was the source of many of the storms, as he'd found that the Fey-demons of the air responded most powerfully to his commands. He'd order a Binder to draw unseen victims to him, and when the air-demons were firmly trapped within the Binder's chant, Vald would focus his will and begin the slow, delicious process of stripping sparks of life from them, forcing them through his Crafting into eruptions of frenzied pain. They couldn't harm him or escape, but in their desperation to free themselves they created the most fantastic storms in Eromar's history—at least until the stormy night that Tarsa'deshae toppled the tower.

The witch's face was burned into his memory. It wasn't so much that he cared about the tower—it was a trivial matter in comparison with his current goal—but he resented her strength, and the clear knowledge that those air-demons didn't destroy half of Gorthac Hall out of fear or pain, but out of rage. The green-skinned creature didn't force them to do anything; she had awakened them, and they responded out of desire, not hers, but their own. And the power that resulted was unlike anything the Dreydmaster had ever experienced in all his years of endless study and toil as a Reaver. The demons never responded like that to his own pleas, entreaties, or bribes, and although they followed his commands when torture was applied, it had always been a ruthless struggle of wills.

Here he was, undeniably the most powerful Man in the Reach, a political leader whom even the great Reachwarden hesitated to openly challenge, a Dreydmaster who had reached the highest ranks of learning and daring among Men, and yet even he was forced to watch as a snake-headed Unhuman witch commanded powers that were, until now, still far beyond his reach.

In another time it would have been galling beyond tolerance, and he would have sent Seekers and other minions to bring her to him, bound and humiliated, so he could slowly unlock her secrets and show her just how futile it was to defy the iron will of Men. But however appealing such leisurely pursuits might be, they were also a distraction of both time and energy. Why hunt her down when she would be walking right to him? The Not-Ravens had followed her throughout her journey and kept Vald informed of her movements, and although he'd been surprised that she survived the razing of Sheynadwiin, he knew that her eventual fate was just as certain. If anything, her approaching death would be more useful to him than if she'd died before the preparations for the great ritual were finished. Her commitment to her broken and ragged kind was an admirable but predictable weakness. It was a shame that someone so strong would be so unimaginative.

Vald turned to the figure who sat on the long sofa across from him. There were others among the witch's people who were far more interesting, others who knew well the pains and joys of sacrifice. He held up his empty crystal cup, and a trembling Goblin crept out of a corner of the room with a steaming silver decanter.

«Would you care for more moché, Lady Shakar?»

The copper-haired she-Kyn held up her hand and smiled wanly. «No, thank you. I haven't the taste for it, I'm afraid.»

Vald waved the Goblin away and returned his gaze to the window. «An acquired taste, perhaps. It is one of the few vices in which I freely indulge—far less disruptive and far more invigorating than the fermented filth so popular among the Unpurified. My wife prefers hers with cream and honeyed chacatl, but I enjoy the honest bitterness of the undiluted seed. It is too easy to get lost in the weaknesses of the senses, and such a bite keeps one's mind clear and undistracted.»

He took a sip of the black liquid. «You have changed much since last we met; I nearly did not recognize you. I trust, however, that you are still committed to the cause?»

Shakar nodded. Her flowing copper tresses were gone now, cut short to just a few fingers' width past her scalp. Her sensory-stalks were covered by delicate white lace netting that draped down to her shoulders. Each cheek was lined with three bright scars, and her face was harder and slightly gaunt, making her violet eyes seem larger and that much more striking. But it was her robes that had changed the most. Shakar no longer wore the white robes of a Shield; she now wore silken robes of azure and midnight blue. The Kyn colours of mourning.

«If I have changed much, it is because I have lost much, but not because of you, Dreydmaster. Visionaries are often called upon to challenge the world's blindness, even at the cost of comfort and rightful recognition.»

«Yes.» Vald put the cup to his lips again and inhaled the acrid steam. «And your new name?»

«A term of shame among my people.» Her eyes narrowed. «I wear it now as a badge of honour.»

«The nations of Men will look kindly on you, Lady Shakar, even if your own people do not, for it is in the histories of Men that your future is ensured.» Vald set his cup on the table but never took his eyes from the window, through which he scrutinized her using the reflection of the glass. He knew that she was fully aware of his facade of lethargic distraction, but she seemed resigned to let him continue with the masquerade, so he turned his back to her and continued his double gaze: first looking to the storm, then to the she-Kyn's reflection.

At length the Dreydmaster grew tired of the game and motioned for the Goblin to clear the dishes. After the creature left, he turned his attention to Shakar.

«You truly *are* a visionary among your people, my dear Lady, and that is why I am so pleased to have you join me on this journey. You above all creatures understand what it is to sacrifice all that is precious to you for a cause that is even greater still. There are few, Man or Kyn, who can say the same.»

Shakar gave him the hint of a smile, but Vald could see the shadow of doubt in her eyes. «*Sad beast,*» he thought to himself. «*She still stings from their rejection. They are only common animals, and she is so much more than they are now, but she cannot free herself from her roots. No matter how far she travels, no matter how much her people despise her, no matter how honoured she is among Men, she will always be a tainted creature at heart…and she fears this unyielding truth.*»

Vald walked over to Shakar and sat beside her on the couch. He leaned in, his leonine face taut and suddenly hungry. His voice was low, little more than a growl. «The world will soon change, Lawmaker, more than you can imagine. And you have been a part of that. You alone of all your kind have understood the inevitability of the changes that are to come. Although your help was scorned, you alone freed them from blind superstition. But it is not over yet, not quite. There is still much that must be done.»

Shakar's eyes glowed in the bursts of lightning that illuminated the room. It was as if the world outside was on fire. «What would you have me do, Authority?» she whispered.

The Man smiled. «Among the exiles there is one who still holds great power over the backward and superstitious of your kind. She is much loved by the people, and they will no doubt turn to her in their doubt and fear.»

«She is dangerous, then?»

«Dangerous? Yes, she is certainly that. But she is also…useful. The old Tree was a powerful symbol, but it was but a tree, and its fall was seen by few. But this witch—she carries an uncommon strength with her, and that can be helpful in showing your people the futility of defiance. Until they come to fully accept that truth, they will be unable to free themselves from the shackles of the past toward a more certain future. Symbols are more powerful weapons than any blade, and they can be used for any purpose, vile or virtuous. It is up to you, my brave, wounded friend, to finish the task to which you committed yourself those few short months ago. It is not too late to find favour among your people and to give them an honest future unclouded by superstition. It is not too late to find your redemption.»

The she-Kyn's wounded face was radiant. «What must I do?»

"Wielder, you mustn't leave!" Sinovian says, his face torn between rage and grief. "You are needed here!*"*

I shake my head and look at the crowd, three hundred strong and growing: Kyn, Tetawi, Gvaergs, Ferals, and others, even a few allied Humans who chose to be fugitives rather than surrender their friends and freedom to the grasping hand of invasion. They are all survivors of the siege of Sheynadwiin, all who somehow managed to avoid capture or death by the mercenaries and militiamen, the ravenous land-seekers who even now crawl close to this remote valley. There is little food here now, and precious little hope of more to come, especially with winter on its way and all the storehouses burned by the Mannish horde. Survival will be very, very difficult.

The Heartwood has healed them of physical injury, but there is nothing I can do to ease the nearly-overwhelming grief on their hearts, or the painful memories of loved ones lost and butchered. There is no room for hope here. There is room only for survival. And so many of our people are defenceless on the Darkening Road. It is they who need me most.

Daladir stands beside me, his stalks bound in green wrappings. I can't cover my own stalks, though, as the Heartwood within refuses to be dampened. So my stalks move with a life of their own, charged with strength beyond understanding. I'm fully alive as never before. My flesh, each hair, all of my body sings to the world. It's all I can do to keep my thoughts together, to keep from fading away into the Tree, but for now my will is stronger than the power flowing through me, and I know I can't stay here. In one hand I hold Unahi's staff. In the other, I hold Tobhi's hat, found just outside the chamber of the Tree, next to the cold carcass of his little deer-friend, Smudge. These material objects keep me rooted. They remind me of how much we stand to lose by waiting. The battle for the future of the Folk won't take place in fugitive caves and furtive shadows. The Tree can no longer be hidden from the world, not here, not anywhere. I must go to where the Tree can grow free and tall again, as it was meant to be.

Sinovian sees the answer on my face, and he turns away. He has lost most of his family—his wife, his eldest son and only daughter, his uncle. But he refuses to surrender. He's a Redthorn warrior still, and if anyone can keep these scattered people together, it will be him. His rage will be the fire that warms them.

I desperately want to say something, but words seem inadequate, and the rising tide of anguish that rolls through the crowd is almost enough to make me turn back. I grieve for Unahi, and dear Tobhi, and all the others who disappeared in the chaos. But Daladir is beside me, as are others who understand my task and wish to join me. I'm not alone.

We're moving away from the crowd toward the tree line when Sinovian calls out. He walks to me, and by his side is his lovely sister, Jitani, who let me take her place on the airship to Eromar, who fought beside us in that last terrible battle for the Tree. She is a striking she-Kyn with bronze tattooed skin and forest-green hair. The pain of her many losses must still be immense. But when she looks at me, it's not pain I see, but kindness, and something else, something I also see in Daladir's eyes. They've both given me my life back. I think of her knife; it has saved my life more than once. More than love of the People brings her to me.

Sinovian turns to me. "You bear a precious burden, Wielder. I wish I could talk you out of this madness, to make you stay here with us where you'll be safe, but I can't force you to listen to reason. I can only pray to whatever spirits still watch over us in this blighted land that you know what you're doing, and that you won't forget us if you succeed."

My throat tightens. "I won't forget you, Sinovian. You have my word on that."

He frowns and continues. "I can't make you stay, but I don't have to let you go without good protection, either." He turns to the she-Kyn at his side. "You know my sister, Jitani. She's a respected Thorn Branch warrior and tracker who has travelled widely in the lands of Men. She knows their ways very well." His glance flickers for a moment toward his sister's two savaged sensory stalks. "There's no one braver, or more dedicated. Take her with you. Do this for me, at least."

Jitani draws a wyrwood blade from the beaded scabbard at her side and holds it to her chest. "You asked me once to protect Unahi, and I failed to do so. But I give my blood vow to you now, Wielder, that I will defend you with my life, and with my death, if it comes to that. Will you accept me?"

I'm speechless. Blood vows are rare and inviolate; they demand much of both the giver and the receiver. But the Darkening Road will be long and dangerous, and I'll need every bit of strength I can get. It's not just the mortal dangers I fear; I also dread the loss of myself within the Heartwood. To know that others are depending on me may be enough to keep me sane and safe. Besides, I'm drawn to her smile, to the curve of her hip and the easy, unhesitant way she balances the blade in her hands. She intrigues me.

"I accept your oath, Jitani of Thorn Branch. Be welcome at my fire."

Sinovian embraces his sister, turns, and walks stiffly away. Jitani watches him for a moment. When she looks at me, there are no tears in her golden eyes. Just acceptance. They have both lost so much, and yet they're willing to take this chance, too, with the hope of something better on the other side of the journey. Finally, I take her strong hand and lead her to the small group.

"It is time," I say, and we begin the long walk west.

"Garyn."

"Beloved, get up."

"Garyn!"

Averyn shook hir lover's arm, but the old Governor ignored hir. Garyn was tired. No, he was broken and blasted to the root. The loss of the barge and all the Folk on it was the last horror he could face. Over all these terrible weeks he'd tried to be so strong, and for a while he really *had* been. He'd comforted mothers when their younglings passed into the Spirit World; he'd calmed striplings when their parents were racked with delirious fever; he'd challenged the mercenary policies of the Kateline Crossing merchants, and personally emptied one trader's sour-mash barrels out of fear that the Man would try to cheat some of the easily-tempted Folk of what little they still had; he'd held young she-Folk who'd been brutalized by Men in the night, and helped plan vengeance attacks with such subtlety that they seemed nothing more than strange and bloody accidents. If Garyn Mendiir had been a loved and honoured leader before the Darkening Road, he was doubly so now, for none of his people, nor any of the other Folk, had ever seen his strength and grace falter. They didn't see him, deep in the night, in the darkness of his wagon, when he silently wept in Averyn's strong arms. They didn't see him when he awoke, or the raging grief that choked him with such violence that Averyn often thought the old he-Kyn would die from the power of his fury. No, the Folk saw in Garyn Mendiir, and in many of their leaders, the strength they needed to continue each day's dark journey.

But Garyn wouldn't get up again, not after what he'd seen, not after the sea consumed all those gentle spirits. *Let the others go on if they can. My walk is over.*

"Beloved, you *must* awaken. Someone is here to see you."

There was a strange quality in Averyn's voice that caught the Governor's attention. It wasn't the ever-present grief of these dark days. He couldn't quite remember the sound, but it seemed reminiscent of something like hope.

The old he-Kyn lifted his head from the thin blanket on the floor of the wagon. Averyn was smiling—actually *smiling!*—beside another figure. Garyn tried to make out the other, vaguely Kyn-like shape, but its features were blurred by a burning blue-green radiance that filled the wagon. The thought occurred to him that he ought to feel fear at this strangeness, but it was a soothing light, and familiar, as though he'd seen it a lifetime ago.

A lifetime ago. And then he knew.

"It can't be," he gasped, pulling himself up to his knees, his eyes shining with wonder. "It was dead...I saw it myself. The Tree is gone."

Tarsa held out her hand and led him from the wagon into the open air. "It's come back, Garyn, to all of us." Their fingers touched, and life returned to the he-Kyn. He was reborn.

"Now come," the Wielder whispered. "We must hurry. There's still so very much to be done." She looked to the sky, where distant shadows disappeared into the clouds.

The attack comes suddenly, but it's not unexpected—we knew there would be no easy way to leave the Everland. This small ridge is dense with scrub oak and shaggy pine, their fallen leaves and brown needles blanketing the rock-strewn ground; these Men are loud and ungainly, even in attempted stealth. They're arrogant, too, filled with bloodlust and greed and warm with the flush of their earlier victory against Sheynadwiin. They think that slaughtering the aged and infirm makes them courageous. They think that they're made strong by heedlessly destroying a place of ancient beauty and unbroken history unique to this Melded world. They expect us to flee, to run screaming from them and their murderous weapons.

They are wrong.

As planned, the Tetawi brothers, Jorji and Jothan, turn and kneel, aiming carefully as they unleash a rain of deadly arrows on the Men to cover our counterattack, while Eladrys darts in among her own kind with long knives flashing, drawing hot blood with every swift movement. Daladir and Oryn rush to join the battle, guarding one another's flank as they strike hard with spear and miner's pick. Others take their positions, and the Men are soon pushed to a desperate knot, striking back with more fear than ability.

I'm standing back, at the bracken-filled hollow below the ridge, with Jitani by my side, waiting for the right moment to strike. We can't leave any survivors to warn others of our presence, as we must travel swiftly and without unnecessary delay, but so much killing sickens me now, and I wish we had another choice. Jitani's attention is split between the fight in front of us and watching our surroundings for unexpected dangers. She doesn't seem concerned about the fate of these creatures, and I wonder why I should care so much myself. After all, they've destroyed so much that I love, so much that is woven into my being. How can I forgive that?

But I remind myself that forgiveness isn't our concern right now— life is what matters, and every new death, whether Man or Folk, diminishes what we're fighting to maintain. I'm tired of death and bloody deeds, but at the moment it's a balance: they die, or we do. Too many people rely on us to permit failure. We have to finish this.

Three Men, large and well armed, break through the knot and rush our way. They want to escape, but we stand in their path, and they're terrified and desperate—thus doubly dangerous. Jitani's sword is ready and her eyes have gone hard, as they did when we faced the Shields at the chamber of the Tree. She closes something of herself when in the heat of battle, and although I know that it makes her stronger and smarter, less likely to be swept away by fear or rage, it frightens me, because I don't know what's behind that inner barrier. I wonder if there will ever be a time when she won't be able to return through it. A Kyn distanced from the pains and pleasures of the sensory world isn't fully Kyn; most who've suffered such a mutilation of their sensory stalks go mad from the loss of that deeper tie to the world and its harsh beauty. How has she maintained her spirit for so long? Has she?

I watch as she plants her feet firmly in the red earth and swings her broad-bladed sword in a wide arc around her, catching one of the Men in its path. He screams and falls as another drives forward, his own sword raised high. She steps slightly to the side and meets his blow, staggering slightly from the force of it. He's much larger, and he's in a frenzy—he wants nothing more than to escape, or to bring Jitani down with him.

The third Man runs around them; he's no longer interested in *killing...he just wants to escape. He's fast, but I'm faster. I extend my hands, a glowing green mist flows across my vision, and the wyr goes hot in my blood. I call out to the earth and sky, and a great whirlwind of blinding dust and choking debris responds. It bears down on the Man just as he reaches the top of the ridge, and he's dragged shrieking into the air, rising higher and higher until he's far from sight and sound. There's a thunderous crack above us, as though a great gate has snapped shut in the sky, and then all is silent except for the groans of the wounded and dying, and a sudden thump on the ground behind me.*

My eyes clear, and I turn to see Jitani stagger slightly, her face pale, golden eyes wide in shock. Her attacker is dead just a few steps away, but she's clutching her neck, and blood streams through her fingers. I rush forward, and she sags into my arms. The wound is ghastly; her hand slips away, and the blood spurts like a fountain with each rhythmic heartbeat. She took the wound intended for me—she's already honoured her blood vow, and we're not even out of our tortured homeland yet. I barely know her, but I have no intention of letting her go. She's a warrior of uncommon skill and strength. We need her. I need her.

Her pulse is weak, and fading; her breathing is getting deeper, more desperate. I cover her wound with one hand and draw her close to me with the other. My thoughts extend into the world, and the wyr answers my call. A link is forged between my flesh and hers; our hearts are on different beats for a few uncertain moments, but they soon find a shared strength and rhythm, drumming with renewed power as the slashed skin on her throat begins to knit under my warm palm. Her laboured gasps ease as my lips close over her own, and my wyr- touched breath fills her lungs and pulls her further from death's grasp. We breathe in unison, and as she gets stronger, she finally begins to breathe by herself. But I don't pull away.

This was not how I'd imagined our first kiss. Her blood soaks my hands, the earth, and her wyrweave tunic; dead Men and injured friends are all around us us; our homeland is broken, our people are in exile on a darkening road west. But as her warrior spirit heals and becomes strong again, and as her bright eyes open and grow clear with a welcome understanding, I don't pull away.

And neither does she.

CHAPTER 5

HOMECOMINGS

Society is a fickle mistress, but she is the only thing that survives the decrepitude of age. The bloom of youth may fade, but good station endures. It was a philosophy that Mardisha Kathek followed faithfully for years, and it had served her well most of that time. The Woman had gone from being the envious younger daughter of a mid-level wine merchant to becoming one of the most sought-after socialites in the First Families, the upper ranks of Chalimor's elite High Houses. The journey had been a hard one, but her studied charm, unyielding ambition, and statuesque beauty certainly helped ease the pains of the journey, as did her marriage to Yelseth Kathek, the heir to the much-envied Kathek mining fortune. The Man might be unrelentingly boorish and unimaginative—in bed as well as conversation—but he had money and family connections, and as long as he was well-stocked with fine liqueurs and a good number of dull-witted but enthusiastic mistresses, he gave Mardisha plenty of freedom to follow her own pursuits. Such a situation was far from uncommon in their social circle, but Mardisha and Yelseth had none of the jealousy or bitterness that seemed to poison similar arrangements among their friends and acquaintances: Yelseth was honest about his affairs, and Mardisha was honestly relieved to be freed of the burden of sharing his bed. As a result, theirs had been a truly harmonious home for nearly thirty years.

There had been a time when Mardisha Kathek had an open invitation to every house on Rosewood Hill, the most respectable neighbourhood in Chalimor and the ancestral territory of most of the First Families. All the Woman had to do was ride in her black-lacquered carriage down the cobblestone lanes of the Hill, past luxuriant gardens and marble-columned stone mansions, and she would have a dozen or more invitations to breakfasts, teas, dinners, salons, and other amusements waiting for her when she returned to her own home at the upper end of the Hill. She'd only accept a few of the invitations each week, thus whetting the appetite of those who sought her company and ensuring a steady stream of admirers for months to come.

Yes, Mardisha Kathek had once been the pampered dove in the gilded cage of Chalimor's finest. But those times were sadly past. She'd fallen from grace so quickly, so thoroughly, that she didn't realize she was outside the cage until the door had closed behind her. Such was the way of the First Families. Confrontation was unthinkable; anything other than pleasant decorum and unruffled refinement was carefully purged from the delicacy of the Hill. But while the surface remained smooth, a glance beneath would find a boiling world of intrigue, cruelty, and deception. It was here that Mardisha now saw her life being ripped apart by sharp tongues and unyielding memories, by festering jealousies, long-nursed and well-fed, now released to spread their venom throughout the only world she knew. Gentle smiles often hid sharp teeth. It would be a little while yet before she was fully exiled from the life on the Hill, but that day was coming. In the meantime, the pace of invitations would steadily slow to a trickle; the conversations would get shorter, and eyes once locked in rapt attention would begin to wander with instructive boredom; her staff would drift away to houses of more respectable station. Then the long-feared day would come when the callers disappeared altogether, and her rejection would be complete. She would be like the dead, snuffed out of Chalimor's favoured circles, denied even the courtesy of a wake in her memory.

And all because of the Dreyd-cursed Folk! Their stubborn, selfish refusal to embrace the gifts freely given by the Dreydmaster of Eromar had tainted public sentiment, even though the Reachwarden was still an unapologetic Unhuman supporter; the creatures' outright violation of the terms of Vald's generous treaty was worse than stupidity—it was arrogance and betrayal, and there was no room among civilized Men for such ungrateful, faithless creatures.

They hadn't always been this way. Indeed, she'd once held great hope for the eventual domestication of all the Folk; it had been her life's work. Her charitable service with the Friends of the Folk had brought enormous prestige to the organization. With her contacts, the Friends had become more than just a group of high-minded socialites; they became a political force with growing influence among the Assembly-members and even with the Reachwarden himself. The Friends were now the undisputed authorities on Reach policy toward the Folk. No law passed the Reach Assembly without their consultation and endorsement. Bringing the Folk into the Nations of Men was a gargantuan task, but it was one that Mardisha and her associates relished. It eased their boredom and gave them myriad little projects of character improvement to pursue.

And they could actually see their work making a difference. She had set an example by bringing a number of the benighted creatures from the howling wilderness into her own home, with the hope of teaching them the ways of Men. She'd given them schooling and taught them to read, to speak, to behave appropriately, to do everything necessary for unburdening themselves of the toxic taint of beasts and dark forests. And, on occasion, she'd been successful, so much so that the funds kept flowing, and all the First Families added their participation among the Friends of the Folk as one more measure of prestige on Rosewood Hill. The too-frequent failures were quickly cut away before they could cause a scandal and corrupt their ever-weak companions, and they vanished as thoroughly as if they'd never existed. All she had to do was dress a little Brownie-child in a blue velvet suit with ruffles on the sleeves and collar and black buckled shoes on his tiny feet, stand him in front of a crowd of bewigged and lace-dripping Men and Woman, and have him sing a plaintive chorus of "To the Argent Moon Sang the Pensive Whippoorwill," and Mardisha's virtue would be the talk of the

Hill for weeks on end. The money would always flow.

All these thoughts burned in the Woman's mind as her carriage bounced and shuddered through the rough, shell-strewn streets of the Merchant's Ward, returning far later than she desired to her fading house on the Hill. She could no longer shop in her favoured Rosewood marts and boutiques. She'd placed orders with a different merchant every day for the past week, and each returned a brief, unsealed note with the same message: *We regret to inform you that the items you have requested are no longer available from this establishment.* The ink fairly dripped with sneering sympathy. If Mardisha had doubted her swiftly accelerating fall before, this was all the evidence she would have needed. She was being pushed out of the Hill, and all with poisoned pens and smiles.

She might have sent one of her trusted maids to do the shopping, but most of these Women had disappeared over the past few weeks, and the few who remained were those she desired to see least: backcountry Kyn and Brownies, all trained by the Friends to be dutiful domestics. They were no longer welcome among the other First Families, and, indeed, weren't very welcome in her home, but she couldn't get hard-working Women anymore, so she had to make due with the very creatures that had brought about her downfall. And now she was finally seeing them with eyes unclouded by romantic charity. Where she'd once seen noble Unhumans in need of enlightenment, she now saw surly creatures who turned their backs on all the precious opportunities she'd provided to them; where once they'd been sweet, faithful children with unlimited possibility, they were now selfish, unkempt, and unmotivated brutes no better than the forest beasts from which they'd descended. Mardisha could barely contain her disgust every time she walked into her home and saw one of the creatures pawing over her lovely furniture with a filthy dust-rag. Something would have to be done, and soon, or her fall would be irreversible.

Still, all was not lost, not yet. A week earlier she'd received her invitation to tonight's festivities—the Reachwarden's Jubilee, *the* social event of the year, held in the atrium of the Hall of Kings. It was the celebration of the overthrow of the old royalty and the installation of a more egalitarian republic, that of the freely-elected Assembly and Reachwarden. It would be a time of unsurpassed goodwill and, hopefully, forgiveness. Although most of the First Families had abandoned her, there were some who still held her in esteem, and these would be her greatest hope for returning to the warm bosom of Chalimor society. Today's quick shopping expedition brought the necessary accessories that would make her fully prepared for tonight's festivities; if she made it home soon, she'd be able to put the finishing touches on a penitent but still elegant jade green dress and pearl-beaded turban and still have time for a light dinner before the Jubilee. If she could prove that her former sympathy for these Unhuman animals was firmly behind her, she might be able to salvage her position, perhaps even return to something greater.

The wagon jolted again, and Mardisha slapped the carriage door with her parasol. «Mind where you're going, you black-eyed brat, or you'll be paying for the repairs. You've been careless enough with my property as it is.» She waited for a sullen response from the Brownie driver. Hearing none, she smirked and nestled back into the cushions. Perhaps her husband was right. All these creatures truly understood was a sharp tongue and the occasional thrashing. She'd tried to change them, but most had proven incapable of abandoning their wild ways. Even red-haired Neranda, her most promising and accomplished pupil, had returned to the wilderness of her ancestors, and by all rumours it seemed that the girl had paid a heavy price for such foolishness. Admittedly, she'd wanted to share her education and new ways with her people, but such training was best left to the firmer minds and hearts of Men. If only she'd stayed in Chalimor…. But it was past time for regrets. Neranda made the choice to go back to that lawless world. She could hardly be surprised that the beasts would one day feed.

Mardisha cursed as one of the wagon wheels smashed into something hard, sending the Woman sprawling across the seat. Where had she gone wrong? She'd once been loved among Folk and Men, but now she received resentful glares from the former and cold dismissal from the latter. It was all terribly unfair. Her perfumed world was crumbling, and now her Unhuman driver was trying to destroy the only good carriage she had left. It was all too much.

To her surprise, the carriage came to a stop just as she was about to start screaming again. She pulled up the shade and looked outside. Her face turned red as she watched the Brownie jump down, throw his coat and hat on the ground, and disappear around a corner.

«Petyr!» she screamed from the window. «Petyr! Where are you going? This isn't the house! Come back here immediately, you little brute!» The smell of seaweed and fish was almost overwhelming. She was in an alley at the dock ward. What was he thinking, abandoning her in this low-district cesspool just before dark?

Mardisha opened her door and stepped outside, only to recoil in disgust as her boot and the hem of her dress dipped into a stinking pool of fish grease and water. She tried to back up into the carriage, but the heel of her boot was now too slick, and it slipped off the step. Her arms flew out wildly. There was nothing to grab for balance, so with a high-pitched shriek she plummeted, face-first, into the stinking street. *«Petyr!!!»* Mardisha screamed, her face purple now with rage and filth.

«He's gone, Mardisha,» a soft voice responded, and the Woman pulled the dripping hair away from her eyes to see a curvaceous figure in gaudy silks leaning against the rear wheel of the carriage. «Besides, his name is Pishkewah, or it was until you made him change it. He's gone to find his family, as have the rest of your rather under-appreciated staff.»

«What have you talking about? What have you done with my servants?» Mardisha hissed.

The newcomer's green eyes twinkled. «I just helped them along a little, that's all. I didn't think you'd mind.» She jingled a small silken belt purse filled with coins in front of the Woman's face. «After all, this money was donated for the noble goal of helping the Folk. I guess one could say that it really belonged to them all along. It wasn't doing them much good in that little locked chest in your study.»

The Woman stood up and tried to wipe her face free of fishy ooze. «I knew you were a whore, Denarra, but I didn't know you were a thief, too. The marshals of Chalimor have no love of either, and they'll be quite interested to hear about this latest venture of yours.»

The Strangeling laughed. «My dear Mardisha—you've become such an unpleasant old codfish! You used to be so sweet and condescending; I wonder what happened. Why, I remember when you were so desperate to be seen in the presence of Folk that even a tainted specimen like myself was welcome to hold your clammy little hand to demonstrate your patronising generosity.» Ignoring the Woman's speechless fury, Denarra shrugged. «But I'm not here to argue with you, darling. I've come to have a little talk, just like in the old days, when you were more pleasant and I was naïve enough to believe that you really cared more about the Folk than your own lickspittle reputation.»

Mardisha turned back to the carriage. «I'm not going to trade false pleasantries with a strumpet. Good evening. Expect to hear from the marshals about my stolen property.» She lifted her boot to the coach-step, but she slipped again and nearly tumbled back to the street.

As the Woman caught her balance, Denarra laughed. «Same old Mardisha. I'd almost forgotten what a terrible temper you have! It's almost as distracting as that enormous mole on your forehead. Don't worry, darling—I won't let either of those things get in the way of our little reunion. I'm a forgiving person. You see, I understand that you still have a bit of influence in high places, and I'm ever so eager to go to the Jubilee tonight. In fact, it's most urgent that I attend. If anyone can help me, I just know it would be you…especially these days.»

It was now Mardisha's turn to laugh. «Help you? You've lost the little mind you once had. If I wouldn't be seen in public with one of my own maids, what makes you think I'd be seen with a creature like you? You're tainted, and you've lost whatever worthy reputation you could claim before. I have no interest in wasting my time or what little standing I still have among the good *Human* people of this city by being seen in your demented company.» She looked at the coach. «Damn Petyr and damn you, too, Denarra Syrene. Find a more receptive audience. I wash my hands of all your cursed kind.»

Turning with a sniff of disdain, she shut the door and moved toward the street, stopping short as a group of figures stepped out of the shadows. One was a dark-eyed she-Brownie who held a long silver dagger in her gloved hand, light gleaming along its sharp edge. Beside her stood a grim young Man in purple silks and leathers with a book chained to his right arm; in his left hand he held a long-hafted hammer that he swung with slow menace. The last of the figures was a well-dressed Goblin with two small hand-crossbows, each pointed at the Woman's vitals.

Mardisha looked back to Denarra, who still leaned against the carriage. The Strangeling smiled coldly.

«Mardisha, darling, I think you've misunderstood me. Let me clarify this in terms that even a half-wit like you can understand: this *isn't* a request.»

Jhaeman read the letter again and shook his head in disbelief. The Reachwarden, Qualla'am Kaer, had summoned the guardsman to his private office back to the Hall of Kings. Jhaeman had already served his shift hours, but he'd dutifully crawled out of bed, pulled on his boots and silver-buckled long-coat, strapped on his sword, and hurried to the waiting coach, ruefully scratching his three-day stubble. The Reachwarden placed the letter in his hand the moment he arrived at the White Chamber. Jhaeman wanted to pretend that it said something else, that the words would rearrange themselves into something that made sense and didn't send his stomach into knots. But no matter how hard he tried to wish the words away, they always returned to the same firm message in a tight black script, so precise and forceful that the pen had nearly ripped through the bleached paper:

> *To My Honored Colleague, the Estimable Reachwarden, Qualla'am Kaer:*
>
> *You have made your point well known to me, Kaer—your curious concern for the criminal Unhumans in the "Ever-land" is unfortunate but not surprising. The weak-kneed statesmen in the silken halls of Chalimor have little understanding of the savagery that is the true nature of these creatures here in the western lands. Ignorance, however, is no justification for cowardice, or stupidity.*
>
> *It is well that you remember one thing: you are Reachwarden, but I am Eromar, and Eromar bows to none, especially when we are well within our sovereign rights. This "Ever-land" belongs to Eromar, not to Chalimor, and certainly not to a handful of unredeemed nomads unable to put the land to the uses for which it was intended. We will have what is ours, with or without your blessing.*
>
> *Proceed on this course and you will find fire at your feet. The Law protects Men; it recognizes neither tree nor stone nor beast, except as they belong to the service of Men. Have you the mettle to enforce this decision? Shall we test it?*
>
> *V.*

Jhaeman re-folded the letter and handed it back to Kaer. «So, he's come out and said it directly: He's declared full treason.»

The Reachwarden nodded. His face was drawn and ashen; it seemed that silver had streaked the thick black hairs of his goatee almost overnight. He looked older than Jhaeman had ever seen him before, and the sudden realization filled the younger Man with fear. A former military campaigner himself, with a sterling reputation for bravery and integrity, Qualla'am Kaer was a Man of indomitable spirit and unyielding moral courage, one whom the guardsman served not only willingly but with pride. Jhaeman was honoured by his work as the Captain of the Reachwarden's Guard, and each day brought more opportunities to make the Guard an effective defensive force like no other. Although he'd seen too much death, deception, and cruelty in his life to think anyone worthy of idolatry, the soldier still had enormous respect for the Reachwarden.

It wasn't Kaer's own clear fear that filled the guardsman with foreboding, but rather the sudden realization that peace in the Reach now stood balanced on the narrow edge of a knife...and the blade sat in Lojar Vald's hand. Worse still, public sentiment was clearly on Vald's side, no matter how wrong-headed or dishonourable his behaviour. Hordes of eager young Men and Women had already left the city for the old Everland with the hope of finding land, riches, and glory.

Jhaeman cleared his throat. «Sir, has anyone else read this note?»

«Not yet. You're the first.» He drained a long-stemmed glass of sweet mead and reached again for the decanter. «Of all the nights to do this, he had to choose the Jubilee. I've got to be at the Crystal Court in an hour to begin 'the celebrations of the unification of the Reach under the republican will of the people,' and this is when that viper-tongued bastard makes his move.»

Holding the folded letter up to the oil lamp at the desk, Jhaeman examined a series of sharp gouges in the paper. «Who delivered the note?» he asked.

Kaer grimaced. «You wouldn't believe me if I told you.»

«I've seen some strange things in my time. Try me.»

«Never saw anything like this. It looked like a crow, only much bigger and, well, nastier. But that wasn't the worst of it. It had the head of a child, with seeping black holes for eyes. I only saw it for a moment as it flew in and dropped off the letter, and that was more than enough. It took me a long time to even pick up the letter, let alone open it.»

Jhaeman's brows wrinkled. «Was there anything else? Did it say anything or do anything unusual?»

«Well,» Kaer snorted, «I'm not exactly sure what is 'usual' for such a thing, so I'm not in much of a position to speak to that, but no, that was it. It flew in, dropped the letter, and flew back out. That's it.»

The Reachwarden and his captain stared at the note. Finally, Jhaeman said, «I took the liberty of planning for a quick deployment after your last declaration to the Assembly. Come morning, they can be ready to advance into Eromar.»

«No.»

Jhaeman stared at Kaer. «But you said that the Reach wouldn't allow Eromar to harass the Everland anymore. You promised to send in troops to uphold the past covenants of defence. The Reach has recognized the rights of the Folk to those lands for almost two hundred years, and it has taken sacred oaths to protect those claims. Vald's note has made his treachery clear. What more do you need?»

Kaer turned a sad but firm gaze on the other Man, who wasn't that much younger in years or worldly experience. In political life, however, Kaer was a reluctant master, and his mind saw webs of action and response spreading out endlessly, whereas his friend saw a few clear paths, some easier than others. Jhaeman was an unyielding idealist, but the wearying world had long ago worn Qualla'am Kaer's idealism away. «There's much more to think about now, Jhaeman…much more. If only it were that simple. There's little support in the Assembly for such interference; there's even less among those on the street. It's not a simple world, not anymore, not ever again.»

«But sir, how can you turn away?»

«I haven't turned away. I've got a lot to think about now, and very little time in which to do it. Wait for me outside. I'd like you to accompany me to the Jubilee.»

The guardsman stood and bowed stiffly. He wanted to argue, to shout, to do anything that would lift the despairing pall from the room, but he'd been given a direct order that ended further discussion.

Jhaeman left the room, and Kaer stood. In the White Chamber, by the fading light of a single flickering oil lamp and the crackling ashes in the fireplace, the Reachwarden opened the letter and read it again. Unlike Jhaeman, Qualla'am Kaer didn't hope to find something new among the black lines on the page. All he wanted to find was courage, and there was little room for that in the words of Lojar Vald. No matter what his choice would be, it would mean devastation.

A sudden chorus of trumpets rang through the corridors of the Hall of Kings to announce the beginning of the Jubilee. Kaer looked up, his brown face haggard. Walking to the fireplace, he let the letter fall among the glowing coals and watched as the paper burst into orange flame. He waited until nothing existed of Vald's missive but a slender sheet of ash, then took up his jacket and strode purposefully from the room toward the Crystal Court. His decision was made; it was the only one he could possibly live with. He hoped such conviction would be enough.

Right or wrong, it would have to be.

The Hall of Kings was a fitting testament to the ambitions of the founders of the Reach. In the days before the overthrow of the monarchy and the establishment of the Reach Republic, the Hall stood as a reminder of the military might of the great kings of old. It had been designed to inspire awe and no small amount of fear in those who viewed it, and the six generations of kings who once ruled over the Reach had each made the Hall their own, drawing slaves and resources from throughout the provinces and other lands to enhance their own grand dreams. It was a half-mile-wide rectangle flanked by two massive octagons built of white marble and granite, with a columned central tower—the Crystal Court—capped by a massive dome of cut glass and joined to the rest of the structure by lacy stone arches radiating from the middle like the tines of a sunburst. The dome blazed so brightly on cloudless days that it nearly blinded those imperious enough to look skyward. Marble-topped towers rose high and proud at the apex of every side of the building, but none stood taller than the wondrous vault of the Crystal Court.

The deep and well-patrolled waters of Chal Bay kept most unwanted visitors from the city's centre, while the cliffs of Mount Imor and the outer city walls amply defended the inner wonders of Chalimor, so the Hall of Kings was unmarred by protective partitions. Rather, its open corridors, wide halls, and carved white columns gave a sense of imposing, spacious generosity, even under those kings better known for cruelty than wisdom. It was a hub of culture and law, where the poor and wealthy alike were welcome, though on different floors of the structure. Lush, fragrant gardens and wide green lawns spread out on every side of the Hall as well as in various open chambers throughout the estate.

The Hall of Kings was the greatest treasure of the people of Chalimor, and when the kings were overthrown there was no thought of replacing such a magnificent structure with anything else. It belonged to the people now, and though it kept its former name—in spite of occasional attempts to replace the antiquated term with something more fitting to a republic—the Hall became even more beloved in the new age of the Reach of Men. It was said that the Crystal Court would never fall, not as long as the glory of Men stood strong.

Quill had heard of the Hall of Kings even before she came to Chalimor, but nothing had prepared her for the sight of the great crystal dome at night, shining from the moonlight without and the thousands of candles and torch sconces within. Light danced through the massive central chamber with such a bewildering array of colours and patterns that it was all she could do to keep her thoughts focused on their reason for being at the Jubilee in the first place. Her eyes strayed upward at the terraces that ringed the great atrium, and her senses swam with the smell of flowers in bloom and the sweet spices that wafted from enormous incense braziers scattered through the growing throng. The delicate sound of soft harps and flutes wove through the crowd and gave a calming note to the slow hostility that built around them.

The Dolltender tried to ignore the dark glances and whispered remarks, but it was impossible to pretend that their small group was welcome. If not for Mardisha's admittedly reluctant presence, they would have been stopped at the Hall's great doors. But the Woman's invitation had said *Guests Warmly Received,* and all the guests were dressed in the expected finery: the Strangeling wore a sky-blue dress with a white silk wrap across her shoulders, bright pearls draping her throat and earlobes, and a wide-brimmed white hat trimmed with her signature peacock feathers; a simple but elegant gown of shimmering, copper-coloured cloth adorned the Brownie; Merrimyn cut a dashing figure in a black suit and polished riding boots, his snaring tome hidden beneath the folds of a long, red-lined cape that gave him an air of mystery and slight menace. As the invitation was quite explicit and made no comment about Folk being excluded from the ceremony, the guards were unwilling to make a scene, so they admitted Mardisha and her three strange companions.

The group walked down a long staircase from the front hall to the atrium as the low, incessant buzz of scornful voices filled the air. Mardisha's shoulders fell. When they at last reached the centre of the great chamber, Merrimyn moved to a high spot from which he could see a long distance, and Denarra released the Woman's arm. Fixing the Strangeling with a glare so venomous that Quill stepped back,

Mardisha rushed into the crowd and disappeared from sight.

"Aren't you afraid she'll tell someone that we forced her to bring us here?" Quill whispered.

Denarra grinned mischievously. "Mardisha and I know each other quite well, too well, perhaps; if she says anything about us, the world will learn about how Yelseth Kathek discovered young Mardisha don Haever in a two-shack brothel in the small fishing town of Waterbourne. If not for a popular talent she exercised quite freely with her regular clientele, he probably wouldn't have brought her back with him at all. Her association with Folk has cast a shadow over her reputation, but it's redeemable; this little bit of news would destroy her place in society forever. It would be worse than death for someone like her."

"And what about you, Denarra?" asked Quill. "What about your place in society? Do you miss what you gave up for us...for me?"

Denarra looked down with surprise. She seemed to hesitate for a moment before reaching out to brush a loose strand of hair away from the Tetawa's eyes. "It hurts sometimes, I won't deny it. But I knew this day would come eventually—there's no permanent place of affection when you're a Kyn-sired among Humans. Admittedly, I always thought that the cause of my exile would be some terrible scandal involving me and the virile son of a local politician or other such silliness, not this particular type of smooth-faced nastiness. Still, I'd rather be on the unfashionable side and be welcomed with love by people of good heart than be the slack-jawed pet of fools."

Quill's eyes misted over and she reached out to squeeze Denarra's hand. In spite of everything they'd said to each other in the past few days, all the suspicious recriminations and biting words, there was no doubt now about the Strangeling's allegiance. Now, more than ever, Quill treasured this odd but tender friendship.

"By the way, Denarra," the Tetawa mused as they threaded their way through the crowd in search of the Reachwarden, "how did you know about Mardisha's past?"

The Strangeling cleared her throat and pulled Quill quickly behind her. "Lucky guess. Hurry now; let's get this over with before the wine starts wearing off."

Merrimyn wandered through the crowd for a while, but eventually returned to the top of the great staircase leading down into the lower atrium. He was restless. Ever since arriving in the city, the young Man had seen far more of Humanity than he'd ever expected or wanted to see. As a Binder, he was cursed to always be separated from his own kind, and so many beautiful people and so much grandeur filled his heart with a longing that was easier to deny than acknowledge. Binders had to devote all their energies—physical, emotional, and erotic—to maintaining the alchaemical locks on their snaring tomes. Surrender to passion could be more than just awkward—it could be catastrophic, for the release of the captured Fey-spirits would bring a vengeful death to the Binder and anyone near him. If not for his obligation to Denarra and Quill, and their growing friendship, Merrimyn would have fled the city just after regaining his strength, for there was too much temptation all around him. As it was, he was planning to leave when they were finished talking with the Reachwarden about the Expulsion.

He tried to reach one of the upper terraces to get a better view. All the other stairs were blocked by soldiers armed with muskets and short swords, so he resigned himself to a place at the top of the sweeping stairway. It was the best height he could find, and enough to see most of the atrium floor. He watched the movements of the Strangeling and Tetawa below.

At present he couldn't see the Reachwarden, but there was no doubt where Denarra and Quill were located, because the crowd always seemed to split apart when the Folk were present. A dull knot of rage burned in the Man's throat at the sight. He was young, but he was far from being naïve. He understood all too well the petty hatred that pervaded the Hall of Kings this night, and he despised it. He despised everything that reminded him of the cruelty and pain he'd seen in Eromar City and throughout most of the lands of Men. He despised everything that threatened his strange, brave friends, and he especially hated the stupidity that led to so much bloodshed in the world.

It was a large world with many people and possibilities, but in the many lands he'd travelled during his twenty-one short summers, he'd found very little that gave him much hope for a future free of death and destruction. Yet below him, winding their way through an increasingly hostile crowd, walked vibrant vessels of that slim hope. It wasn't just that Denarra and Quill had saved his life and brought him along on their quest to save their people; it was also that they considered him a friend—family, even—and trusted him with their lives, just as they trusted each other. Trust was a rare thing these days. Even if he didn't survive this grand adventure, it was enough that he knew that such hope existed.

Trumpets blasted above the young Man, and he looked around to see what was happening in the atrium. His eyes scanned the crowd below and moved upward. Suddenly, he froze. The Reachwarden had entered the Crystal Court with his entourage and guards, but it wasn't this group that caught Merrimyn's attention. His gaze was fixed instead on a short, solid Man in travel-stained leathers and a wide-brimmed black hat on one of the upper terraces, a Man who prowled past the columns lining the chamber's edge and watched the milling crowd with burning intensity.

Vergis Thane had found them.

"He's here!" Denarra shouted over the roar of the crowd. Quill could barely hear anything, but the sudden noise seemed to be a good indication of the Reachwarden's arrival. The Tetawa was too short to see anything other than the well-padded posteriors of Men and Women, but Denarra shoved through the crowd with abandon. The press of bodies seemed to shift slightly; there was less hostility now, as most attention was focused on something happening ahead of them.

Denarra held tightly to Quill's hand as she pushed, prodded, and sometimes kicked her way through. She didn't know how long the Reachwarden would be there, and she wasn't much in the mood for trying to come up with another clever scheme to get into his presence. It would be this chance or none.

The trumpets rang again, and then a voice echoed through the chamber. They couldn't hear much of his speech, and they doubted that anyone else could either, but the energy of the crowd grew, and the Humans seemed to be enraptured by whatever the Reachwarden was saying. The excitement was contagious. They could feel themselves caught up in the thrill that raced through the throng.

"Hurry, Quill," Denarra called out, pushing through a tight knot of bodies, and then they stood at the front of the crowd, looking upon Qualla'am Kaer, the fifth Warden of the Reach of Men, who stood upon a stone dais speaking to the assembly before him. He was a tall, dignified man, with silver streaks in his tight black hair and well-trimmed goatee, and broad shoulders that spoke to his military past. Kaer glanced over at them and his brown face flushed slightly, but he continued his speech for a few moments, occasionally interrupted by exuberant shouts of assent. Finally, his address finished, Kaer bowed low and turned to walk swiftly out of the Crystal Court.

"He's leaving!" Quill wailed. "We're going to lose him!"

Denarra cocked an eyebrow. "No caterwauling yet, please!" The Strangeling rushed shouting toward the Reachwarden's guards, followed closely by Quill, who pulled off her belt and jumped free of the binding weight of her lower dress. Although taken by surprise, the guards were well trained, and they met Denarra's desperate lunge with swords drawn.

«No!!!» a voice roared through the chamber, and the blasting smoke of a musket erupted from the edge of the stairs to strike a columned terrace above. A few small chunks of marble rained down on the crowd. Denarra looked back to see Merrimyn wrestling with a soldier on the stairs, each trying to keep a smoking flintlock from the hands of the other. More troops rushed in to restrain the Binder, and the mood of the gathering shifted instantly. A scream echoed in the atrium, followed by hundreds of babbling voices. As though of one mind, the crowd surged toward the exit, and guards hustled the Reachwarden from the Crystal Court. Others leaped on Denarra and Quill, who surrendered without resistance.

"I hope you know what you're doing," the Dolltender gasped before being led away into the dark recesses of the Hall of Kings.

"Don't worry!" Denarra called back with a grin. "I'm making it up as I go!"

Tarsa slept at last, though fitfully. She lay beside a small, flickering fire that gave more smoke than heat. Like all the wounds she'd suffered since becoming the guardian of the Heartwood, the cut on her head had healed completely, but Jitani still stared at the spot, unable to look away, and unwilling to try. It gave her comfort to know that the Wielder was still mortal enough to be wounded and bleed. Each day that passed brought the Tarsa she knew closer to the edge of oblivion, and Jitani could only watch helplessly as the distance between them grew.

She stretched a knot from her back and looked around. Tobhi sat at another campfire talking with an old he-Kyn Shield that he'd befriended earlier, during the hardest part of the Darkening Road. Oryn and some of the other Humans had gone to help search for bodies from the wreckage of the barge. Most of the other fighters who'd travelled with Tarsa from the Everland had gone off to find their families, hoping that they were among this group of exiles, but Jitani stayed beside the Wielder, true to her blood vow and a deeper need that grew stronger with each passing day.

She wasn't the only one. Daladir sat there too, his careworn face turned away toward the darkness, his hands clearly aching to reach out and stroke the Wielder's tangled hair. He and Jitani rarely spoke to one another. There was little need, for each knew what the other desired. They had no reason to put those feelings into words.

So it came as a surprise when Daladir walked over to sit beside her. They regarded each other warily. "She's getting worse," he said at last, his voice low.

Jitani nodded. Tarsa was fading into the Tree, slipping away from everyone, even—*especially*—those who loved her the most.

He frowned. "It's going to be bad very soon. We'll need to be ready...for whatever happens."

"Yes."

His green eyes shone brightly in the dull firelight. "You fashioned your brother's warrior lock, didn't you?"

Her eyebrow rose. "I did. And he fashioned the one I wear."

"Will you help me with mine?"

It was a simple request, but one that shocked the she-Kyn. A warrior lock was an ancient symbol of a Kyn's dedication to the defence of the people. It was painful, especially for he-Kyn and zhe-Kyn, for it required a plucking or shaving of most of the hair from the head, all save for a long topknot of hair at the crown, which was bound, greased, and braided. She-Kyn had a longer stripe of hair that stretched down the centre, from the forehead to the back of the skull, like a horse's mane with a long braid at the end. For all Kyn, however, the fashioning of the lock involved a scarring of the temples by the warrior's most trusted friend or closest family member, generally a sibling. None were permitted to bind their sensory stalks during the ritual; it required full awareness, no matter how extreme the pain.

That Daladir would ask such a thing of her was unheard of. He either didn't know what he was asking, or....

Then she understood, and she didn't hesitate. Turning to him, she pulled out her hunting knife—not quite the quality of blade that she'd given to Tarsa, but suitable enough for this task—and began scraping it across the side of Daladir's scalp. He flinched at the pain, but even when his head was slick with blood from the shaving and the three angular gashes cut above each eyebrow, he didn't move away from her. Jitani went about her task with swift efficiency. When she finished, she unwove her own dark green braid, cut a long strip of hair, and wrapped it around the base of the he-Kyn's topknot. She nodded approvingly as she re-plaited her braid.

Daladir wiped the blood from his head with a dirty cloth. "*Tsodoka.*"

"It will be dawn soon," Jitani said. "We'll need to wake her before the guards begin to move."

He sighed. "She'll be annoyed that we let her sleep for so long. She's still strong."

Jitani glanced at him. "She's remarkable in *many* ways."

"She's never given up, not once, not in all this time." Daladir tensed, then whispered, "And I can't surrender."

"Neither can I. My decision was made long ago."

They looked at each other again, warrior to warrior, eyes warm and tangled in emotion. They were both scarred and weary, covered with grime, blood, and the heavy burden of loss, wounded by a thousand aches that filled both their waking lives and dreams. They didn't know how it would end, but they were connected now in a way that neither had ever expected or wanted. It was enough to know, beyond any doubt, what mattered most to the other, and to know that it gave them both purpose in a world that was falling to jagged pieces around them.

It was enough. For now.

It had been a long, long time since Mardisha had been in such a place, and she resented the intusion of that long-buried world into her new life. She'd once thought that those days were far behind her, but history was hard to escape. This time, however, would be the last, one way or another. Either her new acquaintance would be able to help her regain her rightful place among the First Families on Rosewood Hill, or she'd reach the unhappy end of the shameful path that her more reputable friends were so skilfully setting before her. It was her last hope.

She'd been close enough to Denarra's pet Binder to see that the boy wasn't a political assassin; he'd grabbed the musket and fired *above* the Reachwarden at someone else. The figure vanished, but only briefly, reappearing in the middle of the fleeing crowd moments later as naturally as if his ragged clothing belonged among the jewels and fine fabrics of the First Families and their respectable guests. Twenty years of high living hadn't erased her ability to identify a skilled mercenary; she'd known many such Men in her old life, and this one moved with the easy, predatory grace of the best of them. She'd watched carefully and followed him from the Hall of Kings, hoping that he wouldn't expect pursuit in such chaos. Whoever he was, his goals seemed to match hers this night. Her social salvation was close at hand.

Mariner's Quay was a nasty place, especially for a Woman bedecked in finery. But delaying to change was absurd; she couldn't risk losing him in the stinking streets and back alleys of the city, because there was no way to know where he'd disappear. She had to stay with him, no matter the risks. She was terrified, of course, as any sensible Woman would have to be, but she feared what would happen if she didn't take the chance far more than any thugs in the shadows.

Now she was in what had to be the most disgusting tavern in all of Chalimor, lit by nothing more than a mass of stinking peat in the smoking fireplace. There weren't many people in the common room—not surprising, given the rancid stench that filled the air. The few who were there seemed far more interested in pawing at the pockmarked serving girl than in the well-dressed Woman at the door. Mardisha took a deep breath, choked back a bubble of bile that rose up in her throat, and moved toward a dark corner, where a plainly-dressed Man sat staring at her, his single blue eye glinting in the dim light.

«I have information for you,» she whispered as she slid beside him on the bench. «Are you interested?»

«Not in the least,» he said, sliding a knife blade against her ribs. «Go away.»

Swallowing deeply, Mardisha pulled a small piece of paper from her handbag. «We share a problem, and I think I can help you take care of it to my satisfaction as well as yours.»

«And what problem would that be?»

The Woman smiled. «Let's just say, her mouth is much bigger than her brain.»

A small smile curved at the rough ends of Thane's lips. «I'm listening.»

«Now then,» Kaer said, turning his brown eyes on Merrimyn, who sat in the White Chamber with his hands and snaring-tome chained immovably. Denarra and Quill sat elsewhere in the room, each wrapped in leather restraints. «You say this 'Thane' is a trained assassin? How do you know this? *You* were the one with the musket.»

Merrimyn sighed. «I told you. I'd seen him a few times when I was a Binder for Dreydmaster Vald. He visited on occasion, and always with someone in custody that Vald wanted to…speak with.»

A red-haired Man of average height turned to Quill. "And you, small one? Do you want to add anything to the tale?" he asked in Folk speech. The Dolltender looked at him with more suspicion than surprise.

"It's just what they said. Thane's a killer. We didn't know he'd be here, but it was a good guess." She turned away from the Man, hoping that he'd let the matter drop. It was clear that he didn't believe them. All she could hope was that Denarra's charm would work on the

Reachwarden, and at present, it didn't look too good.

«I see.» Kaer looked at the trio and frowned. «There's some truth here, of that I'm quite certain, but it's not what you're sharing with me.» He leaned toward Merrimyn. «I'm going to ask you this only once, and you'd better be honest with me, or you and your friends will spend the rest of your short lives in the Trollmaw—which is a place I honestly *don't* recommend. I know something about Vergis Thane, and he's most definitely a dangerous Man. I also know that whatever else he is, he's not a paid assassin. He was here for a purpose, and it didn't have anything to do with me. What was he doing here?»

Merrimyn narrowed his eyes and pursed his lips but stayed silent. Kaer's gaze was unwavering. Finally, his patience at an end, he turned to the younger Man. «All right, Jhaeman, take them away. I don't have time for....»

«He was after me,» Denarra called out from the sofa.

Kaer folded his arms and leaned against his massive oak table. «Ah, I see. And why is that?»

«We have a bit of recently resurrected history together. Our last meeting didn't go too well, so I imagine he was here to finish what he'd started.»

«So, we have a loose Binder from Eromar City and a half-breed Kyn witch who's being hunted by one of the Dreydcaste's most notorious Seekers. Your defence isn't looking too good.» He turned his cold eyes on Quill. «Now, what about you? What's your story?»

The Tetawa looked at Merrimyn's chains and Denarra's tattered dress, and tears sprang to her eyes. Although her facility with Reachspeak was still somewhat rough, it was enough to be understood. «I came to ask for your help. I came to ask you to stop Vald from killing my people.»

The Reachwarden stared at her. "What did you say?" he asked, reverting to the Folk trade tongue.

"Please, don't be angry with my friends. They're here because of me. I left home months ago to tell you how Eromar is taking our lands from us, to tell you how much we need your help. I never would have made it here if it hadn't been for Denarra and Merrimyn. They've saved my life more than once. They gave up everything, just so I could be here with you today. We've tried for weeks to see you, to talk to you, but you wouldn't see us. Coming here, tonight, was the only way to do it." She fell to her knees in front of the table, and the tears streamed down her face as she sobbed. "Please, help us. You're the only one who can stop them. You're the only one who can save us."

Kaer looked at the small figure on the floor. He stood and walked around to the front, where he reached down and ran his big-knuckled fingers through her hair. She stiffened for a moment, but the pain and fear and sorrow were too much, and she collapsed in another wave of tears.

"Be strong, Tetawa—be strong. You have my deepest sympathies," he whispered, then he pulled away and stood up. "But I can't help you."

Quill looked up through her tears, her face stricken. "What?"

Kaer walked swiftly to the door. "As much as I want to help you all, there's nothing I can do."

Denarra stared at him in horrified disbelief. "But *why?* We came all this way to get your help. There's no one else who can help our people! Would you let Vald drive us to extinction?"

The Reachwarden spun around furiously. "*Your* people? Did you ever stop to think about *my* people? Vald is threatening civil war if I intervene, the destruction of the Reach as we know it. The result would be devastation, famine, and death beyond reckoning. And we all know that the Man is more than willing to honour his threats. I could send soldiers after him, but our forces would be stretched beyond endurance, even if they were able to reach him in time. It's useless, anyway, because no Human army is going to fight and die for

Unhumans, no matter how righteous the cause."

Kaer opened the door to leave. "Jhaeman, release them. That, at least, I can give." He turned and shook his head wearily. "I didn't make this choice lightly. I'd help you if I could. But the world is against you now, and your enemies stretch beyond Eromar. You have few friends even in Chalimor. Saving you would bring devastation on us all, and I can't risk the destruction of the Reach. I *won't* do it."

The guardsman stepped forward and placed his hand on the Reachwarden's shoulder, shifting tongues to express the full depth of his dismay. «Would you trade their people's lives so easily, Qualla'am? Would you turn your back on your oath, on all the decency that you've sworn to defend? I never thought you were that kind of Man. I'm sorry to see that I was wrong.»

Without turning, the Reachwarden said, «If it saves the Reach, it's a small price to pay. Let it go, Jhaeman—it's done. I have spoken. *Chalimor* has spoken.» Shrugging off the younger Man's hand, Kaer left the room and slammed the door behind him.

The small group sat in stunned silence—all but Quill, who wept anew.

CHAPTER SIX

AWAKENING

The soldiers couldn't understand it, but *something* was clearly happening among the prisoners. It started slowly, and most of the Men didn't even notice that the comforting familiarity of the journey seeped away, to be replaced by a growing unease. It might have been the gradual revelation that the creatures weren't walking with their heads bowed and shoulders stooped in despair. Maybe it was when a female refused to follow one of the soldiers into his tent, or the fearlessness in the eyes of her family as they joined in her rebellion. Maybe it was the long-forgotten sound of children's laughter, or the gentle songs that rippled through the ragged crowd at night. In spite of the increasingly brutal weather, the lack of food and fresh water, and the relentless pace that was exhausting even for the Men on horseback, the Unhumans weren't dying anymore, not like they had before the terrible barge accident a few days past. In spite of whippings and more thorough beatings, the creatures were no longer weighed down with resignation. Their eyes were clear of death's shadow now, more every day. The troops were worried; the balance of power had shifted, and they found their pain-enforced authority slipping away with each new dawn. Insurrection was inevitable.

«What would you have me tell the Men, Authority?» asked Vorgha, his thinning hair still dishevelled after his recent Dragon-borne trip to the largest of the exile groups. The Goblin skiff had encountered unceasing turbulence among the storm-ravaged clouds on his return to the makeshift camp, but Vorgha was a faithful retainer and knew his duty well. In spite of an aching desire to sleep, and his dry-mouthed fear of Vald's response to the news, he'd staggered off the airship and hurried to the Dreydmaster's regal tent, bedecked in canvas of purple, gold, and black, to give his report.

Vald remained in his seat, seemingly unsurprised by the news, and continued to read from a small, well-worn book in his hand. This troubled Vorgha more than any outburst, especially now that the goal was so close. So much could go so wrong. How could the Dreydmaster be so calm at such a time?

His fears overwhelming his good sense, Vorgha cleared his throat. «Authority, what would you have me do?»

Vald flipped a page of the book and kept reading. «Nothing.»

«Nothing, sir?»

The Dreydmaster's bristling brows narrowed. «Did you suffer a head injury on your journey, Vorgha? A deafening blow, perhaps?»

«No, I...forgive me, Authority,» the thin Man sputtered and bowed low. «I did not mean to question your wisdom.»

Vald returned his attention to the book. «All is as it should be, you can be certain. There will be no uprising. Return to your tent. The troops have their orders, as do you. I will send for you shortly, so rest while you can.»

The attendant bowed again and backed out of the tent into the dry mountain air of their present campsite. He shaded his eyes and looked around. The camp was located on a wide shelf of stone high on a sandstone mesa overlooking a rocky valley. Thirty or more Men from the other Goblin airships—mostly paid mercenaries, but some Eromar militia soldiers, too—were finishing the construction of a rough-hewn log palisade around the camp. It was a precaution more than a practical necessity, as the Pit Fields were generally devoid of anything that might pose a threat to such a large and growing population. But seeing the devastation around them, Vorgha was still comforted by the presence of the wall.

There was no place in the Reach more blasted and bleak than the doom-haunted Pit Fields of Karkûr. It was in this land of shattered stone and storm that the ancient Dreyd had drawn down the power of the Eld Green into the world of Men. The Dreyd lost their bodies in their ascension during the Melding, and the once-lush land of Karkûr became a desolation of broken mountains and columns of ruddy sandstone now twisted into grotesque shapes like nothing before seen in the world of Men. Vorgha shuddered involuntarily at the sight. Their camp was on the periphery of the Pit Fields, looking over the crag-ridden valley pass that led into the broken red peaks surrounding the region. It was as if all the fiends of the Netherworld had risen from their stinking holes for obscene frolic under the stars, only to be turned to monstrosities of rock with the sun. In towering, blasted stone shaped by catastrophe and the unceasing gnawing of a thousand years of wind and weather, Vorgha could see mute testament to the unbound ambitions of Man.

A strange shadow, like a vague grey storm, hung over the western horizon. It was their destination. It seemed to draw all light into itself, but Vorgha couldn't tell exactly what it was. Each time he tried to focus his gaze on the shape he felt a burning tug at his vision, as if his eyes were losing their ability to see anything other than that awful, uncertain shadow. He turned away from the sight and scuttled back to his tent.

Vorgha knew, better than most, the dangers that now faced the world of Men. The Dreydmaster had taught him much over the years. But he knew, too, that there was only one way to truly bring an end to the dangers, and that knowledge, more than anything else, was why he was here in this horrible place. Lojar Vald's great crusade wasn't just for himself; it was for all Men and their posterity. The ancient Dreyd may have succeeded in throwing down the old order and establishing another, but they had been blinded by their pride; their victory was incomplete, and impurities corrupted the full potential of their grand ideal. Their Melding had been only partial; unnatural remnants of the savage world remained behind to torment, tempt, and bedevil the lives and dreams of untold good Men. And although driven back into the shadows for a thousand years, the Unhumans and their ilk had stubbornly refused to fade away.

But their time had, at last, come to an end. Like any good alchaemical doctor, the Dreydmaster had patiently observed the nature of the illness and tested various treatments, to finally conclude that only surgery could fully cure the patient of such a persistent poison. It had been a long, painful, and bloody ordeal, but it was swiftly nearing its inevitable end.

Such a noble, necessary task was well worth the turmoil and trauma of the many years Vorgha had served as Vald's most trusted attendant. It was worth the blood he'd drawn, the pain he'd felt and inflicted, the family and friends he'd lost along the way. It was worth anything, and everything. Vald's ascension would mean the end of the Unhuman taint.

And then, at long last, Men could breathe free in a world fully their own.

Molli Rose leaned back with a sigh. "I en't never felt nothin' like that before," she said as the green glow faded from the Wielder's skin. "It's like all of Creation is swimmin' inside me."

"That's how it was with me, too," said Tobhi. He adjusted the pillow behind his elder's head to make her more comfortable.

"*Mishko*, Etobhi."

"*Ju'uba.*"

Tarsa sighed deeply, pale but contented. "That's all I can do for now. Give me a little while and I'll be ready for the next few."

Molli Rose looked at the she-Kyn intently and said, "What's it like, Wielder? What's it feel like to have the whole world inside ye?"

Tobhi had wondered the same thing many times, but it always seemed too big a question, one that could never be answered in a lifetime of ease and reflection, let alone in the chaotic mix of exhaustion, hunger, and hurried conversations under the watchful eyes of the enemy.

It seemed that Tarsa was having the same trouble with the question. Her brows knitted in thought and her sensory stalks caressed her cheeks. "I'm not sure how to explain it—I can't even remember what it felt like before. The *wyr* is so much a part of me now; I *am* the *wyr*. It's in everything I see, everything I touch. I can feel its rhythms and songs even in this spirit-hungry land of Men." Her voice grew soft and distant, as though coming from a remembered conversation, not the living part of her that sat, tattooed and cross-legged, on the matted dirt of the makeshift camp. "I hear voices in my dreams, thousands of them, all singing the same song, but I don't understand the words. The drumbeat is familiar, as are the songs, but they're in a language I no longer understand, if I ever did. The song gets louder as we move westward, and I get closer to knowing it, to hearing what's truly being said. But the voices escape me now. And I'm getting so tired."

Her stalks slowed down and her eyes grew heavy, but she jerked awake just as her head bobbed downward. Tobhi reached over in concern. "Don't worry," Tarsa said with a reassuring smile, "I'll be fine. I just need to walk around a bit and stretch my legs. You stay here with Molli and enjoy your talk. I'll come find you later." The Tetawa started to protest, but Tarsa waved away his concern. "Really, Tobhi, I'm fine. I just need a bit of air to clear my thoughts."

He watched her pull a worn wool shawl tightly around her shoulders before she disappeared into the crowd. "She's workin' herself too hard. She's gonna end up sick if she don't take start gettin' some rest."

Molli laughed. "That one can certainly take care of herself, little worrier! I'm glad she went with ye to Eromar all that time ago—I can't think of nobody better. If she can carry the essence of the Eternity Tree halfway across the Reach, I doubt there's anythin' that can cause her much trouble." She shifted the weight on her wrapped leg.

Seeing the Leafspeaker's eyes travel to the grimy bandages, she laughed again. "And don't ye go worryin' yeself about me. I en't a Wielder, but I en't goin' nowhere. Good brains will serve me just as

good as the *wyr*, I reckon. Besides, ye've been lookin' more than a bit
wore out yeself, so maybe ye should be thinkin' to yer own health and
stop yer frettin' over the rest of us."

"I s'pose so. I en't been able to get much sleep at night."

Molli Rose's face darkened. "They en't nobody who sleeps well these
days, cub."

Tarsa walked slowly through the camp and breathed in the thin
smoke from the few fires allowed the exiles. Wood was scarce in this
broken land, mostly strange, stunted pine and brush oak that burned
fitfully at best. Groups of four, five, and six were scattered in all directions for a half-mile or more, up nearly to the edges of the jagged valley that surrounded them, but no further, as the soldiers were
increasingly vigilant. The Men might be more watchful, but they were
also frightened, so the nights were less dangerous than before. There
hadn't been a beating or a death in the last few days. Although food
was scarce for all, there were no more threats of withholding the
wormy flour and rancid meat. It wasn't an ideal situation, but it was
growing tolerable.

At least it was for the rest of the Folk. For the young Wielder, the
journey was becoming more frightening. She could feel herself fading
into the Tree. At first the power was invigorating, but then came the
voices, and the gradual realization that her memories and emotions
were growing more distant. She knew they were there, could sometimes touch and recall them, but with every passing day she felt more
space between herself and the life she knew and wanted. The Tree
would survive, and with it the Folk, but what about her?

A hand on her shoulder brought Tarsa back to the present. It was
Jitani. They exchanged weak smiles.

"I promised to look after you, Wielder. You haven't made it too easy
for me," the warrior teased.

"No, I suppose I haven't. I'm sorry."

"Don't be. I'm glad you're not too easy to catch; I enjoy a bit of adventure."

An awkward silence fell as they continued walking, now with a bit of distance between them.

Tarsa cleared her throat. "You gave up a lot to be with us."

"No more than anyone else here. Some have lost much more than I did." Her golden eyes were deep and warm. "Tell me more about Unahi."

"What do you want to know?"

Jitani turned her gaze eastward, to the Everland that now lay so very far away. "My brother admired your aunt very much. She taught him a lot about the Deep Green, and he shared it with me. I was on my travels before I could get to know her very well, and during the Council she was so busy with the other Wielders. By the time it was over, it was too late."

A heavy weight seemed to settle into the Tarsa's stomach. "I wish I could tell you everything you want to know about her teachings, but I can't. I didn't know her long enough to receive them all. There's still so much I have to learn, so much I don't comprehend yet. But I can tell you that she was brave, and defiant, and loving, in her own way. I miss her, more than I would have ever expected. She'd have been able to help me understand what's happening to me now."

They walked together in silence to one of the fires, where a few of their fellow travellers sat huddled together. Tarsa recognized Oryn and the short-haired Woman, Eladrys, as well as some of the Ubbetuk. The two Tetawi brothers had found some of their kinfolk. Someone was missing.

"Where's Daladir?" she asked.

Oryn pointed to a large boulder at the far edge of the camp. "He went to meet with the Governor and a few others over there."

Tarsa thanked the Man and started toward the rock, but stopped to look back at Jitani, who stood hesitantly beside the fire.

"Well, my green-haired guardian," she smiled teasingly, "let's go. We have enough troubles as it is without adding my disappearance to your burdens." She reached out and took Jitani by the hand, as she had the day they left the Everland.

"It's a good plan," Garyn said. "But much will depend on our Jaaga friends. They know the land; they know what plants grow here and what animals are best for food and clothing." He shook his head sadly. "Our days of bounty are far behind us."

Daladir shrugged. "For a while, perhaps. But don't forget that we have many friends in the Reach. They might not have been able to strike against Eromar with force, but they won't abandon us here. Our trade partners in the Allied Wilderlands have always valued our weaving skills and other arts, as have many in Dûrûk and Sarvannadad. It might take some time to open up the trade routes again, but we won't be without options forever."

"Much will depend, of course, on whether the other Folk will agree to the idea," said Averyn, as Tarsa and Jitani joined them.

"What idea is this?" the young Wielder asked.

"We've been thinking about the future, now that it seems likely we'll actually have one," Garyn said. "We know that life will be different and very difficult in our new home. It will be hard, for all of us. Even when our enemies gone, our needs will be great, and there is a grave danger that we will fall upon each other in a starved fury for the meagre resources that remain."

"I've tried to avoid thinking about it," Tarsa said.

"Well, we've got to start, because it will likely get bad very quickly," said Daladir. "There's a lot of rage building out there, and when the Men are gone, our only target will be one another. We have to channel that pain and anger and fear and frustration into something useful, something that will give us reason to live, not an excuse to die."

"What's your suggestion?"

"A confederation of the free Folk, not unlike the Sevenfold Council," Averyn said. "Only this time it would be permanent, rather than being brought together only in times of great crisis. Each nation of the Folk would still remain independent; we'd all choose our own leaders and decide our own community concerns, but we'd be part of a larger group, an interdependent league of peoples dedicated to the creation of another strong homeland, linking ourselves to one another in an alliance belt for both conflict and peace. Perhaps together, with a hopeful vision we can create and share as kith gathered around the same fire, we'll be able to stop our people from disintegrating when the Darkening Road is over. Without that hope, it won't be Men who will destroy us; we'll do it to ourselves."

They'd all felt the slow, silent slipping away of those deep connections that had kept the Folk strong since time immemorial, even during the catastrophic Melding. With so many of their people dead and dying, with so much pain and trauma, the ties of kinship and tradition were slowly but certainly unravelling. It started with the little courtesies, the small observances of honour and respect, and then escalated to beatings…and worse. Too many younglings now knew the pain of a beating at the hand of family; some who were once loved and trusted stalked she-Kyn and younglings in the darkness.

With his consort's help, Garyn stood and bowed to the two she-Kyn and Daladir, who stood up to bid him goodbye. "I must go to think about this idea some more. Molli Rose will be most interested, as will others. There is still much to be done." He leaned heavily into Averyn. "Now, beloved, will you…."

The Governor stopped abruptly as Daladir slumped to the earth. Tarsa rushed forward. Daladir was still conscious, but his face was gaunt, his breathing shallow.

"What's happening to him?" Jitani asked.

"He's tried to be so strong, to deny himself the help he needed." The Wielder held the he-Kyn's head up. "He didn't want me to waste my strength on him, so he pushed himself, harder than anyone, until he couldn't do it any longer. I've got to help him."

"Bring him to our wagon—night has fallen, and you risk revealing yourself too much in the darkness," Garyn said, ushering them into the crowd. Tarsa nodded in agreement, her throat tight, as Jitani lifted Daladir into her strong arms and followed the others.

"You shouldn't have done it, Tarsa. I was just a bit dizzy. It would have passed." He looked at the Wielder in mingled irritation and gratitude. "Why do you have to be so Dreyd-damned stubborn all the time?"

She stroked his cheek with her fingers. "Do you feel any difference?"

"How can you ask that?" He closed his eyes and sighed gently. "It's like nothing I've ever felt before. The pain is gone, the fear, all of it. My whole body is singing."

"Then enjoy the song," she whispered. "Sleep now, Daladir. I'll be here when you wake."

The he-Kyn smiled. "I couldn't sleep if I wanted to. It's been so long since I've felt anything but endless exhaustion. I just want to lie here and enjoy it, and think about the future." He became more serious. "I hope it's a future with you."

Tarsa hesitated for a moment. "Daladir, I...we...."

He took her hand. "I don't want to bind you to me, Tarsa. Different fires burn inside us, but I do love you. And I know you care for me, too, though I'm not the only one your heart desires. If you'll have me, I want to share in your future, in some small way."

"Even though it means that you won't be the only one at my side?" she asked, looking back at Jitani, who sat nearby, uncertain, with her arms wrapped around her knees.

"Even then. Your love for her is part of who you are—I wouldn't divide your heart between us."

The Wielder turned to Daladir with a look of surprise. He smiled again. There was no guile or hesitation in his expression, only love and the rising flush of desire.

An unexpected weight on her spirit slipped away. For now, the burden of the Tree was forgotten. Her love wasn't a finite, limited thing; it expanded and grew with the giving. She could let go of her grief and fear; these two brave and passionate Kyn didn't demand that she hide her difference or push it aside—her strangeness was part of her, and they both loved it, too. They saw beauty when they looked at her, not the monstrous thing she so often saw in herself. In their loving eyes, she was complete, not fragmented and broken, as she'd so long feared. The choice wasn't between these lovers and those of the past; it was a choice between sharing love today or letting it wither into something small and cold and fearful. She felt her passion flow through the world, and she made the choice.

She would be whole again.

Tarsa slid over to Jitani. The warrior's face was flushed but remote, as though she was preparing herself for a long-feared rejection, but the Wielder could feel a pain there that required a different kind of healing than the green glow of the Heartwood could give.

She reached out a hand to Jitani's temple, hesitating before softly resting her fingertips on the copper bindings of the severed stalk-trunks that lay nestled in the warrior's mossy hair. Jitani stiffened, and a flash of panic swept through her golden eyes. To touch another's sensory stalks was an act of unequalled intimacy. To lose a stalk through intent or accident was tragedy, as the loss drained the world of sensual possibility and connection. The world was poorer now without two of her stalks; the air lost much of its perfume, fruit its sweet delight. In all the years since her loss, no one had ever touched her injured stalks before.

But Tarsa's touch was gentle. She gave more than she took as her fingers loosened the copper bands and let them fall to the earth, revealing the pale, wounded beauty of the remnant trunks. Jitani had longed to know that touch since she first saw the young Wielder speaking defiantly to the Sevenfold Council in defence of the Old Ways of the People, dreamed of it since the day Tarsa saved her life with a healing kiss.

This moment, too, was part of the Old Ways. It was right and good. In all of Jitani's dreams and visions, the warrior-Wielder's touch had never been so tender as it was now.

"It happened...a long time ago," Jitani whispered and pulled Tarsa's hand to her lips. "But I remember pleasure, and passion."

Tarsa's eyelids fluttered as Jitani's kisses trailed down her wrist and inner arm. She embraced the warrior and kissed her deeply, then moved back to Daladir and slid atop his trembling body. Her shawl fell to the floor. As their sensory stalks intertwined and wove together, their hunger rising beyond the thin and fragile limits of their flesh, a soft groan escaped the he-Kyn's lips, and he rose up to meet her, hard and warm, sliding his hands beneath her blouse and pushing the garment from her shoulders. Tarsa's own hands pulled at Jitani's belt, drawing it away, letting the breeches fall to reveal flushed bronze skin gleaming with fragrant sweat. The golden-eyed warrior hesitated, but only for a moment, and then her remaining stalks slid outward, strong and bold, as she knelt, smiling, to join the moist and tender caress.

"Let there be a healing," Tarsa sighed, and she slid into their waiting arms.

CYCLE SIX

THORN AND FLOWER

This is a story of the Tetawi Folk, from a time long before the Expulsion, when they and all their Sevenfold kith still lived and loved in the sheltered shadows of the great wyrwood trees and white-capped peaks of the place once known as the Everland.

It is a teaching.

In the old days, before the Melding separated the Everland from the Eld Green, the greater spirit-beings walked the world among their children. Granny Turtle—old Jenna—would often dance around the fire with in the form of an age-worn Tetawa granny with turtle shell leggings wrapped around her calves, pounding out a rattling rhythm as she moved, teaching her grandchildren the songs of thankfulness and celebration that would strengthen them for the hard times to come. Kitichi, the mischievous Squirrel-spirit, lived and loved among the small Folk, his foolish self-indulgence and laziness becoming part of the lessons that young cubs learned as they navigated the world in their growth toward maturity. Tetawi delighted in the exploits of Jippita, the whistling Cricket, and her dreamy but slow-witted Moth friend, Theedeet the Whisperer, and wisely avoided crossing Mother Malluk, the strong but foul-tempered Peccary who so often ended up the object of Kitichi's poorly-planned trickery. The Clan-heralds of all the Tetawi travelled among these brown-skinned Folk, sharing their lives and wisdom as best they could, always giving honour to the Eld Green and its bounty.

There were other spirits, though, who were rarely encountered by the Tetawi, for their purpose was not to walk among the Folk. Formed by the combined efforts of the Mothers of the Folk, these spirits came into being for one single purpose: to guard and protect their world and its inhabitants. One was Guraadja, the winged and antlered Bear-Snake. He was unlike the other Clan-heralds, in that he resembled no other creature that walked the living world; there was no Clan named for him, no mundane versions of his kind inhabiting the deep forests or high peaks. Later, Human scholars studying the Tetawi story-cycle would say that Guraadja and his kind were abominations, the result of confused memories and corrupted stories of the most ancient times.

But Tetawi know differently. True, Guraadja was the only one of his kind, but he wasn't alone, for he and the other Anomalous were kindred to all the Tetawi—indeed, to all the Folk. They belonged to all the worlds, not just one, and could travel freely between the skies and the greenlands and the dark underworld, serving the People with all their varied gifts and talents. Yet first among them was Guraadja. Thus it was that the powerful upper body of a great brown bear and the broad rack of a noble stag of the Middle Place were joined with the shimmering scales and massive lower form of a snake of the Lower Place; Guraadja's kinship to the Upper Place was represented by four majestic wings, iridescent like a celestial rainbow. His swift friend and ally, Saazja the Dreamer, the winged Stag-Rabbit, travelled through the Eld Green bringing news of the other spirit-beings, the Folk, the Beasts, and the leafy peoples, understanding the ways of their homeland and its relationship to the worlds beyond. The other Anomalous and their rare descendants were tied to the three realms—the Upper, the Middle, and the Lower—and journeyed between them to keep them balanced, and to keep them safe, but most powerful among them were the Bear-Snake and his small but keen-eyed companion.

Saazja had seen Kaantor, the proud and greedy Man who would usher in the catastrophe of the Melding, and warned Guraadja of the visitor's strange ways, but the great Bear-Snake dismissed his friend's concerns, seeing little danger in a frail and solitary creature without wyr powers or family to strengthen him. Saazja was more insightful— he knew from experience that the seemingly small and weak could harbour hidden strengths, and he'd seen a frighteningly insatiable hunger in Kaantor's dark eyes. So he watched, and waited, and was ready when Kaantor revealed his ravenous self.

Too late Guraadja realized his folly, and as the Eld Green began to dissolve beneath the power of Decay, and the worlds of Men and the Folk collapsed into one another, he rushed to undo what his negligence had permitted. Yet there was nothing he could do to stop the Melding, and he raged against the collapsing worlds in a fury never before seen in the three great worlds. His great roar was thunder across the cosmos, and his claws were lightning that tore the skies apart. All of Creation trembled from his struggles, and from his blood rose Skyfire and Thunder, the Storm-Born Twins, who bore on their Tetawi-shaped bodies the wings, antlers, and scaled flesh of their three-world father. Yet even their efforts added to those of great Guraadja could not stop the Melding.

All was not lost, however, for as the Eld Green broke apart and the Everland became fused to Peredir, the world of Men, Saazja returned from his travels with most of the Eld Green's great spirit-beings following closely behind, unified in their fear and uncertainty. They gathered together beneath Guraadja's protective wings—turtle and squirrel and tree and moss and eagle and serpent-kind and boulder and others all shielded from the worst of the devastation—and watched in horror as the world they'd known disappeared into the cosmic maelstrom of the Melding.

What happened to the rest of the Eld Green is unknown. Some spirit-beings vanished with the Melding, others were broken and weakened by the experience, while yet others struggled to recover and guide their now-mortal children and grandchildren in the ways of their scarred and wounded new world. Granny Jenna, Kitichi, and most of the Clan-heralds of the Tetawi survived, as did the forebears of the Kyn, the Gvaerg, and most of the other Folk. But brave Guraadja and his faithful friend Saazja were lost in the chaos, their sacrifice ensuring the continuity of their exiled kith.

Of all the Folk, it is the Tetawi who remember the Bear-Snake and the Stag-Rabbit in their stories and round-dance songs. Some say that these and other Anomalous died in the Melding, torn apart by the strange energies released through Kaantor's betrayal. Others claim that they did not die, but that they were lost in another place, a strange and lonely shadow pocket between the Eld Green and Peredir, still fighting to ensure that Decay is not fully victorious, that when they are triumphant in their battle they will return to live among their kith in the green lands of their creation. No one has seen or heard from them in the long thousand years since, but their story is remembered in song, in spirit, and in dream. Theirs is a lesson of vigilance, of sacrifice, of endurance, no matter how great the struggle, no matter how terrible the cost. Theirs is a living legacy, for as long as the Folk live on.

This is a teaching, and a remembrance.

CHAPTER 7

SECRETS

Meggie Mar was a Woman who cherished order above all else. In her world, all things had their place and function, and it was the duty of all right-thinking people to challenge chaos in all its manifestations. Some people fought such battles with swords or speeches; Meggie's own crusade was on a smaller field. Her household was the first line of defence against anarchy, and her weapons were broom, cloth, needle, and ladle. Even Denarra's eccentricities were muted in Meggie's domain. Those who threatened the peaceful routine of the clean and orderly house found in the narrow-eyed Woman an implacable foe, one who wouldn't rest until the known reaches of her world were brought back into the eternal harmony she desired. Love, for Meggie Mar, was expressed by commitment to this cause, and her love and commitment were boundless.

Thus, it was the house matron who suffered the most under the despair that descended after the Reachwarden rejected Quill's plea for aid. The Tetawa was inconsolable and refused to leave her room, even to eat. Meggie's strict rule about shared meals crumbled, and the maid Ellefina took food to Quill's room in spite of the older Woman's grumblings. Denarra remained in her dressing gown all day long and rarely got out of bed, further disrupting household custom. She did come to the dinner table for her own meals, but Meggie almost preferred the Strangeling's absence to the grim, puffy-eyed spectre that appeared. Denarra even stopped styling her hair and never asked once about her beloved peacocks, which heightened Meggie's already significant concern.

Even the young Man, Merrimyn, was wreaking havoc in the household. He'd taken to staying out all night, only to appear in the morning, drunken and bruised. After a few hours of fitful sleep and minimal sustenance, he'd leave again, followed closely by poor Padwacket, who spent each night keeping the young Man from mortal danger. The valet was wearing down as a result, and his own health and work were suffering.

The insanity had gone on long enough. Although Meggie rarely involved herself with matters beyond her little domain, she'd worked with Denarra for many years and knew well the best available resources. Life was changing much too quickly for her liking, as swiftly in the household as in the world outside, and if she didn't do something she knew that the chaos would rule the day. So she found paper in Denarra's study, wrote a short note and sealed it, and called for Padwacket. The Ubbetuk had been sleeping and was barely coherent when he arrived, but Meggie assured him that their troubles would likely be over if he agreed to deliver the note. She couldn't trust the errand to the maids, as Padwacket alone had access to some parts of the city enjoyed by no one else in the household.

When the valet was gone, Meggie replaced her dusty apron with a clean one, and took a broom to the front hall. If the forces of chaos expected an easy victory in this house, they were greatly mistaken.

A piercing shriek ripped through the air. Merrimyn shot upright in his bed, but the pain in his temples sent him sliding back to the pillows with a whimper.

Padwacket entered the room and drew the drapes away from the window to fill the room with blinding daylight. Another scream echoed down the hallway. It was coming closer, but the Ubbetuk seemed unconcerned. "What's happening?" Merrimyn choked out through the thick paste that coated his tongue and sent his stomach churning.

Before Padwacket could speak, Merrimyn saw for himself the source of the terrible sounds. Meggie Mar and Ellefina were dragging Denarra backward down the hall toward the downstairs bathing chamber, the matron's face set in an expression of patient efficiency, the maid's in a silly grin. The Strangeling fought and howled like a wounded panther, but the Womens' grip on her legs was firm, so Denarra could do little more than curse unintelligibly. Merrimyn was shocked to see how dishevelled the ever-fashionable Wielder had become. He swallowed hard, trying to push down his sudden grief and nausea.

"What's been happening?" he groaned as Padwacket tidied the room. The Binder looked down and realized that he still wore his Jubilee clothes from days ago. The sudden, stinking tang of cheap alcohol and other less savoury smells in the fabric overwhelmed his control. He threw himself out of the covers toward the bedpan and crouched with streaming eyes until his clenching stomach was empty. Without any sign of emotion, Padwacket carried the pan from the room and returned with a hot wet rag, which he used to wipe the young Man's face. Merrimyn leaned back against the foot of his bed, breathing heavily, waiting for the world to stop spinning.

The sounds of what seemed to be an epic battle in the bathing chamber filled the house, and in spite of his raging headache and swollen throat, Merrimyn smiled.

Padwacket raised an eyebrow. "Don't be too smug," the valet said. "Meggie's coming for you next."

«What you are proposing is, well, utterly unprecedented.»

«Yes, it is.»

«And you understand the consequences and complexities of such an act, I assume?»

«No. That's why I'm here to talk with you.»

The old Man chuckled. He finished pouring a cup of tea for his distinguished visitor before returning to his own plush chair that stood in a small semicircle of cleared space among dozens of precariously high stacks of books, tablets, scrolls, and sheaves of papers, like a strong tower in the ruins of a once-great civilization. Though it was already midmorning, the First Magistrate's chamber was dark, lit only by a single oil lamp; the velvet drapes on the great leaded glass windows were rarely pulled away, as direct sunlight threatened the delicate pigments on the maps and tapestries on the few areas of wall without bookshelves packed nearly to bursting. Even in this unnaturally hot late summer, the Jurist Temple of the Sovereign Republic Court was frigid, for its stone walls were thick and ancient, and the fickle warmth of the strange late summer beyond never reached the squat structure's heart.

Kell Brennard didn't mind the cold. He was used to it by now, having served in the Jurist Temple for nearly twenty years. He'd long ago taken to wearing ornate, fur-lined dressing gowns and slippers in his private study, and though he was older and more susceptible to the humid chill beyond the building, the stale cold of these wood panelled walls was familiar and almost comfortable now. Leaving the Temple for any reason these days was always unpleasant for Brennard, as protocol and good taste forbade him from wearing the dressing gown in public, and the moth-eaten but familiar garment kept him far warmer than the thin fabrics of his ceremonial jacket, breeches, and hose. Here he could dress in whatever way he wanted, fashion and protocol be damned.

«Well, if it's advice you want,» he said, «I'm happy to provide what guidance I can. But I tell you, Qualla'am, this is new ground for me. I'm not at all sure that I can be of any help.»

The Reachwarden wrapped his brown hands around the teacup. He respected his host too much to wear his overcoat in the study, but he was grateful for the warmth of the drink. «Don't be modest, old friend—it doesn't suit you.»

Again the First Magistrate laughed. He was bent and aged, with a thick mane of silver hair and trembling, blue-veined hands, but there was fire still in his watery green eyes, and a firm set to the jaw that even his ill-set porcelain teeth couldn't diminish. «True, too true. I've always struggled against pride, all my life. You'd think by now that I'd be old enough to not care what others think, but those old habits are too hard to surrender, and even the false veneer of humility is preferable to the unrelenting arrogance of the young clerks and solicitors who strut down these halls. At least I always had the talent to justify my haughty self-regard.»

He slid into his chair and took up his own teacup in hand. «Enough about my own endless and rather uninteresting inner struggles. You have a far more pressing struggle of your own. So what do we do about the Everland, Qualla'am? You've made a rather bold suggestion.»

«Yes.»

«You know that a declaration of war against an allied province without Parliament's approval is utterly illegal, of course.»

The Reachwarden sighed, almost imperceptibly. «Yes, I know that, too. But I was hoping that....»

«That there would be a way to circumvent the Code of Confederation? That you would be able to assert absolute authority on a matter as important as the unity of the Republic itself? No, Qualla'am, it's quite impossible. You made an oath when you were selected by the Reach Assembly to serve as Reachwarden, and that oath was quite specific: 'I will honour the obligations of my office to ensure the stability, integrity, and expansion of the Republic of the Reach of Men, with no higher duty than to the Reach and its peoples, and with acknowledgment that I share these responsibilities with the Assembly and Sovereign Court and will defer to their respective powers.' *With no higher duty.* The Reach is what matters, Qualla'am. It's what brought us peace and prosperity after centuries of petty royalist feuds that soaked the land with blood and left the people poisoned with the hunger for vengeance. It's what we've fought to keep secure for nearly forty years, since the old monarchy was thrown down and a new government of the people themselves was installed. We cannot afford a civil war, and certainly not for such a cause, no matter how righteous. The Reach will endure, but only if you keep true to the oath you gave. As long as you are Reachwarden, you must honour that pledge.»

Kaer slumped back in the chair, his tea forgotten and quickly grow-ing cool. He wasn't surprised that Kell Brennard knew the words of that oath by heart, for he had once said those words himself, having served two controversial terms as the third and thus far most expan-sionist-minded Reachwarden. Qualla'am Kaer was the fifth in the line of leaders of the Republic, and to date his term had been the most peaceful of all his predecessors. «It's not right, Kell, and you know it,» Kaer said, his words echoing the sentiment of his guard captain's dis-appointment when the Reachwarden refused to help the little Brownie maid and her friends. He hadn't talked with Jhaeman since, and the younger Man's dismay over his hero's apparent moral failure still haunted him.

Right was right. It had to be, otherwise what was the point of all this glory and grandeur? He couldn't accept that all the sacrifices he and others had made for so many years were hollow, without purpose beyond expedience and the ambitions of powerful Men. «We can't just sit back while Vald destroys them. The Repubic is a virtuous ideal, not just cold reality. If anyone understands this, it's you.»

The old Man nodded. «I've been a Jurist for far longer than I was in your position, Qualla'am, but in my deepest dreams at night I remain the Reachwarden who single-handedly doubled the territories claimed by the Reach. I'm the one who used both politics and pressure to extend our influence over the western lands with funds seized from Andaaka when we brought the province to heel after the last near-rebellion—a campaign in which you served quite bravely and with true distinction, as I recall. I knew that we couldn't survive as a nation if we didn't have unfettered access to both the eastern and western waters, and Andaaka was the test. Had we failed then, the Reach would have shrivelled and died.» He frowned at the memory, but his features softened, and he smiled. «Yes, I know what an ideal can do for a people. I saw freedom in those new lands, a great people growing even greater with the wide expanse of our possibility. Even so, the yammering Assembly balked at my actions, saying that I'd overstepped my authority and risked our economic stability; the Sovereign Court hotly deliberated the legality of both the seizure and the purchase, but the people rallied to support me and my vision, and, eventually, protests faded. My legacy and the future of the Reach were preserved.»

He leaned back in his chair and sipped at his tea. «Yes, I was bold, and it served us well. I was elevated into the Sovereign Court after the end of my second term, and I've been here ever since. It's been a good life, and I have no regrets. But this is a different cause altogether, my friend.»

«Not entirely,» the current Reachwarden corrected. «It was the expansion west that first put the lands of the Folk under scrutiny. Their lands stand between us and the western sea. It was just a matter of time before the pressure to surrender the Everland became overwhelming.»

Brennard shrugged. «It was inevitable anyway, Qualla'am. The Reach must be the sole sovereignty on this continent; any other claims to autonomy must be eliminated—through peaceful integration if possible, by force if necessary. If the Everland were to remain free, it would embolden every other disaffected region to take up arms and declare their independence. Andaaka will always be a problem, for the Dreydcaste hold the alliance in contempt, and it is only their rather feeble military position that keeps them from rebelling; the people who inhabit the Allied Wilderlands are far too enamoured of their freedom, and they chafe at their subservience to the greater Reach; Eromar is one step away from armed insurrection; the Lawless and Dûrûk are only nominally part of the full alliance. Whether by Eromar's doing now or Chalimor's doing later, the Everland was always fated to become part of the Reach. It cannot be a symbol of resistance, Qualla'am. For our own survival, the Everland as it exists has to die.»

«No,» Kaer said, setting his cup on the table beside him. «I don't accept that. I *won't* accept it. Is our nation so fragile then, our vision so frail, that allowing others to live freely as they have since time out of mind threatens us so much? Can we not live as allies with a shared purpose and destiny, rather than always be perceived as inevitably self-ish potential enemies, facing each other with false smiles and poisoned daggers behind our backs? The Folk themselves manage to respect their differences and still work toward harmony and consensus; is it unthinkable that we might do the same? Is brutal selfishness really what you believe to be at the heart of the Republic?»

«You and I both know you're not that naïve, Qualla'am, so don't pretend to be shocked.» The First Magistrate had no anger in his voice; this was an old and well-worn debate between the two, grown more urgent with the political events of recent months. «Men are fundamentally different from their kind. I, too, mourn the loss of life, and if this was a world in which ideals could survive self-interest, I would advise you to gather an army and march against Eromar on your way to liberating the Everland for its ignorant and idolatrous inhabitants. But you will not find an army willing to kill Men on behalf of Unhumans, nor will you find the Parliament in any mood to support this cause. And while the Sovereign Court would likely find Vald's actions to be illegal and a gross presumption of authority belonging to no provincial prefect, we can't realistically enforce our ruling without you and Parliament, and you don't have the political support to do so either. At any rate, the Folk have no legal standing in the Republic: they are neither citizens nor slaves, and thus outside laws of civil society and property. They don't exist, as far as the laws of the Republic are concerned, except in that they are recognized as having been the first inhabitants of the land. Their continued presence on those lands is at the Republic's pleasure, and as the political mood shifts, that pleasure can be withdrawn at any time. I understand and share your desire to help them, Qualla'am, but you would serve them better by encouraging them to become citizens of the Reach and to abandon their failed dreams of independence. Whatever their past and present, their future is with the Reach, or not at all.

Beyond that, there's nothing else you can do within the laws of this country and the terms of the oath you took at Reachwarden.»

«I didn't accept this office to be party to the wholesale degradation and slaughter of an entire race of people, Kell. That's not why I fought for the Republic for all those years.»

The First Magistrate shook his silvered head, and he looked at his world-weary successor with genuine sympathy. «Of course it is, my friend, though you may not have known or believed it at the time. How else do you think great nations come into being? The Reach stands for many fine and beautiful things, and its light is bright among nations in this world, but the more light we see, the more shadow stretches behind it.»

They talked for a while longer, on topics far removed from the one burdening the Reachwarden's heart, but it was a courtesy conversation only, and Kaer was soon ready to go. The room was too cold, his mind too confused. But before Kaer left, Brennard placed a firm hand on his shoulder. «You look upon the long shadow of the Reach of Men, Qualla'am. To destroy the shadow, you would have to destroy the light. Every Reachwarden comes to know one unhappy, inevitable truth: there are many shades of grey in this world, but in the end, you don't have grey without black and white.»

"Quill, are you there?"

The answer was long in coming. "Yes. Come in."

Denarra entered the room, freshly scrubbed, perfumed, and dressed in a pleated green skirt with a puff-shouldered white blouse embroidered with gold and maroon glass beads. There was no evidence of the strain of the last few days, other than the dark circles under the Strangeling's eyes. Meggie had even taken care to braid and wrap Denarra's undyed brown hair in a respectable crown around her head, tied firmly with a maroon ribbon.

Quill looked up from the side of the bed where she sat looking out the window. Her three dolls sat on the windowsill, their faces drawn, their heads bowed in mourning. The Dolltender gave Denarra a slight smile, but her face was still swollen from crying. She, too, was clothed, having been the first one subjected to Meggie's special brand of therapy. Her plain brown dress was unadorned, except for a yellow belt with black spiders woven into the fabric.

There was so much to talk about, but neither wanted to bring the grief back to the surface, as the present semblance of normalcy was still very new and fragile. Yet they'd been brought out of their solitude for a reason. "You look lovely," Denarra said as she sat beside the Tetawa. "Brown clashes terribly with my complexion, but it really suits you, especially with your hair."

"Thank you."

Silence. The night of the Jubilee was an unwelcome subject for conversation. It had become a cruel, unhappy joke, and a wound best left to heal on its own.

"Have you eaten? I'm absolutely famished. Should we go see what Meggie's made us for dinner—that is, if she had time to make anything in between driving us all into a scalding tub with no warning and precious little tenderness. My neck is still raw."

Quill shrugged. "No, thank you. I'm not really all that hungry."

"Darling," Denarra said, pulling Quill to her, "you can't surrender to despair. It's just not like you. You've come too far to stop now."

The Dolltender bit her lip. "What's the point, Denarra? It's done; it's over. The Reachwarden has turned his back on us, on everything we came here for. You have a good life here, but my life was with my people. When Vald is done with them, the Folk will be gone, and there'll be no reason for me to be here anymore. He's won."

"*NO!*" Denarra shouted. Quill stepped back as the Strangeling jumped to her feet. "I will *not* allow you to surrender! We haven't fought shape-shifting cannibals, Seeker assassins, and hundreds of miles of bad food and worse fashion to surrender to a petty tyrant with more bile than brains! Vald hasn't won *anything* yet, and he's not going to. Our people might be fighting for their lives, but they're not dead yet, and we're not going to let them die." She grabbed Quill by the shoulders. "Between you, me, and Merrimyn, we can shake this Melded world to its twisted roots. All we have to do is be smart about it, and be courageous enough to fight on, no matter what the cost. You're braver than you think, Quill. It's time now to be brave for your Tobhi, if not for yourself."

The Tetawa sat in silence. Memories of her last night with Tobhi came flooding back. He became a part of her on that night, not so long ago, and she him. After that love-bonding, she was certain that she would feel if he was truly dead. She felt pain and loss, but not emptiness. Tobhi still lived. Of that simple fact, and that fact alone, the Dolltender had no doubt.

Denarra sighed and moved toward the door but stopped as Quill hopped off the bed. "Wait," the Tetawa said, smoothing the wrinkles from her dress. "I think I'm starting to get my appetite back."

They walked together to the dining room, where Merrimyn, Meggie, and Padwacket sat together with a new visitor. The she-Folk stopped short. The figure sat framed in the golden light of the doorway. For a moment a flash of fear raced through Quill, as the shape resembled the hunching silhouette of Jago Chaak, the Skeeger who'd tried to kill her. But it was something else entirely, an elderly Ubbetuk in white robes and cap, a frilled lace collar around his neck, with a wasp-headed walking staff in his withered hand.

Blackwick, the Ubbetuk Chancellor, looked up at Denarra and reached out a hand in greeting. The Strangeling had regained her composure, but her eyes were wide in amazement. "Denarra Syrene, you are a vision of loveliness, now as always. We have never had the pleasure of a formal introduction, but I have seen you at many social functions, and young Padwacket here has kept me informed of your many exploits." He smiled. "I was most pleased to receive Meggie's note through my kithsman this morning."

"And this, I assume, is the remarkable gate-walker you wrote me about?" he asked the house matron. Meggie nodded, refilling his mug of tea. The Chancellor's large eyes turned to Quill. The Dolltender had the feeling that his very presence was reaching into her, ferreting out the secret places and fears that she kept well hidden in the recesses of her mind. She felt indescribable relief when he turned away.

Blackwick pulled a small silver whistle from a hidden fold of his robes and blew on it. Within moments the front door of the house opened and a small group of Ubbetuk in tasselled blue caps and long greatcoats entered with a large wooden box that shook and shuddered. The box was wrapped tightly with iron cords; from within came a high-pitched scraping sound. A foul scent seeped out from between the boards. The Chancellor nodded to the Bluecaps, who returned outside, and drank deeply from his steaming mug as if nothing had happened.

"The news, as you know, is grim," said Blackwick as he sipped his tea, ignoring the loud rattling from the box. "It gets worse each day. I will spare you news about the Darkening Road, as you are already well aware of that dreadful event. Instead, my information goes beyond that, to Vald's true reasons for claiming the Everland. My most recent information from the Ubbetuk borough in Eromar City is that Vald has seized all the airships in the city, as well as their crews, and is using them for the transportation of himself, many Binders, and a wide variety of alchaemical instruments to a remote site in the Pit Fields of Karkûr. We estimate that he has at least thirty ships at his disposal, including twelve galleons that are easily converted into warships."

The Chancellor's face grew grave. "I have woefully underestimated Vald, and the price of that mistake has been terrible."

"What mistake?" asked Denarra, her voice tight with sudden fear.

"When Vald first made his intentions toward the Everland known, I, like others, believed that it was a greed for land that was at the heart of his crusade. It was a reasonable inference, given the history of land-theft among the nations of Men. Reasonable, but mistaken. Land was always part of the plan, but it was the surface only. No, Lojar Vald's dream reaches far deeper. He wants nothing less than godhood."

A hissing giggle leaked out of the box, and Quill jumped nervously. The Chancellor looked searchingly at Merrimyn, who nodded. "Yes," the Binder said, "but it's the way of all the Dreydmasters. They all desire to ascend to the ranks of the Dreyd, to break the bonds of this world and move into realms beyond, just like the first Dreyd priests of long ago."

"True, such ambition is not limited to Vald," Blackwick conceded. "But only Vald has discovered the surest path to ascension beyond the Veil Between Worlds."

Not sure she wanted to hear the answer, but unable to restrain herself, Denarra asked, "And what would that be?"

"The eradication of the Folk, and with it, a new Melding."

Stunned silence blanketed the room.

"It can't be true," whispered Quill at last. "Nobody could do something so awful, not even him."

Blackwick shook his head. "Sadly, young Tetawa, Vald not only *could* do such a thing, he is in the final preparations of doing so even as we gather here. He need not kill all the Folk to accomplish his goal, but most will suffer grievously at his hands. If he succeeds, the new Melding may well result in our total destruction, and perhaps that of Humanity itself. As long as we all still live, it is a hopeful sign that he has not yet finished his task."

"He's right," Merrimyn said, his voice so low that they had to strain to hear him. "Of course. This is what Vald was doing with all of us."

Denarra put a hand on his shaking arm. The chain to his snaring-tome rattled loudly. "You remember?"

Merrimyn gripped the Strangeling's hand. "This is what he was doing all along, though I didn't know it at the time. It's so simple, and so perfect. He was collecting Binders from all over the Reach, praising us, giving us gifts, making us part of his inner circle. And when the Seekers started bringing in the Wielders, I knew something awful was happening, but I didn't know that he was planning something like *this*."

"What is it?" Meggie asked. "What is Vald planning to do?"

"The Binders store power within their snaring-tomes," Blackwick explained to the house matron. "It is similar in principle to a dam on a powerful river. The higher you build the dam, the stronger the material and the more cunning the design, the more of that precious resource you can control. If you have enough, you can release the waters to flood the parched world, or refuse to surrender it and turn the lands below into a desert. Wielders, above all other Folk, possess great strength; if they are killed, that strength—what Kyn call the language of creation, the *wyr*—is dispersed throughout the few remaining Thresholds, to go back to the ancient world from which it first came. Binders are trained to draw that strength not just from the spirits of their own world, but also from the spirits of the Folk. And, like a dam, the snaring-tome becomes a dangerous tool with enormous potential for devastation."

Meggie looked at Merrimyn. "So you could release that power on us at any time?"

The Binder shook his head. "No. I can only absorb spirits—I can't control them. I can sometimes let out small bits if I'm very desperate, like steam escaping from an over-heated kettle, but there's no way of knowing what would happen or…who would get hurt." His shoulders sagged slightly, and a shadow crossed his face. "The only members of the Dreydcaste with that sort of will and strength are the Reavers; only they can channel and focus the bound spirits with any hope of success. And of all the Reavers in the Reach, Vald is the greatest."

The implications of Merrimyn's words sunk in slowly. Denarra put her head in her hands. "So Vald sent out his Seekers to kidnap Wielders and steal their strength. Simple, but brutally effective. Why didn't he just stop there?"

"They were never his main goal," Blackwick replied, laying a hand on the box at his side. A low, muffled whine sounded from within, and then silence. "He had a much greater ambition. Yet he could not hope to win against the Everland if the Wielders were still strong, so he slowly stripped away their power. Wielders were rarely the only victims, so they were never identified as the primary targets of the early raids. The Purging of the Kyn Wielders by the Celestial Shields, though not of his doing, was advantageous, as it weakened some of the most powerful Folk who most threatened his plans. So, slowly, inexorably, the Wielders vanished from the Everland, until all but a few of the most powerful of their kind remained."

He held up his empty mug, which Meggie promptly refilled. "The Wielders gave him great power, but there was much more to be had, and it was found in one place above all others."

Quill's eyes grew wide. "The Tree. Vald knew about the Eternity Tree."

"Yes. The Tree was the heart of the Everland, the pulsing centre of the ancient life of the Folk. It tied the people to other worlds, to other ways of being, and gave them strength to withstand the ravages of the world of Men. More than anything else, this was the single greatest source of power in all the Reach, perhaps in all of this Melded world itself. It would be all he needed to become Dreyd at last."

"But he didn't succeed," protested Padwacket. "By all reports, the Tree was destroyed, and he still didn't ascend."

"True, but the power of the Tree was rooted not just to the land—it was, to Vald's apparent surprise, also rooted to the Folk themselves. As long as the Folk exist, the Tree's strength remains whole and thus inaccessible to Vald. For whatever reason, the travellers on the Darkening Road have not died under their torments but have, strangely enough, lately become even stronger. This confirms what we know about the *wyr*—it is woven into the very essence of the *people*, not just to the land itself. The Everland is impoverished without the Tree and the bulk of the Folk, but pockets of the old country still maintain their strength, because scattered groups of Folk remain to honour the green world and give strength to the spirits abiding with them. As long as they endure, those small bits of the Everland will endure as well."

"Forgive the bluntness of my question," Meggie said, uncharacteristically sombre, "but if this is the case, why didn't Vald just slaughter all the Folk right in the Everland? Why drag all those thousands halfway across the Reach to dispose of them?"

Blackwick smiled. "What do you know of ancient history?"

The Woman shrugged. "Not so much. But I've read Tempest Sparks's *History of the Everland Folk and their Legends and Hearth-Tales.*" Denarra and Padwacket exchanged glances. They'd never seen a book in the house matron's hand before, let alone such a rare and notorious volume by a renegade Tetawi genealogist and amateur historian whose pro-Folk scholarship was dismissed by many established Human historians. Meggie pointedly ignored their surprised looks, and Blackwick showed no response either way.

"Then surely you remember the circumstances surrounding the Melding. In what part of this world did the Dreyd ascend?"

Meggie thought for a moment, and then she shook her head in grim understanding. "Karkûr. They ascended in Karkûr, and in doing so turned it into a wasteland."

"Precisely," the old Ubbetuk said, taking another deep draught of his tea. Now that his hand was away from the banded trunk, whatever was inside began to move around again. Blackwick ignored it. "And for a thousand years, the Pit Fields of Karkûr have remained a ravaged blight. One would think that in all that time growing things would have found a way to reclaim the land, but they remain a rarity in Karkûr. The land is sick, and not simply because of the Melding of a thousand years past. It remains, like the Everland, a remnant of another world, but this one is blasted to its heart, and its poison seeps out to burn away all green life around it. It is a great Darkening, a pocket of shadow and death, the mirror-twin of the Everland, with a revenant oak at its venomous heart. The Veil Between Worlds is weakest there. Break the dam, unleash the power, and the Veil is sundered."

It took a while for Denarra to find her voice, and when she did, it was small and trembling. "So Vald drives the Folk to the Pit Fields, butchers them all, and uses their *wyr*-born essence to cross the Veil and join the Dreyd."

They sat in silence for a long time, all lost in their own nightmares. The sudden revelation was too terrible to fully contemplate. It seemed so impossible, but now that they could see the pattern, it made horrifying sense.

The box rattled, its iron bands straining hard against an unseen pressure.

Suddenly Quill looked at the Chancellor. "But if all this was hidden from us for so long, how did *you* come to know all this?"

His shoulders slumped. "The knowledge came slowly…and with no little pain." He sighed. "I am older than I appear, Tetawa. Indeed, I am older than any of my kind, and I have learned many things over those years. Above all else, I have learned that enemies come in many guises, both from within and from without, and the only way to survive is to be ever vigilant. The danger that threatens your people endangers mine as well—it threatens us all." A bitter smile crept across his wizened face. "Many years past, my people abandoned the greater teachings of the Deep Green and embraced instead the magics of iron and steel, machines and industry. But even in doing so, we did not turn away from the wisdom of the past. It continued among a small, select group of scholars and intellectuals who maintained that knowledge and integrated it into the new ways that were ensuring our people's survival. I have kept those teachings. They give me strength today. And they give me other ways of knowing than some might expect." He glanced at the box.

Denarra and Quill backed away from the iron bindings. The Chancellor motioned for Meggie and Padwacket to help him remove the cover. When they pulled the heavy wooden plank away, Quill cried out in horror at the creature that lay within, its humanoid head and feathered body wrapped in blood-spattered metal bands. It was a Not-Raven, and its fanged maw gaped wide in fury as it thrashed wildly for escape.

"The cold-eyed Man will kill you all, yes, he will kill you!" the creature hissed and giggled through bleeding lips. "He will crush your bones and suck dry the marrow. You will weep, but oh, death will come slowly. None escape. None ever escape."

Blackwick's face darkened. He raised his wrinkled hand over the box, and the Not-Raven let loose a shriek of half-heard curses before crouching into a trembling ball.

"You know me," the Chancellor said, his voice suddenly deep, ancient, and terrible as winter thunder, "and you know what I will ask. You have fed on your master's blood, and you know his thoughts. What do you see?" The creature squirmed and whined pitifully, as though it was fighting a devastating battle with itself. The old Ubbetuk's fingers curled slightly. The room grew cold. Denarra, Quill, and Merrimyn felt a frigid surge of power roll into the room.

"You know your master's mind. Tell me!" Blackwick growled. The Not-Raven twitched a bit, and a stream of black bile tricked from its mouth. In spite of herself, Quill felt a great swell of pity for the creature.

"The ascension is at hand, yes," it whispered at last, its voice broken and weak. Blackwick's fingers curled again, and the Not-Raven gasped, "The Wielder, she is the source…she is the key. Within her is the power, oh yes, and when she dies, the master rises. He rises…he…." A low hiss escaped its mouth, and its head lolled to one side.

"We are not yet too late, but we are running short of time," Blackwick whispered as he slid back into his chair.

"You're a Wielder," Denarra said with amazement.

The Chancellor smiled weakly and shook his head. "No. The Wielders of the Ubbetuk died out long, long ago." His eyes grew hard. "You understand? There are *no* Wielders among us. None. I am simply an old politician with an interest in the arcane histories of my people."

Denarra nodded. The other Folk suffered greatly from the ignorance of their neighbours, and the Way of Deep Green was generally considered to be witchery among a good many Humans in the Reach. The Ubbetuk, though victims of other kinds of suspicion, were at least spared this one. If it was known that they had *wyr*-gifts in addition to their already distrusted mechanical genius, vague fear would become burning hatred, and there would be no safe place for the Ubbetuk in the Melded world.

They sat drinking their tea, no one willing to break the silence, until the bell at the front door began ringing. Blackwick smiled. "Ah, at last. I have taken the liberty of inviting some other guests to join us, now that the greater measure of our personal discussion is finished."

They heard a gasp from young Ellefina as she opened the door. Two familiar Men entered. One was of a middling height, with red hair and beard and sombre brown eyes. The other Man moved with an easy authority. He was older, taller in stature and broader in the shoulder than his companion. His tight black curls and silver-streaked goatee were trimmed close to the dark skin, and his dark eyes looked at the gawking group with grave respect. Both wore the faded longcoat side-laced breeches, and oiled leather boots of soldiers, and though the taller Man hadn't been an active campaigner for many years, the warrior's regalia rested as easily on his frame as a second skin, far more comfortably than the fine silks he'd worn when Quill first met him.

Blackwick stood. "I am sure you all remember the Reachwarden, and the captain of his guard, Jhaeman?"

"*Former* Reachwarden," Qualla'am Kaer responded in the trade-tongue. "Or will be, soon enough, when news of this gets out."

Denarra shook her head, her face lighting with sudden joy. "What...how...what are you doing here?"

Kaer smiled apologetically. "I'd taken an oath as Reachwarden to preserve the Reach at any cost. As long as I was bound to that oath, that was my first and only duty. But some things aren't grey, and some costs are far too high, even under the bonds of duty. We're here to help, in some way, if you'll have us. And if you'll forgive my earlier cowardice."

It was the first time Quill had ever seen the Strangeling struck speechless. Denarra's mouth snapped open and shut, but there was no sound. At last, her voice returning, she jumped up with a whoop and threw her arms around the startled politician. "Forgive you?! Oh, you beautiful, gorgeous, glorious Man, you're entirely forgiven! Why, I'd even give birth to your first-born whelp, if I actually had any interest in bearing one of the squalling little parasites!"

Amidst the laughter, the Chancellor patiently waved them all toward the door. "We must go now—Vald is nearing the end of his preparations, and you have many long miles to cover before he is finished. I have ordered all available airships in the region to prepare for any eventuality; my own ship is ready for you now."

Quill shook her head. "But we might be too late, even with the airships. There's no way we'll be able to get there in time." Her own mouth dropped open as the group turned to stare at her expectantly. "Oh, no...you don't think...I can't...."

Blackwick smiled strangely. "I was most intrigued by the story of your arrival in Chalimor. Are you willing to test those skills again?"

"I...I don't know if I can," the Dolltender whispered. Her body began to tremble. They had no idea what the smaller ceremony had already cost her; she could only imagine what another one would demand.

Denarra knelt down. "You can do this, Quill—I know you can. You were born to do this. These teachings were given to you for a reason, and I'll be right there with you." The Strangeling embraced her. "This is your chance to save our people."

Denarra didn't know. Quill hadn't told her about the blood-debt she'd paid to save their lives. She thought back to their earlier argument, when she'd chided the Strangeling for keeping news of the Expulsion from her: *"That kind of secret is still a lie. It hides your heart from the people who deserve to know it."* Now, at last, she understood why her friend had made the difficult choice to hold back the truth, at least for a little while. It wasn't unkindness—it was mercy, and love.

They were all looking at her, waiting. Her friends, who had already sacrificed so much. These new friends and allies, who were willing to give up their comfort, security, and possibly even their lives to help in this quest. Great deeds required great sacrifice, and not just from one, but from many. They were willing to give more. Could she do any less?

Quill's eyes glittered and her face was very pale, but she stood tall and squared her shoulders. Turning to the Chancellor, she said, her voice trembling only a little, "All right; I'll do it." She stopped and smiled apologetically to Meggie. "But I think I'm going to need a *lot* more apples."

CHAPTER 8

WRONGNESS

Truly the old Winter Witch, Shobbok of the Ice-Pierced Heart, reigns supreme. Her malice is clear in the murderous blizzard that has raged for weeks and shows no sign of slowing. She's long been jealous of the Eld Green and its bounty, and now that the Veil Between Worlds has been sundered, her long-harboured resentment rises up in carnage as burning ice and blinding snow sweeps like a blanket over the lands of Folk and Men alike. Shobbok can feel each death as the inner fire sputters out, from the candle-flame of the songbird to the bonfire of the great ocean whale, and she laughs in triumph as the world falls before eternal winter. The ragged old spirit rides through the snows upon the back of a skeletal polar bear, accompanied by her pack of life-stealing skriker hounds, great black beasts with the faces of those slain by their fangs and claws. They are all ravening hunters now, seeking out the last flickering fires of resistance, driven by a hunger that none can explain or defy. The world, at long last, is dying. And the Dreyd watch over all.

I shouldn't be here. I should be as dead as the rest of the world, and yet I still stand before a blazing fire-pit in the middle of a wyrwood grove. The howling winds still rage around the trees, and snow piles up ever higher, but there is safety among the lichen-crusted trunks and moss-draped limbs, perhaps the last of their kind in this world. I'm here for a reason, and only for a short time, because the branches are creaking under the strain of the screaming wind and snow. The storm is getting fiercer: Shobbok is coming.

I'm not alone. The fire is surrounded by she-Kyn, all dressed in long robes of soft owl feathers, their hair pulled back away from their faces and sensory stalks, strings of abalone shells and copper disks hanging from their necks. Each wears a wooden mask like those that circled the guardian of the Eternity Tree. When I enter the circle, five of the she-Kyn remove their masks, and I look upon my proud aunt Vansaaya and gentle aunt Geth, who exchange a sad glance between them, their faces waxy in the yellow firelight. My diplomatic companions on the road to Eromar, sour-faced Imweshi and sweet young Athweid, nod curtly when they remove their masks. But it is the fifth who makes me tremble in mingled joy and grief: Unahi, auntie, friend, and guardian through the chaos of Awakening, teacher of thorn and thunder, the ways of Deep Green. Unahi smiles warmly, but she stands back, as though reluctant or unable to come near. She points her chin to the two last masked she-Kyn, and I rise.

Both are still masked, and they stand still as I come near. The first mask is painted red and black and is lined with a crackling mane of dried grass. Squares of bright copper cover where the eyes should be, so I can't see her eyes. The other she-Kyn wears a mask painted blue and white, with ragged black ribbons streaming down from the head and chin, and black-stone eyes that hide the face behind.

Something snaps overhead. I look up. The branches are covered with motionless white owls who gaze down without fear or emotion. A blast of wind sends leaves raining down into the fire, and I hear something else through the noise of the storm, something that sends my heart beating in terror. Something is howling in the darkness beyond, a noise like nothing of this world, the voices of Men and Folk emerging from feral throats. The skriker howl.

The seven she-Kyn dance around the flames, slowly and with great dignity. They lift their voices in a song that I've heard before, a language that I don't understand any more now than when I first heard it. It is the bloodsong of my Awakening, the war-chant that rose above the shattered trunk of the Eternity Tree, and yet something else. The dancers are trying to speak beyond words, beyond my waking mind, but the words are just out of reach, and I grit my teeth in frustration.

Whatever they are singing, it isn't for me this night.

The figure in the red and black mask steps out of the circle and stops in front of me. "Don't worry. There's still time," she says. The voice is strange. It has the ring of familiarity to it, but distant. The stranger lifts her hands and removes the mask. It is Lan'delar, my mother. Turquoise blue eyes gaze into my own.

"You've grown so brave and beautiful, my daughter," Lan'delar says as her fingers slide a stray hair away from my face. "Such a strong, proud warrior."

The howls grow nearer, and with them the screaming laughter of Shobbok.

"Mother, what is it?" I ask, seeing the sadness in her eyes.

She doesn't respond. Instead, she moves toward the circle, and when she turns back to me, there is fear in her eyes. "There's one other who you must meet, and you must be brave again. You mustn't turn away until you know what's coming. Only then will you understand, and only then will you be prepared."

A branch falls from the trees above and smashes into the flames, sending ashes and sparks into the air, where they are swallowed by the storm. Some of the owls above are growing restless; they flap their wings and snap their beaks in annoyance, throwing clumps of snow from the branches down on the dancers.

I want to grab my mother, Unahi, Geth, to hold them all in my arms and never lose them again. I want to stay here with them forever, in spite of the storm and all the horrors that are so swiftly approaching, but Lan'delar shakes her head and joins the dance as the last of the masked she-Kyn steps out to meet me.

The figure has a familiar stride. Her blue and white mask seems to waver strangely in the fading firelight. I know without any doubt that I've seen this she-Kyn before. The feeling troubles me more than the approaching skrikers or the terrible storm. I'm supposed to know something here, but it's still just out of reach.

Suddenly an owl bursts out of the darkness and swoops down toward us. I duck, but the other she-Kyn stands still, and the owl's talons strike out to catch the upper edge of the mask and lift it into the air. As the bird vanishes again in the night, blue-green light explodes from the figure's exposed face, and horror fills me as I finally recognize the figure and understand, at last, what is expected. Yet before I have a chance to even scream, a wave of black fur and glistening fangs rolls through the grove as the skriker hounds descend upon us. The seven dancers disappear beneath the ravenous creatures, and both the fire-light and the green glow vanish in swirling snow and blood.

The last thing I hear before falling is my voice raised at last in song.

The Wielder awoke with a jolt, sweat dripping down her skin. Except for her copper armbands and choker she was naked, and the early morning air was cold on her skin. Her heart pounded painfully. She took a few deep breaths and remembered that she was in Garyn's wagon, wrapped in the arms and legs of Daladir and Jitani, who both slept on undisturbed.

She lay between her lovers for a while longer, pleased that they'd both finally found restful comfort in slumber, but the dream was still so clear in her mind, and sleep was far away. Perhaps a bit of movement in the fresh air would lift the shadows from her thoughts. With infinite care she slid from their tangled embrace, and pulled a woolen trade blanket over her shoulders before stepping from the wagon.

She knew instantly that something was terribly wrong.

The camp was deathly quiet. She heard nothing: no coughing, no rustling, no crying or soft whispers. Even the Men's horses made no noise. Tarsa could see sleeping bodies everywhere. Their chests moved up and down with breath, so she knew they weren't dead, but it did nothing to ease her unease.

Everywhere she looked lay Folk, Men, horses, dogs, and even a few scavenging birds, all trapped in deep, dreamless sleep. It would be impossible for *everyone* to be asleep at the same time, no matter how exhausting the journey. The air was strangely heavy, and it had an odd feeling, as though a trace of the *wyr* had been drawn out and stretched beyond its limits, like a layer of ice spread too thinly over deep water. Taking a heavy breath, Tarsa closed her eyes and reached out into the air, but the feeling was elusive, and it slipped out of her grasp. Whatever had done this, it was alien to the *wyr* as she knew it.

The Wielder was so focused that it took a couple of heartbeats for her to notice that not *all* sounds had stopped, as a single tread of soft footsteps approached her through the camp. She looked up and was stunned for a moment into silence.

Shakar.

The Shield's violet eyes examined the threadbare blanket wrapped around Tarsa's shoulders. "Apparently *all* the Old Ways endure," she sniffed in disdain. "Even with our people abused, degraded, and dying all around us, you still revel in the flesh. I should hardly be surprised."

The initial shock of the Shield's appearance faded. In the past Tarsa might have become wild and attacked with heedless abandon, but not this day. She was the keeper of the Heartwood of the Eternity Tree, more than either a warrior or a Wielder, and the *wyr* tempered her rage as it filled her with cold resolve. "Every step of the Darkening Road I've waited for this day, traitor," she said. "Every time I walked past one of our kith lying dead at the side of the road or soothed the cries of a youngling cast alone into the world I've thought about what I'd do when I met you. Your death won't bring our people joy, but it might give them comfort."

"You presume too much, Wielder. I did what was necessary, no matter how unpleasant…as I am doing now."

The Wielder's eyes narrowed. "What are you—?" she began, but fell back with a guttural scream as a blast of blinding agony consumed her senses, sending her writhing to the ground.

Denarra had seen many things in her lifetime, but this had to be the strangest, most impressive sight of all. She stood on the deck of the Chancellor's own wasp-headed airship. Knowing that this would be a momentous event worthy of a fashionable entrance, Denarra dressed in her finest scarlet skirt, pleated at the flowing bottom and draped with pearls of many sizes and shapes. She wore a tight-fitting, forest-green jacket with broad shoulders, long sleeves, and a wide, upturned collar; it enhanced the tightly laced bodice that revealed just enough to border on scandalous. The protective iron-ward girdle, although rather drab in contrast to the shimmering silks and muslins of the rest of her attire, added a touch of earthy simplicity with its flecked brown and grey surface. The crowning touch, however, and the one of which Denarra was most proud, was the sweeping green hat, with bold peacock feathers in the brim that lay at a jaunty angle over her curled hair. She was going into great danger that she very well might not survive, but she'd be doing it in style, and that knowledge eased her doubts considerably. Death was painful but short; bad taste lingered forever.

The ship hovered low above the city in the twilight before dawn, as did the two dozen other Dragons that dotted the skies around them, summoned by the Chancellor and prepared for the journey to come. From her lofty position Denarra looked down at the open plaza on the ground below, where Quill was making her final preparations. The Reachwarden had ordered the Chalimite marshals to clear one of the city's smaller market squares for the massive ritual to come, likely one of the last commands he'd be able to make after the Assembly heard of his participation in this extra-legal operation. Jhaeman was organizing the marshals in their tasks, helping them keep curious bystanders away, a surprisingly difficult task given the early hour. Surrounded by Ubbetuk Bluecap guards and a wide circle of dolls, Quill paced back and forth nervously in preparation.

"She's pushing herself much too hard," Denarra whispered to no one in particular, but the Reachwarden stepped to her side and looked down.

"It's hard to believe that someone so small could accomplish such a great task. Are you sure she'll succeed?" Kaer's tone wasn't mocking or condescending; rather, his voice carried a depth of sympathy that Denarra still found rather surprising. Much of his behaviour was unexpected, especially his participation in this adventure. He'd gone against popular opinion by supporting the Folk's claim to the Everland, and though he refused to embroil the Reach in a civil war by declaring Eromar's actions illegal, his willingness to risk censure and even possible impeachment by helping Blackwick and the others was both unexpected and impressive. With this single action, Qualla'am Kaer had committed political suicide, but perhaps it would give them the time they needed to stop Vald, or at least to be with their people when the end came. Either way, it was a brave and honourable act, and it gave her a bit of hope for the possibility of understanding between Folk and Men. Not much hope, but some was better than none, for she'd become far too used to being disappointed by the weaknesses of Men.

Reflecting on Kaer's sacrifice, Denarra bit off her initial snide response. "Darling, there's more fighting spirit inside that little Doll-tender than in all the Men of the Reach combined. I don't doubt for a minute that she can do it. I just worry about its effects. She's only just discovered this skill, and now she's been asked to do something that even great Wielders would find terribly difficult. The last gate-walk was bad enough. She'll do it, certainly, but…." Her voice trailed off, and Kaer didn't press the issue further.

There were many stories about Wielders who'd been consumed by their dabbling in the Spirit World, falling prey to madness or worse. Quill was strong, and the teachings she'd received were rooted in a deep wisdom and respect for the spirits, but many things could go wrong with a Wielding such as this, and the young Dolltender was largely untrained in the finer points of her inheritance. Besides, Denarra wasn't so self-absorbed after the gate-walking experience that she hadn't noticed the way Quill rubbed the pain from her lower belly when she thought no one was looking, or the sad look in the *firra*'s eyes when she'd see laughing younglings chase each other in the cobblestone streets.

The Man and Strangeling lapsed into silence. Denarra wanted to be down in the square with her friend, to share in the dangers of this moment. But the *wyr*-fed energies that would be pulsing through the ritual site would be incredibly powerful, and the presence of other Wielders or Crafters might upset the delicate balance that Quill required to create this gate. If she failed to maintain her concentration, if she stumbled in the dance or forgot a word in the song, she might bring catastrophe upon them all. So rather than risk such dangers, Denarra and Merrimyn had agreed to stay on the Chancellor's own Dragon floating above the ceremony, watching from a reasonable distance, while the Bluecaps remained below both to protect the Dolltender and hurry her onto a small skiff at the end of the full ritual, which would bring her to the Chancellor's galleon for the journey. Yet it was difficult for Denarra to do nothing but watch, and even the knowledge of her own elegant appearance did little to ease either her fear or her impatience.

Merrimyn joined the Strangeling and Reachwarden at the railing as a Bluecap horn blared below. The ritual was beginning.

Although she'd left her own gourd-shell rattle in Denarra's old travelling wagon on the night they fled Vergis Thane's attack, Quill had managed to find another suitable rattle in one of the market stalls of Chalimor that morning. It didn't have as nice a sound as hers, as it was a composite of thin wood and dried seeds rather than the more musical gourd or turtle shell rattles, nor was it as cheerily painted, but it would suffice for today. Green Kishka approved, and of all the dolls she was perhaps the most unrelenting about the precise requirements of this particular ceremony.

Although none of the three old dolls were happy about the

Tetawa's decision for reasons no one had to mention, they all agreed that the alternative was too terrible to consider. Their kind had been created by the Dolltenders of old to bring wise counsel and aid to the Tetawi. There had never been a time when that wisdom was needed so desperately. Yet in the morning, when Quill brought them to the open square near Denarra's house, they looked with dismay at the twenty-eight makeshift dolls that the Dolltender and her friends had hurriedly put together the night before. Such figures were little more than mind-less automatons without personality or even recognizable facial features or wrinkles on their air-browned apple heads. Cornsilk complained that these things were smelly and half-naked, while Kishka groused about the emptiness of their dried-pea eyes. Mulchworm simply pursed his lips and clicked his white-bead teeth with frustration.

Carefully prepared with prayers, tobacco, and other precious med-icinals, each painted on the forehead with a drop of Quill's own blood, the half-formed dolls would be touched by spirits, but they would be conduits only, not creatures with thought and will of their own. It would be the three old dolls and the Dolltender herself who'd have to carry the biggest burden. Such a task would be difficult enough with a hundred of the true dolls. But there were only three, and that would have to do.

Quill looked at the circle of dolls that surrounded her, and her opti-mism sank when she realized that so much depended on so many odd, ugly, unfinished mannequins. She'd always taken great pride in her doll-craft, and such shoddy work grieved her. Yet at the sound of the horn, she turned her mind to the task at hand.

She lifted her head and called out to Green Kishka, who stood across the circle, and slowly shook her rattle four times. Kishka sang to Mulchworm, who stamped his corncob feet on the flagstones in response. Cornsilk took up the song, and as her high-pitched trill rose high, the half-made dolls stood jerkily to their feet, their cornhusk dresses crackling as they moved in a westward-moving circle.

When the dance begins, Spider-child, Cornsilk had told her, *ye mustn't stop. Don't stop until the song is over, or the gate will close, and we'll all be lost. The dance must continue...no matter what happens. There will be pain, cub. Lots of pain. But don't stop dancing.* It had seemed like such a simple thing then, but Quill now understood how difficult it would be, as a hot, heavy weight fell upon them, like the rising blast of a furnce, and the twisting ache began in her lower abdomen. It was nothing like the last gate-dance. This time they were too ambitious, attempting something that they had neither the strength nor the ability to do. The air seemed to be sucked away, leaving Quill straining for breath as she lifted her feet in time with the rattle and rhythm of the dance. The pain pulsed in time with the beat, growing sharper with each step. Sweat poured down her face. She wanted to look around, to see if the Bluecaps were feeling the strain, but inattention could be worse than fatal here, so the Dolltender gritted her teeth against the heat and pain and swift exhaustion and followed the dolls in an ever-widening circle. And as they moved, a small globe of darkness opened in the air above them. Shadowy filaments streamed out from the shimmering mass, a celestial web stretching across the sky.

Shukka, shukka, shukka, shukka. Shukka, shukka, shukka, shukka. The half-formed dolls moved in unison, following the others without hesitation or delay, and the dancing circle grew wider still. The withering heat seemed to do nothing more than wrinkle the apple-flesh of the new dolls, but Kishka, Mulchworm, and Cornsilk felt the strain. Their faces grew crimped and pained, while bits of fabric and cornhusk slipped to the stones as they moved. And still they danced.

Another horn blared below, and Denarra turned her attention to the massive, star-shimmering portal that began to open in the sky. The first of the Dragons slid delicately toward the gate to test its stability. The air seemed to buckle slightly, but the gate held, and the airship slid into the prismatic shadow, followed swiftly by others. The ceremony was almost over. It wouldn't take too long for the small armada to be through the gate and on their way to the Pit Fields of Karkûr and the terrible new dangers that awaited them.

The Strangeling looked down again and nearly swooned from the blistering heat that radiated upward. Quill and her three small dolls had stumbled out of the circle while the other dolls continued to dance. The gate above quivered for a moment but remained largely stable. A dozen airships had disappeared into the gate, and most of the others were moving toward it, filling the air with the sound of whirring gears and wheezing gas bellows and whistles.

Quill's tawny face had gone a ghastly yellow, and she was bent and sweating from the pain. She seemed to be on the edge of collapse as she picked up the old dolls in shaking hands and placed them in her belt-pouch. Yet she managed to stagger toward a Bluecap, who handed her an iron-ward belt and led her gently toward the waiting skiff.

As Quill and her escort turned, the small airship suddenly exploded in a blinding ball of flame, shredding its Ubbetuk crew and sending bodies and debris into the air. Quill and the Bluecap fell stunned to the ground, and a few of the dolls in the ceremonial circle vanished under the rain of flesh and rubble. The gate in the sky shuddered again, this time more violently. Alarm horns on the remaining Dragons filled the air with warning, and everyone rushed to the railings, peering through the flames and smoke to see what was happening below. That it was sabotage was certain. An accident was nearly impossible, as the Dragons were crafted with extraordinary care, and each possessed various mechanisms to isolate potential problems and prevent such a catastrophe. Ubbetuk sharpshooters with stout crossbows slid wicked bolts into place and waited for the smoke to clear. Whoever had destroyed the skiff wouldn't find the other ships such easy targets.

"We've got to get them up here, before the gate collapses!" Merrimyn shouted over the chaos. Their own vessel was the closest to the ground, but it still floated over a hundred feet above the market. Yet lowering the ship was impossible if they wanted to travel through the increasingly unstable gate, as the gas bladders required most of their fuel for lifting off the ground.

"If we try to land now, we'll never be able to make it to the gate before it closes." Denarra looked around in desperation. "Over there," she cried, pointing to a rope ladder hanging from the inner edge of the large cast-iron railing. She and the Binder lifted it up and over and watched the lower edge trail nearly to the ground. The Strangeling grabbed her skirts in her hand and started climbing over the rail.

A hand on her shoulder stopped her. Qualla'am shook his head. "I'll do it. I'm faster, and you're needed here."

"What are you talking about?" Denarra shouted, furious at the delay.

The Man pointed to the ground. She looked down and covered her mouth to stifle a scream.

Vergis Thane emerged from one of the buildings on the edge of the square and moved toward the little Dolltender, who lay unconscious amidst the smoking rubble of the skiff.

The Reachwarden crawled over the edge of the ship and slid swiftly down the ladder.

CHAPTER 9

SACRIFICE

"Flesh-addled child," Shakar hissed as she walked toward the fallen Wielder. "Have you forgotten your history so soon?"

The pain faded, and Tarsa lifted a shaking hand to her forehead, expecting blood. She took a breath and pulled her hand away. Nothing. No blood, no bruise—nothing but a deep pounding throb in her sensory stalks. Her whole being ached, as if she'd fallen from a great height onto rocks, with every limb askew.

The Shield lifted her blue skirts to avoid stepping on an old Tetawa who lay sprawled and snoring on the ground in front of her, yet her violet gaze remained fixed on the Wielder, who struggled to stand. "Have you never wondered why it was that your kind fell so swiftly in the Purging? Have you never wondered why your precious *wyr*-witchery was of no avail against the power of the Shields? The Wielders were trapped in the weaknesses of fragile flesh. We chose the higher path—that of the mind, pure, unyielding, untainted by lower desires. We bent our thoughts to our wills, shaping and honing them into tools...and weapons. Yours is the way of flesh, Wielder, of all things frail and transient. Mine is the path of eternity. The pleasures and pains of flesh are a distraction, a sad reminder of our earth-bound forms. There is so very much more to what we can be."

Tarsa glowered as she looked around for a weapon to defend herself. Her wyrwood staff was still in the wagon. "I have no interest in the teachings of a traitor with the blood of hundreds of her own people on her hands."

Shakar's eyes were cold and emotionless. "Still singing that sad song, Wielder? Here—let me teach you another." A brittle smile crossed her lips.

But Tarsa was ready this time. The *wyr* surged through her body, and the mind-shattering blast dissipated before it could cripple her. She staggered back, feeling the Heartwood recoil from the alien force. Whatever this poisonous power was, it didn't have its origin in the Deep Green. It continued to skitter like a thousand spiders around the edges of her *wyr*-shield, trying to find a weak spot to pierce.

"Impressive," Shakar said as she stalked around the young Wielder with the focused ease of a hawk circling a wounded rabbit. "Most impressive. Not many Wielders have withstood the first strike without falling into gibbering madness; fewer still have had the wits to defend themselves for the second wave. But you are still very young, and flesh is weak. You cannot withstand me forever."

"True," Tarsa groaned. "But I won't need to." She dropped the barrier and, in the same heartbeat, released a whirlwind of her own, a surge of pure *wyr* that burned through Shakar's attack, catching the Shield with its full force to toss her through the air. The Lawmaker smashed into the rocky ground and lay breathing heavily, her dirt-stained silks tangled and torn around her.

Yet the Wielder had made a mistake. The sudden surrender of so much of the Heartwood's strength opened something else within her. The overpowering voices rushed in and filled her head again as they did on the day the barge sank in the storm-ravaged waters of the Shard Ford. The song tore through her thoughts. The voices were desperate now, trying to force understanding upon her, but the cacophony engulfed all thought, all feeling but pain. Her sensory stalks thrashed wildly, and she fell to her knees and screamed.

Shakar stood and wiped the dirt and blood from her hands. The sleeping Folk began to stir, freed from the Shield's influence by Tarsa's defensive attack, but it hardly mattered now. She now had what she came for. Turning to the pain-wracked Wielder, Shakar brought her fingers to her temples and focused her thoughts, stripping her mind of all emotion except for pure, undiluted rage. A pulsing cone of invisible fury bore down on the green-skinned she-Kyn, and Tarsa collapsed without a sound.

The Shield clapped her hands together and Vald's servant Vorgha rode a brown mare out of the rubble on the edge of the camp, heedless of the shouting, sleep-bleary Folk who scrambled to get out of his way. He led a pale grey horse behind him. The Shield lifted her hands and watched dispassionately as Tarsa's limp body rose into the air, lifted by the power of Shakar's mind, and fell roughly over the grey's saddle. Swinging up behind the Wielder, Shakar spurred the horse forward, a small smile creeping across her weary face as the alarm went up.

The Folk would awaken to the knowledge that their savage saviour was gone. As always, the flesh collapsed before the power of a disciplined mind. And when at last all hope for the return of the Old Ways of the wilderness was lost, the people would at last see the truth, and she would return to lead them in patient wisdom and grace. Only when the Deep Green was finally erased from the memory of this Melded world would the Folk have a place among Men.

Something soft and wet touched the Shield's face. She held out a hand. Snow. Winter had come to the Pit Fields at last. This would make her task that much easier, as ice and cold sapped at a defiant will better even than hunger. There would be little to fear now.

She drove the horse toward the rising storm and disappeared into a blinding curtain of white.

Denarra screamed in frustration. She couldn't touch the elemental spirits with the iron-ward around her waist, but removing the belt would expose her to the Dragon's debilitating poison. She grabbed an empty crossbow from a nearby stand and tried to crank it back, but her agitation and lack of skill made the task impossible, so instead she lifted the weapon over her head, took aim, and threw it over the edge of the ship. It didn't come close to striking Thane.

A handful of Ubbetuk sharpshooters were more successful, how-ever, and sent a barrage of missiles toward the Seeker, hoping to keep him from approaching Qualla'am Kaer, who'd finally reached Quill. The Dolltender seemed to be coming to her senses, but her Bluecap escort lay unmoving, either dead or unconscious. The remaining dolls continued their dance, but their movement was growing as erratic as the gate between worlds. Their time was growing short.

In spite of the skill of the archers from above, their bolts met empty air, for they were no match for Thane. Nor were the surviving eight Bluecaps on the ground, who raised their weapons and fired at the man. Drawing on all the Dreydcraft defenses he knew, and fuelled by long-tempered fury, Thane's sword was a cyclone of silver fire. As the bolts shattered into splinters and dust, the Man was among the Bluecaps, his dark cloak blurring his form like the mantle of Grim Death. One Ubbetuk charged with his sword held out like a spear. It was a foolish, desperate move. The Seeker brought his own blade down to block the attack. As the Ubbetuk staggered back from the impact, Thane's left hand disappeared into his belt and appeared again with a small dagger that he hurled into the Bluecap's belly. Rushing past the gurgling creature, Thane slid his boot under the Ubbetuk's fallen sword and kicked it into the air, grabbing the hilt with his empty hand and moving in on his other opponents with two blades now at the ready.

Thane closed in on the Bluecaps so quickly that those above had to hold back, afraid to strike their own. Unaware of their vulnerability, and refusing to be cowed by a single Man, three of the remaining Bluecaps stepped out to meet him, swords drawn, and moved in a small circle. They were strange, deadly dancers, darting around like silent hornets, stabbing outward and then retreating out the reach of the Man's blades. With other opponents, such movements were unnerving, but Thane seemed more annoyed about the delay than intimidated. He lunged at the nearest one, who hopped away and blocked the sword. But Thane was faster than he looked. As one of the other fighters zipped in to take advantage of the Seeker's feint, Thane spun back around and brought his sword down hard on the Bluecap's extended wrist, neatly severing the hand. Ignoring the spurting blood, Thane ducked and rolled into the shrieking Ubbetuk, hurling it against its companions.

The Seeker was on his feet again in an instant, swords twirling, and he dispatched the fallen attackers with twin throat thrusts, leaving the lesser blade embedded in the neck of one of the dying soldiers. A bolt flashed through the air. It slowed down as it neared the Seeker, whose free hand flew up, and the Bluecap archer watched aghast as Thane caught the Craft-slowed bolt in mid-air, the force whipping him around as he sent it winging back at full speed, all in the same fluid movement. The archer didn't even have a chance to think before the bolt plunged into his open mouth. He was dead before he hit the paving stones.

The last three Bluecaps faced the Man, eyes desperately seeking escape. Although they were the elite warriors of the Ubbetuk Swarm, they'd never faced such an enemy. He was a born predator, or worse, for he had no fear, and he clearly had Craft-power. They forgot the steps of their deadly dance, and that lost memory was fatal. Thane reached under his cloak and pulled out a black-muzzled hand musket. There was a flash of fire, a roar, and one of the Bluecaps lurched forward with a cry. The others turned and tried to flee, but Thane dashed in, sliding the point of his sword behind the knees of the first and smashing the other Bluecap on the head with the butt of the musket. Both fell and twisted in pain, trying in vain to avoid the blade that slashed across their flailing arms and through their throats, leaving them gasping in their own lifeblood.

The great galleon buckled in the air. The filaments stretching out of the gate began to unravel and weaken. One of the ship's crew cried out, "We've got to go—*now!*" The Dragon moved ponderously into the air toward the gate.

"Kaer's got her!" Denarra screamed. "Just a moment longer!"

The Reachwarden had watched Thane's efficient carnage with horrified fascination. Although widely considered an expert with the blade, the former soldier had never seen such swift and unemotional destruction, and the knot of fear at the pit of his stomach moved up and squeezed his heart. In one hand he held his sword. He dragged Quill toward the ladder with the other, but he quickly realized that one of the two would have to go. He'd had the sword since his elevation to captain of the Republic Army, over thirty years now. It had served him well and saved his life a thousand times. But he couldn't defend himself against Thane and climb to the ship with the stunned Tetawa at the same time, and given the Seeker's skills and uncanny powers, even then Kaer wasn't sure the weapon would do him much good. He looked up just as Thane dispatched the last of the Bluecaps. The Seeker lifted his dripping knife and turned his single cold eye to Kaer, smiling with grisly satisfaction as he identified the Reachwarden's dilemma.

In the face of this menace, only one choice was possible, so Kaer tossed the injured Dolltender tightly over his left shoulder and ran at top speed toward the rope ladder rising swiftly off the ground. With a twinge of regret he flung the sword away to clang sharply on the cobblestones, threw himself forward, and caught the third rung of the ladder. Quill, dazed and nauseated but now conscious, reached out weakly and grabbed the rope.

They weren't alone. Ignoring the bolts that crashed into the flagstones around him, Thane dashed forward like a panther and threw himself at Kaer's legs, clutching tightly with one powerful arm. The Dragon thundered upward into the sky, slowly picking up speed as it flew ever higher above the city. Kaer kicked downward as hard as he could, but the Seeker's vice-like grip was unbreakable.

Thane ignored the Reachwarden. His eye was fixed on the Dolltender, whose own terrified gaze was locked on the long knife in Thane's free hand.

The gate was collapsing, and the air trembled and warped with the strain. The great Dragon groaned as a massive blast of wind smashed into its side. Denarra clutched at the railing and watched the rope ladder spin out of control, its passengers straining desperately to hold onto their one small chance for survival, one that was growing more precarious with every passing moment. The ladder wasn't meant for this kind of strain. Already the rope was fraying on the airship's rough hull.

"We've got to pull them up before we get through the gate!" Merrimyn yelled.

Denarra shook her head. "Are you completely out of your senses? We can't bring Thane on this ship—he'll kill us all!"

"Then what are we going to do? We can't shoot him off and risk killing the others."

The ship shuddered again. They were almost at the gate, the last ship to pass through, but most of the filaments had disappeared into black fire, and the great gate seemed to be vanishing even as they watched. A wave of bitterly cold wind rushed outward to surround the ship.

Denarra stood still at the railing, her white-knuckled fingers wrapped tightly around the metal bar. She was like a bronze statue, beauty frozen in time. Quickening in the east, the light of a new blue morning rose to life in bright contrast to the storm-ravaged gate that quivered before them. She'd never seen a dawn quite so lovely before, with feathery clouds of lavender, blue, and pink glowing softly against the deep gold of the rising sun. It was almost as if it was the first dawn the Strangeling had ever really seen. When she finally turned back to Merrimyn and the Ubbetuk crossbowmen, she had a smile on her face, but there were tears in her eyes.

"You won't have much time to get them up here after Thane is gone, so be ready." She began to unbuckle the iron-ward around her waist.

The Binder looked on in momentary confusion that gave way to dismayed understanding. "No...you can't...."

Sacrifice

She reached out and pressed her fingers to his lips. "It's been a bold and grand adventure, darling, but a true lady always knows the best time for a graceful exit. I promised to get her to Chalimor; you'll have to help her get back home to her sweet Tobhi. Do this for me, my friend. Now, get ready." Before Merrimyn could say anything else, Denarra ripped off the iron-ward and launched herself into the air.

"*NO!*" he wailed as she disappeared over the railing.

A burst of wind met the Strangeling on her way down, and although the iron-sickness threatened to overwhelm her senses, she was able to direct the wind toward the flailing ladder. Thane's attention was focused on his loosening hold on Kaer's leg, so he wasn't aware of the Wielder until her arms were wrapped around his throat and free arm. He gasped in pain and amazement, nearly losing his grasp as her knees smashed, hard, into the small of his back. Quill cried out and reached for her friend.

The moment of surprise was all the time Denarra needed to grab the steel blade from Thane's other hand. The metal erupted in crackling mauve flame. The Strangeling's emerald gaze lingered on Quill's grief-ravaged features, and she flashed a merry smile. "Keep the fire, darling!" she shouted as she drove the burning knife with all her remaining strength through the Seeker's hand and into Kaer's upper calf. Thane screamed and his hand shot open involuntarily as Kaer kicked backward with a bellow.

The smoking blade slipped out of the Reachwarden's leg. With Denarra still clinging to his back, the Seeker fell away from the ladder, to disappear in a flash of red silk and brown leather among the clouds as the great airship finally slipped into the gate and vanished with the rising sun.

CHAPTER 10

DECAY

«It is time.»

Forty-seven years, eight months, and nineteen days had passed since the Dreyd first revealed themselves to Lojar Vald, who was then only a struggling young jurist in a lawless land. He had made a lifetime of watching enemies stumble and vanish under their accumulated mistakes, allies grow tired and frail with the years, while the might of Eromar flourished under his firm guidance. And as his fidelity to the Dreyd grew, so did his strength, and so too did that of his people. There was no province in the Reach more feared or more imposing than Eromar; no one doubted the ability of the Dreydmaster to pursue his goals with unwavering commitment. Any doubts that may have once existed had been erased by the fall of the Everland—a military victory unsurpassed in the history of the Reach. No enemy could stand against Lojar Vald. No state dared impose its rule over the people or government of Eromar. They were one, the Man and the State, and as he ascended, so too would Eromar.

Yet worldly ambitions held no appeal except as they could enhance the greater goal on Vald's mind, and now, at last, the two came together in a broken, barbarous land far from the timbered walls of Gorthac Hall. Soon the decades of personal deprivation, endless study, political manoeuvring, and retributive justice would bear sweet fruit, and the Dreydmaster would leave this flawed mortal shell and join the new Immortals, free of the indignities of age and infirmity, free to experience all the delights enjoyed by absolute power. He and his name would live in triumph forever.

Vald surveyed the preparations with rising excitement. Hundreds of Eromar militia troops joined with the Dreydcaste Binders and Seekers on a great broken pinnacle of red stone that rose up from Riekmere Swamp, a boggy, bowl-like valley that stretched for nearly six miles in each direction. Thousands of Unhumans of every unwholesome mixture filled the floor of the valley and milled around in the frigid morass, along with a few hundred of their traitorous Human collaborators. Soldiers with muskets and cannons lined the sharp stone ridge surrounding the valley and kept the exhausted captives from escaping. The last large group of Unhumans would be arriving soon, and once they joined their kindred in the swamp they would find their exit blocked by well-armed mercenaries and slavers, all with experience in keeping these creatures in check. This final rabble included the Unhumans that Vald had been most interested in seeing, for it was among their ranks that the most troublesome of their kind had been found. She had been so arrogant in Gorthac Hall, never lowering her eyes respectfully as a proper Woman would have done, even daring to condescend to him— to *him!*—and going so far as to destroy half of the structure with her witchery. But she was no longer so proud and defiant. She and her people were broken. It was their fate to vanish with the day's last sunset, fading into the oblivion of memory at last. And in their destruction would come the full and final redemption of Men.

«I am ready, Vorgha. Let us begin.» The Dreydmaster turned to his attendant, who bowed his head reverently and stepped to the side. They walked together, Vald in front and Vorgha behind, to the edge of the rocky plateau, from which the Reaver could observe the events as they transpired.

A few hundred Men ringed the ridge valley, with groups clustered around massive copper-capped iron posts driven into the stone every quarter-mile. Chained to each post was an Unhuman witch, brought from prisons and holding pens from around the Dreyd-dominated lands of the Reach, and beside each of these stood a well-trained Binder with snaring tome held ready. Long copper cables rose from the tops of the posts, stretched across the valley, and wrapped around spikes at the top of a narrow iron tower, crudely erected of crisscrossing latticework at the apex of the central stone peak. It was here that the Veil Between Worlds would again be pierced, and it was here that the greatest of the Unhuman witches would have the honour of watching the new Melding take place. Once enough power was unleashed, Vald would move to the centre of the pinnacle and finish the great Reaving ceremony. Dying, the witch would unleash her power, the Veil would open, and he would step into immortality.

Vorgha lifted a small horn to his lips and sounded three piercing blats. Screams erupted from the witches at every post along the valley bowl as the Binders began their delicate tasks. The Dreydmaster turned toward the iron tower, his eyes gleaming with an almost childlike joy. «Bring her to me,» he called to his Manservant. «Bring me the Spearbreaker. Bring me Tarsa'deshae.»

"What happened?" Tobhi yelled as he rushed toward the wagon, his eyes still blurry from sleep. He'd been awakened by screams, then heard whispers that sent his heart racing. Grabbing his hat and pack, he ran to find his friends, but when Tarsa failed to emerge from the wagon with the other two Kyn, he knew that the rumours were true.

Jitani slipped into her boots, her face grave. "They took her, not long ago. They had a Shield with them."

Tobhi glanced at Daladir. "It was Shakar," the he-Kyn confirmed. "All the descriptions are the same. The whole camp was asleep; nobody knew she was here until just before she thundered away with Tarsa."

Blocking the morning sunlight from her eyes, Jitani turned to the west before kneeling to examine the remaining hoof tracks scattered through the camp. "They took her the same direction we're going. We're all a part of the same thing, one way or another. I just don't know why they're in such a hurry—we'll be there soon enough, before sunset if we push on as we've been doing."

"It's not Tarsa that they want as much as what she carries, and Vald has much need of that," said Daladir.

"Well, then," Tobhi frowned and pulled his hat down securely on his head, "we'd best get her back."

"And what are we going to do about them? I don't think they'll let us just walk out of here." Jitani gestured toward a large group of soldiers standing nearby. The Men milled around nervously, clutching their weapons in their white-knuckled hands, and watched the agitated Folk with increasing discomfort. Weeks of brutality and ruthless dispossession had built a murderous rage among their prisoners. Whatever had happened here wouldn't help matters. It would take very little to unleash that fury.

"They will die if they hurt you." A shadow fell across the three companions. Tobhi glanced up to see Biggiabba standing over them, a ragged cloak protecting her body from the worst of the sun's rays, her once-massive bulk worn down to a nearly skeletal thinness, her hair matted and dirt-crusted. Great oozing sores stretched across her grey skin, and the eyes that stared out at the world gleamed with an agony that bordered on madness.

For a moment Tobhi thought that Biggiabba would fall upon them in her pain, but instead the Gvaerg matron bowed her head and croaked, "Men killed them all. Sons, brothers, husbands, fathers. From wide-eyed pebble-child to worn-stone elder, killed them all, hundreds and hundreds. They attacked Delvholme. It was a peace city, a place of sanctuary, and they burned the houses and destroyed the sacred caves. Our he-Gvaergs—they all died, every one. Drove stakes through their bodies, pinned them to the mountainside until the suns rose, then laughed as the sunlight burned them, boiled their blood, turned them to stone from within. The she-Gvaergs, they all tried to fight, tried to stop it, but the Men drove them back, cut them, pierced them, destroyed all hope of help." Her ravaged shoulders shook with suppressed sobs. "I should have been with them. I could have stopped the killing. No Man set foot in my people's mountains while the Gvaerg Wielders stood strong. I came to Sheynadwiin, and my people died. I failed them all."

"No," Tobhi whispered, resting his tiny brown hand on the old Wielder's too-thin arm. "Ye en't to blame. Ye did the only thing ye knew to do. That's what we all did. There en't no shame in that. We en't to blame for the evil that was brought down on us by the greed and hate of these Men. That burden belongs to them, not us."

Biggiabba's eyes narrowed as she looked past the Tetawa to the crowd of soldiers. "Yes, of course—you are right. It was Men who brought this down on us. It will be Men who pay for their part in this evil."

Tobhi jumped back in alarm as the Wielder growled, her mouth ringed with blood-specked froth. "Vengeance!" she roared with a voice that crashed like an earthquake in the rocky valley. "Death to Men!" The binding chains snapped apart, no stronger than spider-silk. Before anyone could stop her, she charged at the stunned soldiers, her massive fists sweeping Men and horses aside so quickly that the survivors' only response was to flee as the sounds of gurgling screams, cracking bones, and shredded flesh filled the air. For a moment Biggiabba was alone, and then other Folk joined her, their pain and hatred finally unleashed.

"Now!" Jitani hissed. She grabbed Tobhi's arm and jerked him toward the rocky ridge and motioned to Daladir, who watched the devastation with horror.

"Daladir, this will be our only chance—look!" The she-Kyn mercenary pointed to the far end of the camp, where another group of soldiers was galloping at full speed toward the uprising. "Dreyd-cursed fool!" she shouted. "Think of Tarsa!" At last the he-Kyn turned, his face pale and troubled, and rushed to the wagon. He emerged an instant later with Tarsa's wyrwood staff in one hand and Jitani's sword in the other, and followed his companions into the rocks at the edge of the camp. They rushed on, heedless of pursuit, until they breathlessly reached the top of the ridge and threw themselves over the edge and out of view.

"Do you think they—" Tobhi began, but his words were lost in a sudden chorus of musket-fire, followed by thin, wailing screams that went silent all too quickly.

They crouched together in sombre silence. "Come on," Jitani whispered at last. "We can't help them now; we'd only die along with the rest. The only hope we have is to find Tarsa and the Heartwood, and quickly."

Tobhi wiped a dirty sleeve across his eyes and followed, with Daladir close behind.

"We've got to go back! We can't leave her!" Quill screamed, throwing herself at the railing again, heedless of the iron-sickness that pulsed through her body. Merrimyn tried to wrap the charmed talisman around her waist, but the Dolltender's struggles made the task impossible. Another seizure struck her, and she crashed to the deck in white-eyed agony, her hands curled into claws.

Qualla'am Kaer snatched the sash out of Merrimyn's hands, pinned Quill to the wooden planks with his right hand, and wound the ironward around the Tetawa's thrashing body, holding her down until it took effect.

Merrimyn looked down at the spreading scarlet pool under the Reachwarden's leg. He swallowed, the memory of the fight too close and painful to speak, and turned to one of the deckhands. "A poultice and some bandages—hurry." As the Ubbetuk rushed away, the young Binder turned back to Kaer, who now held the sobbing Dolltender in his arms and rocked her back and forth gently.

"We've got to find her," Quill whispered, her voice small and choked with deep sobs. "She's going to need our help…we've got to…." Exhausted, and pained beyond endurance, she slipped into a fitful sleep.

The old soldier looked up at the Binder, but neither Man spoke.

When the ship's surgeon arrived to look at Kaer's injuries, Merrimyn sat with legs crossed on the deck, slid his snaring-tome and chain out of the way, took Quill's sleeping body into his own arms, and cried.

The flight of Dragons emerged from the darkness of the gate into the orange glow of the late-day sun. It was impossible to tell how long they'd been between worlds, and few could describe what that nether-realm had been like. For some it seemed like an endless night, with strange stars shining everywhere; for others, it was a grey mist that burned with ghostly hues and vanished as the eye tried to focus on them. Watching the alien sky brought only dizziness and confusion, so those on deck or inside the hold of each ship quickly turned their attention to mundane tasks, uncertain if they would ever emerge from the gate and, if they did, fearful of what awaited them.

The Chancellor was no different, although he watched from the comfort of his well-appointed apartments in Chalimor through one of the many viewing globes he used to keep track of the armada. A few moments of viewing were enough to send him reeling to his quarters, where he shrugged off assistance and slumped into a high-backed chair to settle his nerves with a goblet of silvered mead until the nausea passed and he could return to his scrying.

Such weakness infuriated the old Ubbetuk beyond words. He rarely succumbed to emotional displays, even in private, and his fortitude had by now become the stuff of legend. It was a carefully managed image, one that hid the flaring pain in his joints, the fading eyesight, and the numerous aches that made each morning's awakening more difficult than the last. It was the best defence for an aging politician with the chilly breath of mortality at the back of his neck. His reputation as a pillar of mental and physical immortality was enough to unnerve all but the most desperate enemies, and those few who remained to trouble him were generally dealt with in both decisive and subtle ways.

And yet, for all his wisdom and foresight, the Chancellor had underestimated Vald's ambition, and this mistake had already proven quite costly, both to Blackwick and the Swarm itself. A mortal-minded adversary always needed resources, and the Swarm's unsurpassed talents with advanced machinery and arms gave it economic leverage in every part of the Reach. No province had been a more enthusiastic trading ally than Eromar, but now, too late, Blackwick saw the fatal flaw in the bargain: Vald's allegiance stretched only as far as his celestial ambitions were served. Once enough Ubbetuk resources were in reach to pursue the central focus of his crusade quickly and efficiently, Vald had no further need of the Swarm, and any attempt by the Chancellor or the Whitecap Council to punish Eromar with trade sanctions or a harsh embargo had no effect. Without that threat, the only alternative was war.

The weary Ubbetuk leaned back and slid a thick fingernail against the rim of the glass, taking dour satisfaction from the high-pitched scraping sound that set his teeth on edge. War. It was always his last choice. To declare war was to admit defeat, for the inevitable catastrophe to all involved would demonstrate with painful certainty that there could be no true victory at the end. It would be a gruesome experience, with death and bloodshed unlike any seen since the last Melding.

He hadn't been entirely forthright with the others during their plans for the attack on Vald and his troops. True, Blackwick sincerely wanted to rescue the Folk from their torment, but there was another reason to participate, one that was far more immediately compelling. Vald had presumed to confiscate Ubbetuk airships and take their crews hostage. The Dragon fleet, although not the only weapon in the mostly-hidden arsenal of the Swarm, remained its economic, political, and military lifeblood. If Men presumed to claim for themselves what had emerged from hundreds of years of Ubbetuk artistry and genius, then the Swarm would never be free of danger. This flight of Dragons came, not simply for liberation, but as a lesson to all Men, for all time: Blackwick would see the Dreydmaster's power scattered like autumn leaves in a storm. From this day on, Men would never doubt the power of the wrathful Swarm.

Indeed, it might be the start of a new era for the Ubbetuk, one in which delicate diplomacy could give way to the irresistible certainty of their industrial might.

If things went badly, and the flight of Dragons was destroyed by anything less than another Melding, Blackwick would begin again, secure now in Chalimor. He'd left a few airships in the city, just in case—his long years were the result of leaving many alternatives open, even when the odds were firmly in his favour.

If, on the other hand, Denarra's ambitious friends could help prevent Vald's ascension, so much the better, for both themselves and the Swarm. He'd been sad to see the Strangeling's sacrifice and fall, but wasn't surprised that the Binder and the Dolltender were continuing on. They were certain in their purpose, and that was enough to get them through all but the worst trials to come.

Yet the Ubbetuk had survived the first Melding. They would most likely survive another.

The Chancellor held up his goblet and watched the glistening liquid move across the crystal in soft, delicate swirls. The nausea was passing; he was already feeling better. Standing with care, Blackwick returned once again to the scrying room.

Only in her Awakening had Tarsa experienced pain like this, tongues of blood-borne fire that twisted through her body from flesh to bone and back, jagged spirit blades that tore her apart from the inside, leaving her broken nearly beyond healing. During that time, seemingly so long ago, she'd simply surrendered to the pain, unable to claw her way out of the iron-veined pit to which she'd been exiled by her townsfolk and relatives. Yet now, as the Heartwood pulsed like a drum through her veins and those now-familiar voices sang out in response to the smothering crush of iron that surrounded her, a spark of defiance flickered to life, and she fought back. Though the words of the song were still unclear, the desperation in the voices was unmistakable: whatever the pain, she must survive.

To do so, the young she-Kyn would have to draw again on an earlier strength, the training of mind, body, and spirit that belonged to an ancient tradition every bit as old as that of the *wyr*-bound Wielders. Tarsa was a Wielder now, but she would always be a Redthorn warrior, and there was no place within that tradition for despair. A Redthorn fought out of duty and love—a love of the People, of home and life. The song filled her thoughts and vision, and she joined the chorus, her voice small and broken, but growing. The words seemed to lift her out of her flesh and the pain, drawing her from the haze that clutched at her spirit and into a shimmering blue-green radiance that beat with the pulse of primordial life and resonant awareness beyond comprehension.

Into the Deep Green.

And as the radiance enveloped her body, she felt it burn away the taint of iron that coursed through her blood, and she was left weak, but once again whole. Her body trembled uncontrollably. Even when she'd joined with the Heartwood after the fall of the Tree, she'd never reached the Deep Green. Such knowledge was elusive and unknowable by those bound to the mortal world. Even now, just heartbeats later, the certainty of the experience left her mind, and all that remained was a renewed vigour in her muscles, and the faint but unmistakable scent of deep-woods flowers and moist soil that still lingered in the air.

Tarsa's sensory stalks stroked her face, tenderly drawing her back to the waking world. She lifted her head from the dry stones with a low groan, catching her breath as she gazed into the flat, empty eyes of Lojar Vald, who stared at her with patient scorn, his black greatcoat fluttering like dark wings in the rising wind. Behind him in a hooded blue cloak stood Shakar, her head bowed and face shadowed by the cowl.

Rage surged through the Redthorn Wielder. She flung herself forward but screamed in frustration as the cold chains around her throat, wrists, and ankles dragged her back to the rocky earth.

«A savage to the last, Wielder?» Vald said, shaking his head in amazement. «And at such an auspicious moment. I should perhaps be thankful. Your consistent predictability has made this so much easier for us all.» He clapped his hands, and a group of six heavily-armed Men jerked on the chains. Together they wraped their links around the wide base of an iron tower that stretched high in the air, its open scaffolding gleaming with a dull, bloody hue in the fading light of day. Dozens of stout copper cables stretched outward from the top of the tower, but Tarsa couldn't tell where those led, as the chain bearers pulled her to her knees and thus out of sight of anything but this wind-worn shelf of rock. They stepped away, and Shakar moved in with a small net of a strange grey metal in her hands. This she draped over the Wielder's head, and Tarsa's sensory stalks thrashed frantically under its blistering touch.

An agonized scream split the air from far beyond her view, and one of the copper cables hummed, its length rapidly vibrating. Another scream followed, and another, and soon all the wires above buzzed with wild energy. The she-Kyn watched in growing horror at the pulsating, irregular shadow that streaked across the first wire toward the tower. As it grew near, her skin tingled with familiarity. Tarsa's body buckled, and her own harsh cry joined the others as the mingled life-essence of the shattered Wielders was absorbed by the metal netting and drove down, ripping through flesh and spirit, rooting inward to tear the Heartwood from her thrashing body.

«It is your turn now, my Lady. Begin the extraction, and we will finish this final ceremony. Redemption is at hand.» Vald nodded to Shakar. «Our time is at hand.» The Shield lowered her hood. Her face was devoid of expression, but she trembled as she approached the screaming Wielder.

The Dreydmaster motioned to Vorgha, who lifted his small bugle and sounded three long calls. There was silence for a moment, and then the cannons roared, followed by the thunderous discharge of hundreds of muskets firing into the defenceless Folk in the valley below.

"The Binders are killing them!" Daladir shouted to the others, who struggled up the rubble-strewn slope behind him. They'd rushed through broken canyons and across sharp, narrow cliffs that slashed their boots, knees, and hands until each limped and stumbled with more will than strength, trying desperately to move toward the shadowy cloud without exposing themselves to discovery. Now they were here, close enough to see the terrible events unfolding on the ridge beyond but overwhelmed by the sudden realization that they where hopelessly outnumbered. And there was still no sign of Tarsa.

The trio stood about a quarter-mile behind the ridge and could see a massive promontory stretching out of the deep valley beyond. One of the iron posts that lined the ridge was well within their sight. There, chained tightly to the rust-streaked metal, crouched one of the deer-Folk Ferals, his battered face unrecognizable at this distance. They watched with spirit-sick revulsion as a thin, white-haired Woman with a massive book chained to her right wrist shouted something and lifted the open text high into the air. The Feral Wielder twisted in visible agony with each word. The Woman's voice soon vanished under the wordless shriek that clawed its way from the Wielder's throat, and a wavering blot of shimmering shadow snaked up the side of the post and slid across the wire toward a tall spike of lacy scaffolding that jutted from the top of the massive tower of stone. The scream ended abruptly, and the Feral's body slumped in the chains.

Tobhi fell to his knees. What had become of their world? How could they possibly stop a whole nation of enemies like these? He'd once believed that good intentions and right actions were enough to have a long, love-filled life, even in frightening times. He lived by that philosophy, treated others with care, and tried to bring light to the lives of those around him. But it wasn't enough to stop the Darkening Road, and he didn't know how to make sense of the world again. Sometimes you could do everything right and cruelty would still torment you. Sometimes the only thing to do was just push on, no matter how terrible the world might be, no matter how much one suffered, never depending on hope but never quite giving up on it, either.

Maybe not giving up was the only thing left at the end.

His heart a stone weight in his chest, Tobhi turned to check again that they weren't being followed. There was nothing behind them but ravaged stone and broken earth, but then a movement caught his attention, and his eyes followed a strange pattern of dappled shadows darkening the ground. As his gaze moved upward toward the source of those shadows, his mouth dropped open with a gasp.

"It can't be," he whispered in suddenly rekindled hope.

The sky was filled with Dragons.

CHAPTER 11

SUNDERING

The Feral Wielder's scream was followed by dozens more, each one more terrible than the last. The two Kyn ran forward now, heedless of the danger, quickly closing the distance. The slicing pain of the stones on their wounded feet held no more concern for them, nor did the masses of Men who surrounded each tortured Wielder. Only one thing mattered now: doing something—anything—to stop this madness. The mercenary and the diplomat, side by side, joined by the love of their people and a green-skinned Wielder who was lost, just beyond their reach. Jitani drew her wyrwood sword and started singing her war chant. Daladir glanced at her for a moment, then lifted Tarsa's wyrwood staff and joined in her song.

Suddenly, above the dying screams of the Wielders and the droning chants of the Binders, a familiar voice rose in a wail of torment shattered the air, and both Kyn tumbled to the ground. The voice's owner was connected to them through their past healings, and for the space of a breath her agony was their own. Jitani and Daladir held their hands to their heads, trying to drive out the dread that clutched at them. Although their stalk wrappings were still secure, the intensity of the scream penetrated these defences.

"Tarsa," Jitani groaned, digging her hands through the rough soil, trying desperately to push herself back to her feet.

Daladir lifted himself to his elbows. "We're too late," he hissed through clenched teeth. "We're too far away."

A deep, grinding roar shook the ground and something darkened the sky as a cloud of blinding dust struck the coughing Kyn. They looked up, dazed, to see a small Ubbetuk airship floating above them, its massive, moth-shaped wings flapping furiously beneath a billowing gasbag.

Tobhi stood on the deck, his long black hair whipping wildly in the wind.

"Ye want to try this again?" the Tetawa shouted to Daladir, waving his hat with glee.

Averyn pushed Garyn aside as musket shot splashed in the frigid bog. The Governor swayed and toppled into the muck, narrowly avoiding another blast.

"Run toward the tower!" Averyn cried, jerking hir lover to his feet, but Garyn held back.

"Not there—look!" He pointed to a line of Men at the base of the rocky outcropping who were following the example of the soldiers on the ridge above. "They're everywhere, beloved. We're trapped." The air blazed with screams and the metallic tang of fresh blood and flashpowder. Death surrounded them. There was no place now to run or hide.

They'd travelled hundreds of miles and shared numerous loving years together, side by side. Love found them easily and without ceremony: Averyn had been brought in by the Branch-mothers of Thornholt town as a healer when Garyn, then Firstkyn of the town and representative to Sheynadwiin, suffered a crippling fall. The young zhe-Kyn, then just past hir adulthood rites, stayed with Garyn and gave him medicinals and deep stretches to ease the pain in his hip, taught him of joy and the peace of soft music and gentle speech, and, eventually, remained to teach him of other pleasures, too. And in spite of the years and qualities that separated them, they found strength in one another from then on, even in these days of shadow.

Averyn grabbed Garyn and kissed him deeply, tears streaming unchecked down hir cheeks. They said nothing; words were futile now. They simply held tight to one another, standing tall against the onslaught from above. As their people fell dead and wounded around them, they never let go, even after the musket balls tore into their own flesh and drove them, gasping, into the cold embrace of the swamp.

The sky was alive with cannon fire, and the Dragon tilted precariously to the side. Kaer pointed toward the ridge. "We've got to stop those cannons!"

Merrimyn scrambled back to his feet after being tossed down by the last explosion. Lurching to the edge, his hair askew and eyes wild, he cried out. "Binders—at least a hundred of them! They'll be worse than the soldiers!"

Nodding, Kaer turned to the captain, an immaculately dressed Greencap. "Is this ship armed?"

"Of course it is!" the Ubbetuk said with a harsh laugh. "Do you think the Swarm would travel into hostile territory without adequate defences?" He waved to some of his blue-capped crew, who moved to a series of arched doors in the lower side of the ship, below the portholes. Motioning to the Men, he turned to the observation railing with a strange glimmer in his eyes. "Watch closely," he said. "This will be a story to share for years to come. Witness for yourselves the power of the Dragons."

The sharp peal of bells and whistles split the air, and the airship shifted westward. Suddenly, one side of the hull seemed to fall away, and a series of massive metal tubes extended outward, each carved to look like a monster's screaming mouth, and pointed toward one of the cannons below. Another whistle screeched, and the air exploded in a gout of liquid fire that roared with unerring precision toward the ridge, sweeping downward and incinerating everything in its path. The fiery torrent continued on and on, blasting downward as the Dragon shifted to the north, following along the top of the ridge, unleashing its deadly barrage on the frantic Men below. The fire burned long after the ship passed by, and Merrimyn watched in fascinated revulsion as the militiamen and mercenaries tried hopelessly to free themselves of the clinging fire. They lasted scant seconds before collapsing in charred, smoking heaps.

In the air around them, the rest of the Ubbetuk Dragons sent by the Chancellor unleashed their deadly cargo on Vald's soldiers, assiduously avoiding the release of any fire on the Folk who crouched, wounded and terrified, in the valley beyond. Some of the ships commandeered by Vald's soldiers moved to intercept the Swarm armada, but most drifted in the air, unmoving, as their Ubbetuk crews rose up against their Eromar captors.

For now, at least, the Swarm ruled the skies.

Quill, standing in a shadowed alcove on the other side of the airship, also observed the destruction of Eromar's militia. Though her belly was still tender and her legs unsteady, her insides had quit clenching so badly; now there was nothing but emptiness, a hollow ache to remind her of what she'd sacrificed to be here at this terrible moment. Yet in spite of all the cruelty brought on her people by Vald and his kind, she couldn't look on the scene below without disgust and pity. She tasted thick bile on her tongue.

"So much death, so much pain. Will it ever end?" she whispered, looking toward the east, her thoughts winding back to a vanished friend far away. More had been lost than Quill had ever imagined, and there would be so much more to come.

"We're drowning in blood this day." She put her face in her hands. "Oh, Granny Jenna, Old Turtle, forgive me. Forgive us all."

Shakar focused her thoughts and twisted them into Tarsa's struggling mind. She gasped. The pain was extraordinary, worse than anything she'd ever experienced in her own body, and yet, impossibly, the Wielder still fought against the intrusion. Cocooning her own senses from Tarsa's pain, the Shield marvelled at Tarsa's strength. If it had been another time, a different world, they might have admired one another, maybe even been allies, if never friends. They shared a love of the people and an unwavering conviction of purpose. But in this world, they were destined to be on opposite sides of history. As unpleasant and gruesome as their situation was, there could be only one survivor. In all things, it was the strong who endured, and the Old Ways had no place in the world of Men. It was another age now, and Shakar intended for her people to be a part of that age, even if they had to be dragged into it against their collective will. The only barrier was represented by this raging, tattooed creature crouched and chained before her, more beast than Kyn. The Wielder's death, like that of her mentor, Unahi, would be a small price to pay for the survival of the Folk. Like a rabid wolf infecting others with its poison, the *wyr*-witches had too long tainted their people. And although Shakar's duty was unpleasant, it was the necessary excision to ensure the health of all. There was only one cure for a beast like this.

More Wielders died on the surrounding ridge, and as each one's bound spirit smashed into Tarsa's weakening body, Shakar found the resistance lowering. She could feel thin filaments of the Heartwood begin to spread outward and away from the weakening Wielder, desperate to hold on yet helpless to resist the multiple attacks. The Shield redoubled her efforts as the last of the Binders released their snared powers. The wall began to crumble. The young Wielder pushed against Shakar's mind, but she was too weak, and the nearness of success gave Shakar a tremendous advantage. There would be no failure now.

A thin, tearing cry rose up from Tarsa's throat as Shakar at last pulled the Heartwood free, and the Wielder collapsed in the pile of chains, her face ashen. Backing away from the young she-Kyn, Shakar looked upon the shining green globe in her hands. Hundreds of slender tendrils stretched outward and caressed the Shield's trembling fingers, and the globe seemed to expand and contract with a pulsing life of its own as she held it. The emerald light stretched down her arms and flowed over her body. She staggered backward and turned to Vald.

«Take it!» she gasped, holding the *wyr*-power as far from her body as possible. She could feel the Heartwood flowing through her, changing her, opening doors in her mind that she had thought locked forever. The masks were falling. Layers of certainty and pride fell away, leaving her exposed to herself and the world. What was revealed was nothing she wanted to see. «Please, hurry!»

The Dreydmaster smiled at Vorgha. At last. This was his destiny. He'd been born to rule Men, and now he would be reborn to rule worlds. The Not-Raven spies had told him the truth—the she-Kyn witch was the source of the power. And now, that power was his. He held his hands up to Vorgha, who took a small knife from his belt and cut a long, wicked gash in each of his master's palms.

Turning to Shakar, Vald reached out and took her hands in his own, smearing them with his blood. For a moment the Heartwood recoiled, its tendrils clinging desperately to the Shield's trembling arms, and then it was gone, slipping into the Man's bleeding flesh like water into parched earth.

Shakar stepped away, shaken and sick, and her gaze moved beyond Vald to the valley below, where cannons and musket blazed into the screaming Folk. Confusion clouded her eyes.

«Your Men—they're killing them,» she said, her words slow and uncertain. «You must stop them. You must….» She shook her head, as if to clear it of a nightmare grown too real in waking. Her eyes moved from the carnage below to the great iron scaffolding, following the copper wires to the chained and battered Wielder who lay groaning softly at its base.

«Betrayed,» she whispered evenly, as much to herself as to the Dreydmaster. «This was never what I wanted, I swear it. Oh, Moon-Maiden, please—anything but this.»

Vald ignored her. He stood staring at his hands. Suddenly his body stiffened and his head dropped back, his eyes wide and staring. He swayed slightly, balling his hands into fists and breathing heavily, his mouth working as if repeating words no one else could hear. Unnerved at his master's uncharacteristic behaviour, Vorgha reached out and touched the Dreydmaster's arm. «Authority?» he whispered. «Are you—?"»

Vald's head spun around and his mouth opened wide. Green fire burned from his eyes and mouth. «Mortal filth, you dare touch the Dreyd? You are unworthy! *You are unclean!*» A pale, clawed hand shot out and smashed through the valet's chest, spraying gore in a scarlet fountain across the dusty rocks.

Vorgha's body crunpled to the earth, and Vald dropped the Man's still-beating heart atop it with disdain. The Reaver's own form was growing, changing, becoming monstrous, magnificent. He roared in proud exultation as power rose up within his frail Human flesh, making it greater than even his most fevered dreams could have imagined.

His ascension was at hand.

He turned to the Shield who stood at the edge of the cliff, her lowered gaze still locked on the massacre taking place below them in the valley. «Now, Shakar, we finish the ceremony. This is the end.»

The Shield turned, her violet eyes bright and clear, her lips in a thin, taut line. «That, at least, is true,» she hissed, and her thoughts drove like a blazing spear into the Dreydmaster still-Human mind. He clawed at his head and fell back with a guttural howl, even as the transformation continued unabated. «But I am Shakar no longer. My name is Neranda.»

One small band of Binders gathered on the ridge, unobserved by the fire-spouting Dragons and their armed crews above. Vald hadn't expected an airship armada, but he was sensible enough to keep some of the Dreydcaste hidden in case of unexpected problems. These Men and Women could feel the Dreydmaster begin his transformation. The new Melding was imminent, and their faithful souls might still be spared if they died in his service. They weren't Reavers like him, but neither were they helpless.

As one, they gathered in a circle with arms extended. Calling out an obscure Crafting invocation, trying to keep their voices strong in spite of the acrid smoke around them, they all reached into the snaring-tomes of their neighbours, chanting louder as they felt their own spirits unravel and join the tortured entities within. Their bodies sagged, dripping into the ground like sun-warmed wax, and with a final, screaming burst, their embodied forms changed, shifting from flesh to flame, great spinning rings of yellow fire that shot into the sky to consume a great Dragon galleon in its path. The airship exploded instantly, and burning debris fell to earth like white-hot rain.

Merrimyn rushed to the railing, Quill beside him, and watched helplessly as two of the smaller ships, their gas bladders shredded by shrapnel, crashed with a roar into the swamp. Like all Binders, he could feel every Crafting in the area, and the power of this conjuration burned in his senses. The Binders who destroyed the first galleon were dead, but their success emboldened others, and another group moved into a circle to repeat the catastrophic Crafting of their fellows. And the Dragon they focused on was his own.

Before he knew what he was doing, Merrimyn opened his snaring-tome and held it wide in front of him. But rather than simply call upon the powers within its leathery pages, he sent his soul in search of the spirits of the Folk that flew on silent white wings through the fading light, calling them to his aid. He didn't seek to snare them or force them to his will. He had neither the desire nor the power to control them. He was neither a Wielder nor a Reaver—neither *wyr*-touched nor a Dreydlord—but his need was great, and he sent it spinning into the twilight.

Nothing happened. The air around the Dragon grew heavy, pensive, as though the great airship knew its fate and was powerless to stop it.

And still the young Binder held his book aloft, tears of fear and frustration streaking his face, his soft voice muttering his plea to the anxious air.

And then the floodgates opened, and a wave of glowing white mist washed over him from behind, sweeping down across the deck of the airship to push the young Man hard against the railing, his open snaring-tome pointed at the circle of Binders below. Quill fell back with a shriek as innumerable spirits danced across Merrimyn's body, through his bones and muscles, their sightless eyes finding vision through his own as they became a river of half-formed phantoms, his willing flesh the channel for their ageless vengeance. The snaring-tome shot forward through the air, held back only by the taut chain still shackled to Merrimyn's bleeding wrist, and the spirit wave burst down upon the chanting Binders, a screaming, howling torrent, tearing at the Humans with their curses, cutting soul as easily as flesh. The Binders vanished under the flood, and their destructive Crafting dissolved, its lingering thread vanishing with the last despairing cry.

Quill crept forward to Merrimyn, who lay limply against the ship's railing, his right arm hanging over the side. His skin was cold and waxy to the touch, but his eyes fluttered open when the Dolltender grew near, and he smiled weakly.

"Free," he whispered and slid unconscious to the deck. Quill stared at his arm in amazement. The snaring-tome was gone, as was his hand, the stump healed, skin smooth and clean as a new dawn.

"There!" Jitani nodded to the flurry of activity atop the small butte in the centre of the swamp. They couldn't tell exactly what was happening, but a battle was taking place between a small figure in a blue cloak and a pale, Man-shaped creature that seemed to be growing larger and more terrible as they watched. She looked down. "Tarsa's got to be there somewhere. Maybe she's the one battling that...thing."

Tobhi shook his head. "That en't her. No, that's someone else." He squinted and frowned, his sharp eyes following the wires that stretched across the valley to the iron monolith. "She's there!" he shouted, pointing to the tower's base.

Daladir turned to the Ubbetuk captain. "Get us as close as possible!" The Goldcap nodded and the airship roared downward, but it lurched abruptly as a sharp blast shook the hull. The mercenaries on the ledge below the tower raised their cannons again, and the ship shuddered again as some of the artillery found its mark, some narrowly missing the great wheezing gas-sacks that kept the ships aloft.

Daladir slid the wyrwood staff into the back of his belt and threw the ladder over the edge of the ship. "We're too close to Tarsa to use the Dragon-fire, so we'll have to do this ourselves before the ship is destroyed." His face darkened. "We can't all go after Tarsa. Two of us will have to stop those cannons, or they'll kill her even if we can find a way to get her free."

A flash of pain crossed Jitani's face, slowly giving way to firm resolve. "My sword is ready." She turned to Tobhi. "We'll keep them away from you both as long as we can. It might not be for very long."

Tobhi nodded. "I won't fail ye," he whispered in a quavering voice. "I promise."

Daladir laid a hand on the Tetawa's shoulder and smiled gently. "I know you won't, my friend. *Tsodoka.*"

Swallowing the sudden knot of grief in his throat, Tobhi embraced them both and moved toward the ladder. Daladir motioned to the captain. The airship swept dangerously low, its upper wing nearly touching the tower. Taking a deep breath, the little Leafspeaker threw himself into the air, followed closely by Jitani and Daladir. Muskets and cannons exploded from below, and the Dragon limped away, one of its gasbags pierced and leaking.

Thunder boomed over the valley as a web of lightning streaked through the sky. A swirling hole of shadow split the twilight clouds, opening into a roaring pit of darkness and chaos that grew slowly wider.

For the first time in a thousand years, the Veil Between Worlds began to open.

CHAPTER 12

REMEMBRANCE

Betrayal.

She had surrendered her position, her reputation, honour, and home, even her family, some of whom now faced death below. For years she'd believed their assurances of truth and benevolence, accepted what seemed to be inevitability. The Humans she had known so often truly seemed to care about the Folk; why else would they have worked so hard, so tirelessly, if not for a sincere desire to bring the Folk out of the darkness of savagery? She'd watched the Kyn fade before the onslaught of Humanity, and she'd embraced the ways of Men as the only reasonable alternative to obliteration—change was preferable to extinction. Her mind and body had been trained in the arcane ways of the Shields until it was a keen weapon, but she rarely used its greatest power, for she wanted her victory to rest on reason, not on coercion. Her path was clear, and righteous; it required nothing more. If the future belonged to Humanity, it was as Humans that they must live.

And in all those years, after all the pain and suffering, she'd never once doubted that the Kyn would endure, even if they were transformed beyond recognition. Life mattered more than pride. Men said that the vanishing of the Folk was destiny, inevitability, but there was nothing inevitable about the massacre in the valley. It was the long-planned, deliberate decision of a Man and his minions. They chose each step willingly.

As did she. And now, she made a different choice.

All these things passed from her mind into the thing that was once Lojar Vald, and he roared with pain as her consciousness seared through his own. Grief now fuelled her white-hot rage. She paid no attention to his ever more massive bulk, which now seemed more a bloated jellyfish than a Man, nor did she regard the Dragons above raining fire on the Dreydmaster's troops, the militia's deadly cannon shot in response. Her full attention was focused on Vald, to his torment.

The Dreyd-creature crashed against the tower, and the great copper cables snapped and spun back down into the valley. Neranda's mind was honed to its deadliest now, and she wouldn't surrender. She would break him without quarter or mercy. Vald would not make a liar of her, not again.

She reached deeply into his seething centre and sought the Heartwood.

Tobhi held a shaking hand to the back of his head. Blood, but not much. His hat was gone again, lost among the ruins. He'd reached the tower just as that huge *thing* smashed into it, sending debris down on the Tetawa, who scrambled out of the way to avoid all the big chunks, but not enough to avoid the smaller ones. He breathed heavily, thankful that he still wore the iron-ward from the airship. If not for that, the nearness of all this cold iron might have killed him.

Keeping a close eye on the battle between the monstrosity and the now recognizable Shakar, Tobhi crept over to the pile of chains to find Tarsa crumpled within. Panic seized him. He reached out and pulled on one of the chains. Nothing. Moving closer, he tugged hard on the chained shackle around Tarsa's throat. The Wielder's eyes shot open in wild fear and she gasped for breath.

Tobhi reached around to the back of the band. It had a rusty latch that he unhooked with only a little effort. The shackle sprang open, and Tarsa fell forward, coughing and choking.

Repeating the movement on the rest of the bindings, Tobhi quickly freed the she-Kyn, and she leaned heavily into his arms in exhausted relief. He tried to pull her away from the tower, but both he and Tarsa were weak and wounded, and it was all she could do to move away from the pile of chains.

A battle was raging here on the top of the hill, but screams and musket shots just beyond their view indicated another fierce fight, one with dear friends against dozens of well-armed adversaries. Tobhi tried to push the thought out of his mind. He was here to get Tarsa to safety, and their chances for escape weren't much better here than in the valley.

He looked into the sky and gawked at the sight of the sundering Veil. Light seemed to die as it reached the great fissure, and a bone-cold wind flooded from the roaring darkness. The sky seemed to shift, as though the firmament itself was cracking under the strain of the ever-widening wound.

It seemed that their chances were going to get even worse.

Tarsa lifted her head. She was alive. It was much more than she expected after her struggle with Shakar. But the true struggle was far from over.

"Help me...stand," she gasped to Tobhi, each word catching painfully in her scream-shredded throat. She pushed with the little remaining strength in her legs as the Tetawa struggled upward. They breathed heavily from the strain. She tried to pull away from him, but he shook his head. "You can't stay here, Tobhi," she whispered hoarsely. "It's going to be too dangerous."

He chuckled, then winced from the sudden pain in his wounded head. "Ye think so? Don't seem all that bad to me." He sobered. "I'll be by yer side through the rest of this journey, Tarsa. We started out together, and that's how we'll finish it, to whatever end."

She smiled. "Then that's as it should be." Together they stumbled forward, Tarsa leaning on the exhausted Tetawa, as the growing abomination thrashed around on the ground, its fleshy tentacles whipping the stony ground with frenzied fury.

«*NO!*» Vald howled in a bubbling voice that barely resembled

Human speech. *«YOU CANNOT HAVE IT! IT IS MINE!»*

The Shield moved forward in torn and ravaged blue robes, her hands on her temples, sweat and blood trailing down her face, sensory stalks flailing wildly from the unyielding extension of her strength. The air crackled with unseen power. She pushed on, heedless of her swiftly weakening state and her injuries, unaware of anything but her monstrous enemy. Vald had finally collapsed under her relentless attack. She staggered a bit, then stood straight as she brought her hands together with a swift cutting motion.

A crack of thunder shook the mountainside, and the Shield stood tall, a glowing orb of pulsing green resting lightly in her trembling hands.

Tarsa stumbled forward and faced the Shield. Neranda lowered her arms and gently cradled the Heartwood, no longer resisting the cleansing touch of its tendrils.

"I was honest with the world and never once surrendered to temptation," Neranda said, her voice weak. "None could have ever made the claim that I broke my word, or surrendered to any cause I believed to be less than worthy of honour. And in spite of it all, I have failed beyond measure." Her lips tightened. "No one will remember me with anything but hatred and contempt. I am 'Shakar' now, to everyone. But I am no traitor. I…I never meant to be."

Tarsa was silent for long moments, her turquoise gaze unyielding. Finally, her face softened, and she nodded. She and the Shield saw Neranda's actions very differently, even now, but their war was over.

Neranda took a deep, shuddering breath of resignation. The power that had strengthened her against Vald's Dreydcraft had finally faded away, leaving only a barren space of spirit-deep exhaustion. She would not be returning from this terrible place.

"I do not ask you for forgiveness, Wielder. All I ask that you remember me as I was—as I am, at this moment—even if no one else will do so." Her voice grew thick with emotion. "I do not want to be forgotten."

The Shield held the Heartwood out to the Wielder, but as Tarsa reached to accept it, a grey-white tentacle wrapped around Neranda's waist, jerking her backward, the Heartwood still clinging to her hands. Vald's great bubbling bulk rose high above her, his pallid, vaguely Man-shaped visage twisted in madness. His wide maw opened wide, putrid slime dripping from thousands of spear-like teeth.

«*I hunger, little pain-giver. You will be the first!*» Vald fell upon the Shield and the glowing Heartwood, swallowing both in a single swift movement, leaving behind only a burning pool of black ooze on the rocks. Neranda's single cry of despair lingered in the air a moment longer.

«*You are next, witch!*» His voice was the wet, gasping hiss of a thousand snakes, his form the writhing mass of a thousand nightmares given fiendish shape. His head slid upward and a hideous grin crossed his lengthening face as steaming liquid dribbled down his chin. «*And with you comes the end of an error left too long uncorrected. At long last, this world will be free of your kind. Men will rule supreme, and the Unhumans will be driven from the memory of a world that should never have been yours.*»

The Veil Between Worlds gaped wider. Arching bursts of gold-green lightning radiated through the sky to smash into a few airships, hurling them to the earth.

Tarsa stood motionless and watched Vald roll toward her. The abomination's great body lurched forward on a wave of slime-coated tendrils that had once been legs. There was a strange, distant expression on her face. She could feel Tobhi tugging at her arm, but she ignored him.

She finally understood.

The *wyr*-formed voices had whispered to her for months, their language always just beyond her understanding. From the earliest moments of her Awakening on that night in Red Cedar Town, when she'd watched the Stoneskin's body burn to ash and felt a new world of power and frightening possibility open up within her, the voices and their haunting songs had remained a maddening mystery, ever present but just beyond comprehension.

Yet now, at last, in Vald's triumphant words she'd found the answer.

The dream of my mother, Unahi, and the others, around the blazing fire in that icy, snow-blasted wyrwood grove. The last she-Kyn, the one with the blue and white mask of mourning. It's Neranda. And it's me. We're part of this world. This world is us.

Ours are the voices I've been waiting for.

"It was a memory song," she whispered to herself as the monstrous once-Man loomed above her, blue-black ichor falling in sizzling pools around her feet. "This is no Melded world. It has always been our own. *This* is the Eld Green, all of it. They wanted us to forget, to believe that we didn't belong here."

She looked up. "But I remember now. We will *all* remember." She raised her hands toward the sky, and the mountain trembled from deep within, knocking Tobhi to the ground and sending Vald skittering backward. Bright-eyed eagles with burning plumage the colour of rainbow fire swept out of the darkness and fell upon the monstrous Dreyd-creature, their talons tearing into his still-mortal flesh, and the Redthorn Wielder began to sing in a language strange but beautiful, her voice growing stronger and more forceful.

She sang, and the world responded.

For the first time since the fall of Sheynadwiin and the start of the Darkening Road, Tobhi felt no fear. He heard the song in his blood, felt the rhythm flow through him like the very beat of his heart. It spoke to him in the voice of his ancestors, of the great Clan-beasts and their proud legacy. He heard the voice of Buborru the Badger, knowledge-keeper of the Burrows family, and all the guardians of the Spirit World who had watched over their Tetawi kindred since time immemorial. The song drew Tobhi closer to them all and opened a world of understanding that the lore-leaves had only ever hinted at.

Lore-leaves. He'd almost forgotten them. It had been so long since he'd turned to the leaves for comfort or guidance. But he was a Leafspeaker, and he remembered his duty. The badger-snouted pouch trembled at his side, and he pulled open the clasp. As his own voice joined Tarsa's and the song grew in strength, the leaves came swirling out of the satchel, all aglow with a bright inner fire, dancing joyfully around him like playful dragonflies newly awakened to a deep green world. They wove a new story for the Leafspeaker, one that he'd never before read in their varied and shifting movements. And as the lore-leaves shared this great storyweaving, their ancient symbols burned cool blue on Tobhi's body, seventy-seven bold and painless honour markings that would hold the story in his flesh for the rest of his days. It was a story that renewed the world and realigned the cosmos.

Now he understood what Tarsa meant. The Thresholds had always seemed to be the last remnants of their lost world, but in truth the Folk had never left the Eld Green. The whole of this world—all the Reach and other lands claimed by Men—were the homelands of the Folk. Kaantor's ancient betrayal hadn't brought the world of the Folk into the world of Men. It had simply brought Men into the Eld Green, and they'd laid claim to it. And over the years, as the Folk fell to the tyranny of Men and the lands beyond their Thresholds grew harsh and hostile, many forgot the truth and believed the lies Men told to assure them-selves of the right of conquest.

But the spirits remembered.

Averyn looked up, blood streaming into hir eyes, as the song reached them. Garyn lay motionless in hir arms, bleeding heavily from numer-ous wounds. One of Averyn's stalks had been torn open in the last bar-rage, and zhe could barely contain all the agony as zhe tried desperately to hold the Governor out of the filthy water and maintain some hold on hir own sanity. Others were screaming in pain and ter-ror all around them. It was pure, unrelenting madness.

And then came the song. Zhe gasped as the words wove into hir deepest being. The screams faded, and all zhe heard was the slow, steady throb of hir heartbeat, or of a drum pounding its primal rhythm in the centre of the earth. The zhe-Kyn, like all the zhe-Folk, was a between-worlder, neither male nor female, something other than both. The healer inhabited a space between and among the others, and such a position brought with it knowledge and a responsibility distinct to the zhe. Of all worlds and none.

It was what zhe was meant to bring to this moment.

As the song opened hir spirit and zhe began to understand what had so long been forgotten, Averyn added hir own voice to the chorus. Zhe didn't know what zhe was singing, but zhe knew that the words were right. And as zhe sang, the world changed.

Garyn shuddered and opened his eyes, the song already on his lips as he returned to consciousness. The screaming stopped, and others took up the chant, growing stronger with the words. Musket shot fell harmlessly into the mud. The cannons were stilled, and Men ran screaming as a figure rose out of the darkness and found shape from the zhe-Kyn's song, finding form and strength as others took up the rhythm. It grew larger as Averyn's voice grew more certain, its great rainbow wings stretching across the valley, lightning dancing across its antlers and moon-curved claws, its serpentine body blazing upward like a comet, triumph and fury bright in its dark ursine eyes. The strange shape of a winged and antlered rabbit emerged from the darkness to fly fiercely at his side.

Guraadja roared in fury, a crackling thunderstorm boiling through the sky in his wake. Finally free from his ages-long prison, he and the other Anomalous rose up in the renewed world to strike at the enemies of the Folk.

Great cracks opened up in the earth. The demon Vald laughed and

Rebirth

slime sprayed outward. *«Little green fool, is that all you can do? Sing on, sing on—it will do you little good. I can sing too!»* He lifted his head and bellowed, and from the torn Veil flapped a horde of chattering Not-Ravens. The firebirds joined Saazja and great Guraadja as they rushed up to meet the foul creatures, and the air was soon filled with skyfire, feathers, and blood.

Vald lumbered forward, his glistening, hairless bulk shining in the light of the Dragon-fire that still burned around the rim of the valley. *«Enough of this foolishness. I hunger still. Now, witch, you are mine!»* He rolled toward her but stopped with an ear-piercing shriek as a wyr-wood blade and the sharpened end of a wyrwood staff plunged deeply into his flesh from behind. Tarsa's heart soared as Jitani and Daladir pulled their weapons free of Vald's quivering bulk, but before the monstrous creature could crush the Kyn warriors for their impertinence, the ground shifted beneath his weight, forcing him to once again face the Wielder.

He spun back to see Tarsa standing calmly beside the remnants of the iron tower, her voice and arms lifted high in remembrance and certainty.

Those she loved most were with her now. Tobhi, Jitani, Daladir. Unahi, Geth, Lan'delar. Living and spirit, they all strengthened her. The *wyr* flowed through the world again, other voices answered the call, and the Folk were renewed.

Hunger gnawed at Vald's belly. Neranda wasn't dead, not yet. She would be gone, and with her, the miserable Wielder who had caused him so much trouble. He needed only a little more strength to rise up and pass through the Veil. With a howl of triumph, he surged forward, a seething, flowing mass of slavering menace.

But the hunger inside him suddenly changed. It became something else, moving from an aching emptiness to a sharp, piercing pain that spread out, growing larger and more insistent.

Vald slid to a halt. He felt Neranda's flickering life-spark take up the green witch's song in the brief flash before it was extinguished. Now the words were everywhere: in his head, in his bones, in his quivering flesh. They seared him with an unimaginable pain, as though his very organs were aflame.

The torment inside moved up, then down, everywhere, and the Dreydlord felt something *move* deep inside.

His Dreyd-touched senses knew what was happening. And he knew that he'd failed.

There would be no ascension, not now, not ever.

So close to victory. So very close....

Green fire tore upward through his skin, shredding muscle and blood, twisting outward through pierced and broken bowels and the crackling shards of his smoking bones. He opened his frothing maw wide to spew his bitter hate and fury on the Melded world, a poison to corrupt everything it touched, but his lungs vanished beneath the upward rush, and even the gurgle of blood gave way to blue-green radiance and the rustling of silver leaves as the first branch shot from Vald's maw into the open sky. More branches burst through his pulpy white flesh, sending bile shooting in upward sprays until, as the massive creature convulsed from the pressure of the flowering Heartwood, Lojar Vald split apart, and the Eternity Tree emerged reborn from the shattered remains of the former Dreydmaster.

A high-pitched wail filled the night as the surviving Not-Ravens fled back through the Veil. The great rift between the worlds slowly faded, and another shape filled the heavens, a vision that none of the survivors below ever expected or even dared hope to see again.

The air was filled with the smell of fertile earth and wyrwood leaves, the primal flush of life incarnate. The firebirds wheeled in celebration and Guraadja roared triumphantly in the sky above as the Greatmoon, Pearl-in-Darkness, watched over the Folk once more, its cool light shining down upon the remembered world.

CHAPTER 13

GATHERING GROUNDS

The proper name of the new homeland was Shemshéha—"The Place of the Good Red Earth" in the Tetawi tongue—but most of the survivors simply called it Folkhome. The naming was the first of many steps in the long, difficult task of healing both themselves and their wounded land, which still bore the scars of a thousand years of torment. They went slowly about the task of rebuilding their lives, making homes, towns, and settlements, discovering ways of understanding the spirits of beasts and plants and introducing the animal and plant people who had travelled with the Folk on the Darkening Road, familiarizing themselves with the weather patterns and the flow of waters, connecting with the ghosts who still inhabited the wilder places of this new Everland. Although the reborn Eternity Tree—now known as the Forevergreen Tree—gave them strength, there was still deep grief, for there were none who hadn't lost at least one beloved friend or family member.

. Some had lost far more. Nearly half the Folk of the old Everland had died or disappeared on the Darkening Road. Families were shattered, many broken to the core. Some of Seven Sister nations had suffered more than others: the Wyrnach were no more, and most of the he-Gvaergs had been murdered, impaled and turned to stone on the sun-bleached slopes of their old mountain-holds. But most Branches, Clans, and even some of the Gvaerg Houses survived and opened themselves to new kith, and love expanded to embrace those left alone by the devastation.

Tobhi and Quill married quickly and opened their moundhouse to a trio of Road-made orphans, two Tetawi—Benji, the cub who'd stolen Tobhi's boots one awful morning on the Road, and Anja, who'd watched her mema and siblings vanish into surging waters on the sunken barge at Shard Ford—and a she-Gvaerg youngling named Brigga. Their adoption of the orphans into Quill's Spider Clan was a ceremony of great joy among the Tetawi. Life had changed them, but the Folk continued.

They struggled to build a homeland that would endure, but bitter divisions exploded into bloody feuds between rival groups. The Kyn Shields, although diminished, continued to exercise their influence, although now with more humility under the wise guidance of old Braachan, Tobhi's he-Kyn companion on much of the terrible journey, who had come to prominence in Neranda's disgrace. Rather than viewing the Celestial Path as the enemy of the Deep Green, Braachan taught that the two ways could coexist together, each giving strength to the People, both dedicated to the growth and survival of all.

Yet many of the Greenwalking Folk blamed the Shields for their troubles, and a number of the latter died in midnight executions. A similar fate met a few of the allied Humans who'd walked the Road with them—especially the Proselytors who believed that the Dreyd had put the Folk through this terrible trial for their own good—but as most Men and Women were adopted into Folk families and protected by their kinship connections, their lives were spared. Eladrys had been adopted into Willow Branch before the Expulsion, and she maintained her ties with her Kyn family, so she was protected by that relationship, but those who'd travelled with Tarsa and Quill—Merrimyn, Qualla'am Kaer, Oryn, and the rest—became part of either Cedar Branch among the Kyn or Spider Clan among the Tetawi in honour of their efforts.

But it was still a cruel, bloody time when the Folk turned on one another in their grief and pain. There were conflicts with some of the Jaaga, who were growing increasingly and fairly resentful of the Folk's intrusions into their hunting grounds. The brutal winter that followed Vald's destruction added to the tensions, and in its first few months Folkhome risked falling into chaos.

Yet calmer minds and more forgiving hearts prevailed. Tarsa—now the honoured Keeper of the Forevergreen Tree—said very little in the debates, but when she did speak, draped regally in her restored leaf and feather cloak of office and bearing the worn wyrwood staff of her martyred aunt, her voice carried a weight far beyond her years. Garyn and Averyn joined Daladir, Molli Rose, and at least forty representatives from all groups of the Folk to begin the creation of the much-discussed confederation that would honour their individual traditions and yet give structure and security to the sevenfold nation. Garyn, though blinded by his injuries in the final conflict, was filled with fiery energy that inspired others with its strength.

Through the long, cold winter, the assembly discussed, cajoled, argued, fought, and pleaded, from dawn until long after sunset every day, and by the first flowering of the new spring had given structure to the Free Folk Alliance of Shemshéha. The first Speaker of the new Alliance, elected unanimously by the council and affirmed by the population at large, was Molli Rose, the Tetawa matron who'd spoken so eloquently for the strength of the Folk at the old Sevenfold Council.

After much discussion, those Kyn who had walked the Darkening Road now called themselves the Free Kyn Nation of Folkhome, to distinguish their government from that of the remnant still in the Old Everland. Their new capital was built close to the Tree in the valley, and they named it Dweshamaagamig, "the Place of the Flowering Tree," a peace city and neutral ground, all the more blessed because it had been born from so much blood and violence.

Garyn continued his work as Governor of the Free Kyn with the blessing of all seven Branches. Many of the artefacts and ritual items he'd had hidden from the first wave of invasion in the Old Everland had been lost, but others gradually found their way to the new homeland, where they were quickly returned to their work of rooting the People in land and memory. Garyn's own work ended in late winter, when he took ill after a fall, and he died peacefully with his beloved

Averyn at his side and many friends nearby.

The debate over Garyn's successor was a surprisingly contentious one, but Tarsa's nominee was the one who finally received the Branch-matrons' assent, and the reconstituted Kyn Assembly of Law had little choice but to support it: Averyn, the healer and longtime consort to Garyn, became the first zhe-Kyn Governor. Some of the Celestial Kyn argued against a zhe-Kyn as leader, fearing that the Human disdain for between-worlders would bleed into Folkhome's fragile political recognition and some of the negotiations with Chalimor over their independence from the Everland Kyn. But Averyn proved hirself a skilful leader and formidable opponent to those who would challenge Kyn sovereignty. Many underestimated hir strength, and those who'd once doubted hir ability gradually became some of hir staunchest defenders.

Garyn's peacemaking legacy lived on.

The surviving Wielders and their *wyr*-touched kindred gave guidance to the grieving and provided words of comfort for the dead as their kith struggled to recover from the nightmares of the past and present throughout those dark months. Frail and wounded in body and spirit, old Biggiabba's sharp mind had returned, and she gave much of her remaining strength toward this healing work. And although the whispering boughs of the Forevergreen Tree were now empty of dark-eyed owls, the spirits of the lost were remembered that spring in the strange, small flowers that sprouted up around the new Tree and throughout Shemshéha. Seven pale white leaves radiated from the scarlet centre of every blossom, each leaf tipped with a soft streak of gold. They grew alone or in thin clusters in shadowed undergrowth.

The sevenfold rose came to symbolize the new life of the Folk.

Spring in Folkhome was far different from the same season around Spindletop. In her old home ground, Quill could plant her garden just after the snows disappeared, but here, even with the snow long gone, the soil remained hard and frozen for weeks longer. The growing season would likely be shorter, the plants somewhat strange in comparison to those she was most familiar with. She didn't worry much about the quality of food, however, as the *wyr* that flowed from the Forevergren Tree would ensure a bountiful harvest. It would just take some time to get used to the changes.

She was glad to finally be able to start her garden now. The reborn Tree was strong, but it couldn't make food out of nothing. If not for the Ubbetuk airships and the supplies they brought each week, the Folk might well have starved to death or fallen to illness or the bitter cold that rushed down from the frozen northlands known as the Lawless. Although she appreciated the Swarm's help, she couldn't help but be nervous about the Chancellor's intentions. The look on his face as he ripped information from the Not-Raven in Denarra's house chilled her even now, and she still had nightmares about the fire raining down from the Dragons. As they'd learned to their painful regret in the past year, there were few free gifts in this life. She wondered what the price would be for the Chancellor's generosity.

She shook the shadows from her thoughts and turned back to the task at hand. The garden wouldn't plant itself. For a moment Quill considered bringing one of the apple dolls outside for some advice, but she quickly reconsidered, as the dolls now generally spent their days in pleasant drowsiness, uninterested in mundane domestic tasks like these, unless they involved the new apple orchard that Tobhi was planting down in the valley as a wedding gift to his new bride. At night, though, the dolls often told stories to the younglings, with Green Kishka taking the lead on sharing the teachings of old. The dolls were far from young anymore—indeed, they'd all been given to Quill by her own mema, passed down from her granny—and their adventure and the loss of so many of their fellows had aged them a bit, but they had a new vitality now, especially now that there was a rapt, wide-eyed audience to listen. Young Benji, the oldest of their new cubs, vowed to be the first *fahr* Dolltender, and Quill thought he just might be right, particularly as Anja and Brigga seemed more inclined toward Tobhi's leaf-speaking. Continuity through change, transformation through tenacity. It was the guiding principle of their new life. Not everything had to remain the same to endure.

But it would be a while before she taught Benji to make the dolls. She hadn't had much time or, more honestly, much heart to begin again. It wasn't that she was unhappy, because she had a loving husband and children who filled her life with more joy than she'd ever known, no matter that they weren't born of her flesh. Tobhi was her spirit-mate, and theirs was a healing love. Yet she was different now. She'd seen more of life than she'd ever expected, and much of it was unimaginably cruel. Even now she woke sometimes with the eyes of the dead haunting her dreams.

Fortunately, however, there were other, kinder memories to think on, and friendly faces to welcome into her life and thoughts. Merrimyn lived nearby, sharing a house with dark, lovely Eladrys, who enjoyed teaching the one-time Binder the many joys he'd missed in the forced celibacy of his former life. Quill came to adore Tarsa and her fiery consort Jitani. She could understand why Tobhi had such admiration for Daladir's quiet strength. The he-Kyn was rarely present, as he spent most of his time renewing diplomatic ties to the Reach in Chalimor. Qualla'am Kaer had been impeached and was largely disgraced in Chalimor, though he was now a hero to many Folk-allied Humans through the Reach for his brave defiance of the self-serving bigotry of Reach politicians. He had a home in Shemshéha, not far from their own settlement of Turtletown. He couldn't return to Chalimor without risk of arrest, but he gave able guidance to Daladir and the other Alliance treaty and trade negotiators from afar. To all reports, they seemed to be making progress, though it was maddeningly slow going.

She'd long missed her vanished cousins Gishki and Medalla, but recent news gave hope that they might be part of another Tetawa town founded to the south of Shemshéha, where Men and Folk currently lived together in peace and for mutual benefit. But while she missed these friends, she mourned most for one whose tinkling laugh and emerald eyes left her heart empty and aching. The pain hadn't faded with time. She wasn't sure if it ever would.

She'd hoped for news from Chalimor, that maybe Padwacket or Meggie Mar would have heard something, but when Daladir went to the little brick and stucco house one one of his trips to the city, he found it abandoned, the garden overgrown, Denarra's prized peacocks gone. Only some of the furniture remained, hurriedly and only partially draped with dusty sheets. No one knew when the other inhabitants had vanished, but they hadn't been seen since the day of the Strangeling's long fall.

Quill wiped her eyes, leaving smudges of garden dirt on her face, then cleared her throat and looked up. Where were the she-cubs? They'd been clamouring to help all morning; now that she could actually use their assistance, they were nowhere to be seen. They'd likely be exploring with some of the other Turtletown younglings, while their quiet older brother spent his day helping Merrimyn and some of the *fahr* build a moundhouse for a newly arrived family. The settlement was small, named for the town of the same name in the old Everland, with no more than forty families right now, built into a sheltered hollow at the eastern edge of the Valley of the Tree. It was a leisurely walk to the Brown Lodge, the large, timbered hall of the Tetawi clans, where Tobhi served as official chronicler of Shemshéha and one of Molli Rose's most trusted advisors. The Dolltender had been offered a post in the Speaker's circle, but she much preferred to stay at home and give help to those who stopped by, as in the old days. For her, the hearth was the best place to change the world.

The scuffling of boots on dirt caught her attention, and Quill looked up to see her daughters, dainty Anja and massive, broad-shouldered

Brigga, rush up the hill with eager grins on their faces. Skidding to a stop just before the freshly turned garden, the younglings nearly fell over one another in excitement.

"Mema, see what we found!" Anja said in a breathless rush. "Isn't it pretty?" She held up a long, slightly crumpled shape, waving it back and forth so wildly that Quill couldn't quite make out what it was. Brigga held one, too, but she handled hers with tender care, as if afraid that it would fly off into the air if she didn't treat it gently. She was younger than Anja, but stood nearly three times the little *firra*'s height.

A flash of bright colour caught Quill's eye, and she walked over to Brigga, who smiled and opened her arms to show her new discovery. The Dolltender swallowed a gasp, and tears sprang to her eyes as she took it in her trembling fingers. "Where did you find these, sweet cubs?"

"By river," Brigga giggled. "Come see!" They ran down the hillside with Quill on their heels. It was a short, well-worn path to the water's edge, and there Quill stood weeping silently among the cattails and reeds. She wasn't sure if it was tears of grief or joy that streaked down her cheeks.

Floating leisurely in the sluggish river, playfully iridescent in the light of the bright spring sun, were dozens of blue-green peacock feathers.

CYCLE SEVEN

FOREVERGREEN

Tobhi lifts the last leaf into place and steps away to watch the pattern develop. The symbols on his exposed flesh shine in bright blue response to the gold fire of the swirling shapes. The leaves weave together slowly, carefully, as though momentarily uncertain of the answer to his questions, but they finally quicken their movement to create a clear picture. His eyes glaze over and he whispers quietly to himself until he understands what's been revealed, and then he places his hands against the blurring leaves until they slow down enough to be returned to their red cloth and the small leather satchel at his side. The images on his skin go dark, looking once again like the honour marks of old.

As many times as I've seen this, it's always an amazing sight. Who would imagine that there would be so much wisdom in these light, fluttering things? Who would believe that within each is the life-giving force of the world?

I'm sitting on a rock, not far away from Tobhi. Although I've tried to be quiet to avoid disturbing him, my large, swollen belly is making such sitting rather uncomfortable, and I'm relieved to finally be able to shift into a new position as the leaf-speaking finishes. "Well?" I ask, slowly massaging my sides.

Rubbing the blurriness from his eyes, Tobhi smiles. "She'll be a strong daughter, Tarsa—strong and healthy, just like her memas."

I let out a deep sigh and try to stand up, placing a hand against my lower back for support. "I had the same feeling, but I wanted to hear it from someone else. It's going to be another hard year ahead. And a bit lonely."

He takes my extended hand and leans back, pulling me to my feet. "Ye know ye're always welcome to stay with us. They's plenty of room. Merrimyn's got a place of his own now."

"I know," I say, walking slowly toward the rough path that leads to the top of the narrow peak. "But Jitani will be back soon from seeing Sinovian in the old Everland. She's hoping to make it home before the birth, and we'll need that time alone together. She's as nervous about being a mother as I am! We'll send for Quill and Biggiabba when it starts, and when four nights have passed you and the others can come by to visit. Until then, it's just the mothers and aunties."

Tobhi nods and follows me up the thin trail, watching for any loose rocks that might cause us to tumble. I don't tell him that it's still sometimes hard for me to find comfort or connection with others. A bit more solitude might help me make sense of all the ways I've changed. The Heartwood brought me closer to the wyr, but it pulled me away from those around me, and it's been a longer journey back than I'd expected. I'm distant in ways that I still don't understand. But those who love me the most are patient, and that's reason enough to find my way back to them.

We've been hiking since the day before, seeking the highest point in the area around the Valley of the Tree, and are finally approaching the summit of a red sandstone spur. We'll watch the sunrise and begin the ceremony today. Everyone thinks I should wait until after the little seedling is born, but this is the right time to do it, and they don't fight, even if they do worry. The only company I want is Tobhi's, for both the leaf-speaking and his calming presence.

We don't see each other much these days, as the duties of our new life in Folkhome calls us to different tasks. I'm the guardian of the Tree and keeper of its teachings, and he's the lore-keeper of the new Council, almost giddy in love with sweet Quill and their new younglings. This is one opportunity to bring us closer together again. The last time we spent much time with each other was when we each spoke in the great Gathering of the Law, where the surviving Wielders came together to share the teachings of the Eld Green with the assembled Folk. It's an old tradition that was long abandoned in the lost Everland, but as with many old things, we're giving it a place of honour in our new home-place. With so few of us remaining, we must do all we can to renew these sacred fires and make them relevant to the struggles of today.

Neither Daladir nor Jitani can make this journey with me. She should return in the next few days, and then we'll need to prepare the birthing room. We hope that Sinovian will be able to visit soon. He and Tobhi will each give our daughter a name, as is the maternal uncles' duty and right; with two mothers and two such uncles, she will be doubly blessed. Daladir's new life is largely spent in Chalimor, as much by choice as circumstance. He's there now negotiating a new treaty with the Reach, and it's taking him longer than he'd hoped. Qualla'am and Blackwick are giving him good guidance, though, so he shouldn't be too long this time. We still see each other on occasion, and he'll meet his daughter when his other duties are done. Beyond that, nothing between us—the three of us—is settled or certain.

But those are thoughts for another time. I stop and look around, stretching the pain from my back. "We're here."

Spearbreaker was my warrior name, but I am Tarsa'meshkwé now, the Spearplanter. The spear stands tall in rich red soil, its roots deepening with time. I will be a warrior-Wielder for the growth of good things, a Greenthorn Guardian. Those blooding days I spent as as a Redthorn are done.

My Tetawi brother and I stand side by side on the upper crest of a broad sandstone ridge that extends a few miles to the north of the Valley. Sharp towers of rock rise up high in all directions around us, but from this height we can see above most of them and look off to the eastern horizon, which slowly brightens with the approaching dawn.

We paint our faces red and white—war and peace, strength and mercy in balance—and then I reach into the long leather pouch draped across my shoulder and pull out a tapered golden sphere as large as my hand. It's a wyrwood seedpod, the first one that has fallen from the Forevergreen Tree since its planting. It will be the start of Folkhome's renewal, Zhaia's gift to her tree-born descendants. Wide wyrwood forests filled these valleys before the rise of the Dreyd and the coming of Men, and although the land is broken and battered, it still holds the memory of those soaring trees and singing leaves.

My belly moves, reminding me of the importance of this ceremony. We've suffered much this past year. Red Cedar Town is far, far away. Unlike the great stories of quests and adventure that I loved so much in my younger days, there's no possibility of homecoming, no returning to those hills and the life I once knew. This must be our home now. Many beloved friends died or were lost on the way: Unahi and my aunts Vansaaya and Geth, kind Garyn, Quill's friend Denarra, and so many others. Sheynadwiin is now in ruins. We belong now to Shemshéha, far from the Everland that gave us life and for so long shared its strength with us.

The Redthorn warriors are still here, still the first to defend our homeland against intruders, but they're now joined by other Greenwalkers. We call ourselves the Greenthorn Guardians, a small but growing group of Folk dedicated to the teachings of the reborn Tree, its continued renewal, and its protection. We sing the songs and keep the dances. We plant the trees and restore the waters. We will heal this land, and when we're finished, we'll heal the rest of this world. Seven young she-Folk are training in both Redthorn and Greenthorn traditions to be my assistants at the Tree—it will be ably protected, even when I've gone on, in my time, to the ghostlands.

There are now new gathering grounds again, and even some of the Celestials have started to come to the grounds to keep the Tree alive. Of the Seven Sister Nations, only the Wyrnach aren't present at the Greenthorn grounds. Their arbour stands empty, in rememberance. There are Kyn, Tetawi, Ferals, and even some Gvaergs and Beasts among the Greenthorns, as well as a few rare and honoured Humans. Kinship is so much more than blood. It's a lesson we should never forget.

And we haven't forgotten. We've learned from the Ancestrals of the past, and keep their memories and legacies alive today. Now it is time to look to the future.

I sing and hold the seedpod to the rising sun. Tobhi joins his voice to mine and draws Quill's rattle from his belt, shaking it in time with the song, watching as the golden pod ever so slowly splits apart and thousands of small winged seeds, glimmering copper red, burst outward and float into the air.

"Our memory has returned," I say, watching the seeds scatter on the wind. "We won't forget again. We dance beneath the arbours, sing beneath the moon. The balance endures. Everywhere a seed takes root, the Deep Green will flourish, and so too will we. A healing is taking place at last. This is our home.

"We will change, as all things change, and our future will be no better or worse because of it. We will simply be. The Folk will continue. We'll lose some of what we are, and gain other things, other ways, but we'll endure, and so will the Green. That's the way of life in this Melded world of Folk and Men. It's our blessing and our curse. It's our hope."

Tobhi and I stand together in joyful song, voices proud and clear, and watch the healing seeds rise high with the dawn. They dance on the breeze and swirl eastward, toward the sister suns.

An Ending

Folkhome

Lore-Leaf Symbols

NAMES AND OTHER STORIES

A

ACADEMIES. Human houses of higher learning. Most Academy curricula are separated into the following schools: Rationalism (Moral Sciences), Alchaemy (Natural and Elemental Sciences), Philosophy (Theological and Terrestrial Law), and Manufactory (Industrial Sciences). The Learnèd Academy in Chalimor is the largest and most celebrated of the Academies in the Reach.

AIRSHIPS. The primary military and mercantile transportation craft of the Ubbetuk Nation. These galleons draw elemental energies from the air for lift, causing dramatic atmospheric disruptions and great lightning storms that can be seen for many miles. Called Dragons by Humans; the preferred colloquial Ubbetuk name is Stormbringers. An Ubbetuk armada is known as a flight of Dragons.

AKJAADIT. "The Hummingbird's Granddaughter." The Dragonfly in Tetawi teachings.

ALCHAEMY. The twin Human sciences of physical change, both bodily healing and elemental transmutation.

ALLIED WILDERLANDS. A southern province of the Reach. It is a loose confederation of independent townships inhabited by rugged and self-reliant Human miners and foresters who often trade with and marry among the Folk, and who have little use for either the Dreyd Creeds of Andaaka or the political posturing of the Reach-capital of Chalimor.

ANCESTRALS. The first of the Kyn to emerge from the Upper Place to the Eld Green; the primeval ancestors and progenitors of the Kyn Nation.

ANDAAKA. A south-western province of the Reach best known as the home of Bashonak, the heart of Dreyd-worship in the Republic.

ANJA REDBIRD MEADOWGOOD. The adopted Tetawa daughter of Quill Meadowgood and Tobhi Burrows.

ANOMALOUS. Spirit-beings formed from the strengths of miscellaneous creatures of the three planes of existence—the Upper Place of order (sky), the Lower Place of chaos (underword), and the Middle Place of balance (earth)—and tasked with the duty of protecting the Eld Green and its peoples. The most powerful Anomalous are Guraadja, the great winged Bear-Snake, and his swift companion, the Stag-Rabbit Saazja.

ASCENSION. In Dreyd teachings, the promised rise of a dutiful and deserving Dreyd adherent to the ranks of the immortal Dreyd themselves. The only known true ascension was the Melding that first brought the Dreyd to godhood a thousand years past.

ASHANNA DOL'GRAEVER. Newly married socialite from one of the First Families of Chalimor and acquaintance of Denarra Syrene.

ASSEMBLY OF LAW. The governing council of the unified Kyn Nation in the Old Everland, which replaced the Gathering, an earlier council-meet of the autonomous Kyn towns.

ATHWEID. Young Celestial she-Kyn diplomat to Eromar murdered by Vald before the Expulsion.

AVERYN. Zhe-Kyn healer; consort and advisor to Garyn Mendiir.

AWAKENING. The first emergence of *wyr*-powers in the life of a young Wielder, generally around the time of puberty. It is often a physically traumatic experience; if a Wielder is unguided in the transformation, the uncontrolled *wyr* can lead to madness and/or death.

B

BASHONAK. The capital city of the Dreydcaste in the Reach. It is a massive stone fortress at the edge of the Tuskwood in Andaaka, known as much for its rigidly authoritarian creeds as for the skilled military training of its adherents.

BÉASHAAD. The capital province of the Reach, located on the eastern edge of the continent. Its inland region is a temperate mix of hills, farmlands, and wide prairies, while its coastal waters teem with marine life. The great metropolis of Chalimor is built on the eastern shores of Béashaad.

BEAST-TRIBES. The various communities of animals, birds, and Beasts who called the Old Everland home. Each group has its own chosen leaders, and those leaders often meet in council.

BEASTWALKERS. Tetawi *wyr*-workers gifted with the power to communicate with and sometimes take on the bodily form of animals.

BENJI CORNTASSEL MEADOWGOOD. The adopted Tetawa son of Quill Meadowgood and Tobhi Burrows.

BETTHIA VALD. Dying wife of Lojar Vald.

BETWEEN-WORLDERS. Folk who share characteristics of multiple genders.

BIGGIABBA. Gvaerg Matron and Wielder.

BINDER. The second rank among the Dreydcaste. They draw the essence of spirits caught by Seekers into their snaring-tomes for use by Reavers.

BLACKWICK. The aged Chancellor of the Ubbetuk Swarm.

BLOOD VOW. A sacred Kyn oath of protection.

BLUE SAGE VALLEY. The homestead of Vergis Thane's ranching family in the Certainty Hills.

BLUECAP. The military and defence rank of the Ubbetuk Swarm.

BRAACHAN. Apple Branch he-Kyn elder and Shield

BRANCH. One of the seven clans of the Kyn. Each Branch is named for an ancestral tree-spirit and is known for its gifts in particular spheres of Kyn life: Willow, trade and diplomacy; Oak, leadership and philosophy; Ash, healing; Thorn, defence; Cedar, lore and the arts; Apple, horticulture; and Pine, mysticism and dream-guidance.

BRANCH-MOTHERS. The leading she-Kyn of a particular Branch. They determine Branch law and ensure proper behaviour and ritual observance among their kith.

BREMEN AND CROWE'S MEDICINE SHOW AND REPERTORY OF THESPIAN DELIGHTS. Travelling performance company and refuge for outcasts and eccentrics.

BRIGGA MARBLEMACE MEADOWGOOD. Adopted she-Gvaerg daughter of Quill Meadowgood and Tobhi Burrows.

BROWNBRICK DISTRICT. An area of Chalimor of growing economic and social importance. Not as fashionable as Rosewood Hill, but far from the rough reputation of Mariners' Quay, Brownbrick is home of merchants, traders, and other ambitious professional families.

BROWNIES. A pejorative but widespread Human term for Tetawi.

BUBORRU. The Badger-spirit and wisdom-keeper of Tetawi teachings.

C

CANOPY VEIL. The barrier between the Eld Green and the mortal world of Humanity.

CELESTIAL PATH. The philosophical principles of Luran-worship, descended from Dreyd teachings brought by the Proselytors who accompanied the first Human traders into the Old Everland. The Path is characterized by a denial of the flesh and an emphasis on the power of the purified mind, a commitment to hierarchy and obedience, a rejection of the *wyr* and the relational values of the Way of Deep Green, and an embrace of the individualistic and commercial values of Humanity.

CELESTIALS. Kyn followers of the Celestial Path.

CERTAINTY HILLS. A contested, arid region in Dûrûk, best known for its lush, grassy hills, which are popular among both the cattle of Human ranchers and the wild bison and antelope hunted by Jaaga-Folk.

CHACATL. A dark, bitter bean from the southlands of Pei-Tai-Pesh. When roasted, ground, and mixed with spices and honey, chacatl is a delectable and highly addictive after-meal refreshment. Though enjoyed to excess among the urbane Chalimites, chacatl is treated with ceremonial regard among the inhabitants of Pei-Tai-Pesh.

CHAL BAY. The bright, fish-rich waters of the edge of Chalimor.

CHALIMITE. An inhabitant of Chalimor.

CHALIMOR. "Jewel of the Reach." The capital city of the Reach of Men, named for its location between the white shores of Chal Bay and the rugged slopes of Mount Imor; political, artistic, and cultural centre of Humanity; home to the great Hall of Kings, the Reachwarden, and the Sovereign Republic Court.

CHANGELING. A Tetawa with the ability to shape-shift into the form of her Clan animal. The shape-changing Tetawi witches—Skeegers—are a cursed form of Changeling without the calming Clan influence.

CHANTING SASH. A woven or braided belt, generally of wyrweave or sturdy linen, into which a Wielder sews or beads some of her more powerful prayers, stories, and medicinal formulas. The sash serves as a calming memory aid to help balance the Wielder's mind and emotions as she does her work.

CLAN HERALD. The animal spirit-being from which a Clan takes its name.

CLAN. The primary social and political foundation of Tetawi life, with each being matrilineal in authority and descent. All Clans are named for an animal, which is deeply honoured by all members of that Clan. The most powerful are the Four Mother Clans: Raccoon, Spider, Kingfisher, and Trout.

CLOUD-GALLEON. See AIRSHIP.

CODE OF CONFEDERATION. The foundational political document of the Reach Republic. It defines both the governmental bodies and their respective powers. It is the highest law of the Republic, beyond even the Dreydcaste Creeds.

CORNSILK. Apple-headed spirit doll of Quill Meadowgood.

CRAFTING. The Human use of occult ritual and elemental alchaemy to shape the fabric of reality.

CREEDS. The ruling doctrines and dogmas of the Dreydcaste. Among the most problematic is the Supremacy Creed, which is often interpreted as a justification for the subjugation of all non-Human life to the will and benefit of Humans.

CROPMINDERS. Tetawi *wyr*-workers gifted with the power to communicate with plant life.

CRYSTAL COURT. The crystal-domed centre atrium of the Hall of Kings.

D

DALADIR TRE'SHEIN. Ash Branch he-Kyn diplomat for the Old Everland; stationed for some time in Eromar City.

DARKENING ROAD. The death march of the Folk who were part of the forced Expulsion of the Old Everland.

DARKENING. A pocket of Decay within the mortal world.

DARVETH THANE. Younger brother of Vergis Thane and spurned suitor of Denarra Syrene.

DECAY. A chaotic elemental force that destroys all mortal things.

THE DEEP GREEN. The ancient ceremonial and kinship traditions of the Eld Green; maintained by the Wielders. Also known as the Old Ways.

DEERMEN. Deer-headed Ferals of the Kraagen Mountains.

DELVHOLME. The great underground capital of the Gvaerg Nation in the Old Everland.

DENARRA SYRENE. "Wildflower, Last of Autumn." Eccentric Strangeling Wielder and adventurer.

DOLLTENDER. A Tetawa *wyr*-worker who draws on hand-made dolls—usually with dried-apple heads and corn-cob bodies—for spiritual guidance.

DRAGON. The Human name given to a mechanized Ubbetuk airship.

DREAMING WORLD. The nether-realm to which all beings travel in times of sleep, delirium, and unconsciousness, and from which some can draw wisdom and guidance. It is a strange and dangerous place for those unable to comprehend its distinct logic, which differs much from that of the Waking World.

DREYD. An order of now-immortal Human priests and sorcerers who overthrew the old Immortals of Men and assumed their place, thus causing the cataclysmic Melding.

DREYDCASTE. The rigidly authoritarian and Human-supremacist followers of the Dreyd. Their holy city and seat of power is Bashonak.

DREYDCRAFT. The alchaemical sorceries of the Dreydcaste.

DREYDLORD. A very rare term for a Dreydmaster who has risen to the top ranks of the mortal Dreydcaste.

DREYDMASTER. A leader of the Dreydcaste. There are generally no more than three Dreydmasters in the world at any single time, though the Dreydmaster of Bashonak is widely regarded to be the authoritative voice among them.

DÛRÛK. The westernmost province of the Reach, characterized by broken and blasted lands at its eastern border, wind-swept prairies in the center, and stormy coasts in the west. Its largest settlement—aside from the tent-cities of the Jaaga-Folk—is the notorious Harudin Holt.

DWESHAMAAGAMIG. "Place of the Flowering Tree." The new capital and peace city of the Free Kyn in Folkhome.

E

EATERS OF OLD. The collective name for an ancient group of carnivorous beings best known for their uncontrollable appetites. Stoneskins are among the most powerful of the Eaters.

EDIFIED. Those Folk who have accepted the teachings of the Dreyd Proselytors. Distinguished from SANCTIFIED by the degree of inspiration: the edified are informed, but the sanctified are truly transformed.

ELADRYS. Human knife-fighter and adoptee into Willow Branch who chooses to walk the Darkening Road and remain with her friends and family among the Folk rather than vow fealty to Eromar and the Reach.

ELD GREEN. The lush, ancient world of the Folk before the arrival of Men.

ELLEFINA. Giggling young Human housekeeper in the employ of Denarra Syrene.

EROMAR CITY. The capital city of Eromar, built on a bluff overlooking the Orm River. It is the location of Gorthac Hall, the home of the Dreydmaster Lojar Vald.

EROMAR. A heavily industrialized and militaristic province that abuts the Everland on the north, east, and south. Eromar is the primary political antagonist of the Folk of the Everland.

ESSIANA. Murdered she-Kyn fiddler and one of the Sisters of Wandering Virtue

ETERNITY TREE. The physical manifestation of Zhaia, the first mother of the Kyn, the source of the *wyr* in the Everland, and the living covenant between the Folk and the land.

EVERLAND. See OLD EVERLAND.

EXPULSION. The Eromar-led campaign to drive the Folk from the Old Everland.

F

FAHR. In the Tetawi tongue, the word for a male.

FERALS. Folk whose bodies resemble a union of Humans and Beasts, such as the birdlike Harpies, the antlered and hoofed Deermen, and the sly and furred Fox-Folk.

FEY-FOLK. A slightly pejorative term among Humans for the Folk. "Fey" designates mystery or strangeness at best, evil difference at worst.

FEY-WITCH. The common Dreyd term for Wielders and other *wyr*-workers.

FIRRA. In the Tetawi tongue, the word for a female.

FIRST FAMILIES. The wealthiest, most elite, and most insular families among the upper echelons of Chalimor high society. Social station and propriety are paramount concerns among the First Families, for whom subterfuge is a finely-crafted art.

FIRST MAGISTRATE. The chief jurist on the Sovereign Republic Court. Kell Brennard is the current First Magistrate.

FIRSTKYN. Town chieftains among the Kyn before the separate towns were unified into the Kyn Nation.

FLIGHT OF DRAGONS. The Ubbetuk airship armada.

FOLK. The collective term for those peoples and nations originating from the Eld Green, including the Kyn, Tetawi, Gvaergs, Ferals, Beast-tribes, Wyrnach, Ubbetuk, and the Jaagas, among others. While such an encapsulating term acknowledges the shared post-Melding history of such peoples, it can also erase their significant cultural, geographic, ceremonial, and physical distinctiveness.

FOLKHOME. The common name for the new homeland of the Folk following the Expulsion.

FOREVERGREEN TREE. The name given to the reborn Eternity Tree after the fall of Sheynadwiin.

FREE FOLK ALLIANCE OF SHEMSHÉHA. The name of the Folk confederation, which was formed to give a permanent structure to their shared concern while respecting and acknowledging each nation's sovereignty and independence. The Alliance is a permanent counterpart to the crisis-centred Sevenfold Council.

FREE FOLK. The defiant survivors of the Darkening Road in Folkhome.

FREE KYN NATION OF FOLKHOME. The new name for the surviving government of the Kyn Nation of the Old Everland, used to distinguish them from the now-autonomous government of those Kyn who remained behind.

FRIENDS OF THE FOLK. A group of self-congratulatory Humans dedicated to saving the Folk from their supposed barbarism and backwardness through assimilation into Human values and Dreyd Creeds.

G

GALLERY OF SONG. The central gathering chamber of the Kyn Assembly of Law and the Sevenfold Council in now-ravaged Sheynadwiin.

GARYN MENDIIR. Pine Branch he-Kyn Governor of the Kyn Nation and Speaker of the Sevenfold Council.

GATE-WALKING. Travel between worlds through *wyr*-work. Such work requires long preparation and significant safeguards, for it demands much of the *wyr*-worker's skill and life-force to ensure its success.

GATHERING GROUNDS. The open-air ceremonial centres of the new Greenthorn Guardians and other followers of the Deep Green.

GETH. Cedar Branch she-Kyn of Red Cedar Town and deceased aunt of Tarsa'deshae. Died in the attack on Red Cedar Town.

GISHKI. Spider Clan she-Tetawa of Spindletop and cousin of Quill Meadowgood.

GOBLIN CHANCELLOR. See BLACKWICK.

GOBLINS. The common term used by Humans for the Ubbetuk; often perceived by Ubbetuk as an insult, as it associates them with a mythological race of idiotic monsters common in Human folktales before the Melding.

GOLDCAP. Ubbetuk merchant or trader of high rank.

GOLDMANTLE. Largest of the sister suns of the Everland.

GORTHAC HALL. The sprawling, many-gabled estate of Lojar Vald in Eromar City.

GOVERNOR. The political leader of the unified Kyn Nation.

GRANNY TURTLE (JENNA). Spirit-being and creator of the first Tetawi people.

GREAT ASCENSION. The Human name for the Melding; refers to the rise of the Dreyd over the Old Immortals of Men.

GREAT WAY ROAD. Major east-west travel and trade route through the Reach of Men.

GREATMOON. See PEARL-IN-DARKNESS.

GREATWYRM. Also known as Wyrm. A dragon-like serpent with poison saliva, deer-like antlers, and panther-like legs, which makes its home in subterranean tunnels and deep swamps. Greatwyrms cannot fly, but they can run swiftly and swim well.

GREEN KISHKA. Apple-headed spirit doll of Quill Meadowgood.

GREENTHORN GUARDIANS. Greenwalkers who work as the healing ceremonial counterparts to the more war-oriented Redthorns.

GREENWALKER. An adherent of the Way of Deep Green.

GUAANDAK. The Emperor Triumphant of the Marble House of Kunkattar
of the Gvaerg Nation.

GURAADJA. In Tetawi tradition, the Anomalous winged Bear-Snake and
guardian of the Eld Green.

GVAERG NATION. One of the Seven Sister Folk nations, the Gvaergs are
rough-featured, largely hairless giants who live in vast cave cities
beneath the earth. Their link to the *wyr* is through earth-borne spirits.
Gvaerg society is rigidly divided into proud and pious Houses under the
ancestral authority of aged patriarchs. The suns are deadly, as their light
turns he-Gvaergs to dead stone, but wyrweave wrappings can defend
against that fate.

H

HALL OF KINGS. The residence and forum of the Reachwarden in
Chalimor. Though the leader of the Reach is now elected from the
Assembly, the Hall retains its name from the old monarchies that had
long ruled the territories claimed by the Republic.

HARPIES. The most powerful of the Feral peoples with the heads of wizened
old Women and the bodies of massive eagles.

HARUDIN HOLT. The western-most city of the Reach, second in size and
influence only to Chalimor. It is a tiered and sprawling city built on the
limestone cliffs of the storm-shattered Reaving Coast, and is best known
as a haven for pirates, mercenaries, criminals, and fortune-hunters.
Though it is managed in the name of the Lord Mayor, the Three Guilds
are the true power of Harudin Holt.

HEARTWOOD. The *wyr* essence of the Eternity Tree.

HIGH HALL. The seat of political and spiritual Dreyd authority in grim
Bashonak.

HIGH HOUSES. See FIRST FAMILIES.

HOUSE OF STATES. The public forum and debate chamber of the Assembly
of the Reach Republic.

HOUSES. The primary social and political foundation of Gvaerg life, with each being patrilineal in authority and descent. All Branches are named for a stone, mineral, or type of metal, which is deeply honoured by all members of that House.

HUMANS. The collective term for those peoples and nations originating from the lands beyond the Eld Green, including such diverse populations as the theocratic Dreyd of Andaaka, the fiercely independent miners and foresters of the Allied Wilderlands, the republican aristocrats of Béashaad, and the defiant tribespeople and merchants of Sarvannadad. While such an encapsulating term acknowledges the shared post-Melding history of such peoples, it can also erase their significant cultural, political, and physical differences.

I

IMWESHI. Celestial she-Kyn diplomat poisoned by Vald in Eromar.

IRON. Deadly poison to all Folk but Ubbetuk and Gvaergs. This virulent quality is well known to many Humans, and they use it to their advantage against many of the Folk, particularly the highly sensitive Kyn.

IRON-WARD. Amulets created by the Gvaergs for their Folk kith to protect the latter from the toxic effects of iron.

IXIS. Harpy Mystic and Wielder.

J

JAAGA-FOLK. One of the Folk peoples, descended from the Strangeling unions of Kyn and Humans. Though not one of the Seven Sister nations, the Jaagas consider themselves and are generally considered by other Folk to be kith of the Seven Sisters. They are a musical, largely nomadic, patrilineal people who inhabit the northwestern wilds of the Everland, as well as the sweeping grasslands of the Reach province of Dûrûk.

JAGO CHAAK. Tetawa toymaker and cannibalistic Skeeger changeling.

JEKOBI. Raven Clan he-Tetawa of Birchbark Hollow, Leafspeaker, and father of Tobhi Burrows.

JENNA. See GRANNY TURTLE.

JHAEMAN. Captain of the Reachwarden's guard.

JIPPITA THE WHISTLER. In Tetawi tradition, the brave Cricket spirit.

JITANI AL'DAAR. Thorn Branch she-Kyn warrior and mercenary; sister of Sinovian.

JORJI. Tetawa freedom fighter; brother of Jothan.

JOTHAN. Tetawa freedom fighter; brother of Jorgi.

JUBILEE. The social event of the year in Chalimor, hosted by the Reachwarden himself in the Crystal Court of the Hall of Kings.

JURIST TEMPLE. The stark stone chambers of the Sovereign Republic Court in Chalimor.

JYNNI THISTLEDOWN. Badger Clan she-Tetawa of Birchbark Hollow, healer, and maternal aunt of Tobhi Burrows.

K

KAANTOR. The Human Blood King of Karkûr and treacherous instigator of the Melding.

KAJIA. A long-dead former lover of Tarsa'deshae.

KARKÛR. A once lush and bountiful land ruled by Kaantor, now the desolate and poisoned devastation known as the Pit Fields.

KATELINE CROSSING. The narrow but unpredictable strait at Shard Ford that links the Great Kultul Sea and the Riven Sea between Eromar and Dûrûk.

KELL BRENNARD. Former Reachwarden; currently First Magistrate on the Sovereign Republic Court. During his term as third Reachwarden, Brennard advocated the absorption of the Everland, its people, and its resources into the larger sovereignty of the Reach of Men.

KISHKAXI. Harpy Brood Mother of the North Wind Aerie.

KITH. Family, relations. Depending on context, the term refers to either immediate, extended, or distant relationship through blood or adoption.

KITICHI. In Tetawi tradition, the trickster Squirrel spirit.

KYN NATION. The most numerous and widely-dispersed of the Seven Sister nations. The *wyr* of the Kyn is drawn from the green growing world and elemental forces of nature, although a growing number of Kyn follow the Celestial Path and ways separated from the *wyr*. Kyn have a heightened sensitivity to the spirits of nature through their serpentine sensory stalks. Their matrilineal branches are descended from the seven sacred trees of the Old Everland. Sheynadwiin, the great peace city of the Everland, was their political and cultural capital; it is now Dweshamaagamig in Folkhome.

L

LAN'DELAR LAST-BORN. Cedar Branch she-Kyn of Red Cedar Town and deceased mother of Tarsa'deshae.

LAWLESS. The rugged, snow-swept region at the margin of the Reachwarden's influence. It is without a central government, although there are numerous small settlements scattered throughout the area that maintain their own laws and order. While home to many brigands, out-laws, and petty despots, it is also home to many fiercely independent peo-ple—Folk, Human, and Beast—who settle their own grievances and avoid conflict unless it is forced upon them.

LEAFSPEAKER. A Tetawi *wyr*-worker who interprets the patterns of *wyr*-shaped leaves to communicate with the Spirit World and to preserve sto-ries and teachings. The leaf-reading skills are the Tetawi expression of Kyn teachings, thus highlighting some of the co-operative links between the two peoples.

LOJAR VALD. "The Iron Fist." Prefect of the state of Eromar and ambitious Dreydmaster.

LORE-LEAVES. *Wyr*-working tools used by Tetawi Leafspeakers.

LOWER PLACE. One of the three primary worlds of existence in the Eld Green and, to a lesser extent, the Melded world. It is a realm of chaos and shadow, though not evil.

LOWER RINJ. High-quality smoking leaf with relaxing and slightly hallu-cinogenic qualities.

LURAN. Moon-maiden. The Celestial manifestation of the Human Dreyd entity Meynanine; revealer of the Celestial Path to the Kyn Shields. For most Folk, the Greatmoon of the Everland, Pearl-in-Darkness, is male; the virginal female representation is drawn from Human cosmology.

M

MARDISHA KATHEK (née don Haever). Chalimite socialite and general secretary of the Friends of the Folk.

MARINER'S QUAY. The dangerous docks district of Chalimor.

MEDALLA. Spider Clan she-Tetawa of Spindletop and cousin of Quill Meadowgood.

MEDICINALS. The herbs, roots, plants, bones, insect stingers, animal glands, and diverse other pharmacopoeia used by the Folk for healing.

MEGGIE MAR. Humourless and efficient housekeeper of Denarra Syrene.

MELDING. The catastrophic union of the Eld Green and the mortal world of Humanity a thousand years past.

MEMA. "Mother" in the Tetawi tongue.

MERCHANT'S WARD. See BROWNBRICK DISTRICT.

MERRIMYN HURLBUCK. Young Human Binder and rebel against the Dreydcaste Creeds.

MIDDLE PLACE. The material world inhabited by Humans and Folk.

MOCHÉ. An extremely bitter drink make from dried and ground seeds from the southern mountains of Ardûk-Shei. Used by Humans and increasing numbers of Folk to clarify the mind and energize the body, or as part of rituals of general social interaction.

MOLLI ROSE. Tetawa Clanmother, Spirit-talker, and former leader of the confederated Tetawi settlements of the Old Everland.

MOTHER MALLUK. In Tetawi tradition, the strong but moody Peccary spirit.

MOUNDHOUSE. Stout Tetawi cabin with sharp eaves, cedar-tiled arched roof, interior and exterior carved support posts, and deep-set hearth. Moundhouses generally surround a ceremonial mound at the centre of the settlement.

MOUNT IMOR. The soaring, snow-covered peak that shelters Chalimor.

MULCHWORM. Apple-headed spirit doll of Quill Meadowgood.

MYRKASH THE UNBROKEN. The great elk chieftain of the Everland beast-tribes.

N

NERANDA AK'SHAAR. "Violet Eyes, Daughter of the House of Shaar." Celestial she-Kyn of Pine Branch. Legislator and Shield. See SHAKAR.

NEW IMMORTALS. Another name for the DREYD.

NOT-RAVEN. A malevolent ghost and flesh-eating spy of the Human world.

O

OATH OF WESTERN SANCTUARY. The euphemistic title given by Lojar Vald to the writ of expulsion presented to the Everland Folk.

OATHSWORN. Pejorative term given to the Kyn conspirators who signed the Oath of Western Sanctuary in defiance of the legitimate Folk leaders of the Sevenfold Council.

OINARA. "Strange New World." The Human name for the Melded world, derived from a word in the now-defunct dialect of Pei-tai-Pesh.

OLD EVERLAND. The ravaged remnants of the Everland after the Expulsion. Though most of the Folk were forced from their homeland; some pockets of resistance remain; most of the Kyn, Tetawi, and rebel Humans are led by the Redthorn warrior Sinovian.

OLD IMMORTALS (OF MEN). The gods of Humanity who were overthrown by the Dreyd during the catastrophic Melding. Though displaced, it is rumoured that the Old Immortals did not die and have long plotted their return to ascendancy.

OLD WAYS. The teachings and traditions of the Eld Green that predominated among the Kyn before the rise of the Shields.

ONE MOON PATH. A euphemism for the Celestial Path, which holds a single moon as the supreme representation of Luran's remote beauty and purity.

ORYN OF DELDMAAR. A Human trader who chooses to walk the Darkening Road and remain with his friends among the Folk rather than vow fealty to Eromar and the Reach.

P

PADWACKET. Weed-addled valet and loyal friend to Denarra Syrene.

PEACE-CITY. A site of sanctuary, where violence and physical conflict are forbidden, and where all given refuge. The Kyn capital of Sheynadwiin was the oldest peace-city in the Everland; its successor in Folkhome is Dweshamaagamig.

PEARL-IN-DARKNESS. The Greatmoon of the Everland. He is sole survivor of a trio of celestial night-spirits of the Eld Green; his brothers were shattered in the Melding, but their broken bodies remain in the form of a sparkling silver ring that surrounds the world in both night and day. Pearl-in-Darkness emerges from his grief to show his face to the Everland every thirty days; for most of that time, he is in various stages of mourning for his lost brothers.

PEPA. "Father" in the Tetawi tongue.

PEREDIR. The mortal world of Men before the Melding.

PETYR. The Human name given to Pishkewah, a Tetawa *fahr* in the employ of Mardisha Kathek.

PIT FIELDS (OF KARKÛR). The blighted epicentre of the devastating Melding.

PIXIE. A Chalimite poet of Jaaga heritage and friend of Denarra Syrene.

PROSELYTORS. Dreydcaste adherents dedicated to the transformation of the world through the teaching of the Creeds to the "unsanctified," by reason if possible, by force if necessary.

PURGING. The decimation of the Wielders by fear-maddened Kyn during the last great pox epidemic. Up to two-thirds of Wielders were killed during the three-year campaign of terror, during which time the Shields rose to power.

PURIFIERS. Dreydcaste interrogators and defenders of orthodoxy.

Q

QUALLA'AM KAER. The fifth and current Human Reachwarden and former soldier for the Reach Republic.

QUILL MEADOWGOOD. Tetawa of Spider Clan. Dolltender and *wyr-worker*.

R

REACH (OF MEN). Also known as the Reach Republic. The primary political and economic power in the Melded world, dominated by Humans and their ambitions.

REACH ASSEMBLY. The parliamentary decision-making body of the Reach Republic.

REACH-TONGUE. The common Mannish tongue in the Reach.

REACHWARDEN. The elected leader of the Reach Republic, chosen for a five-year term by a majority of Assembly representatives.

REACHWARDEN'S JUBILEE. See JUBILEE.

REALIGNMENT. According to Celestial doctrine, the final cleansing of the Melded world of all corruption and impurity. Only rigid adherence to the ways of the Celestial Path will provide safety during this tumultuous future event.

REAVER. The highest rank among the Dreydcaste. Reavers use alchaemical formulae and crafting to control the spirits captured by Binders.

RED CEDAR TOWN. A Kyn town in the southern Everland; youngling home of Tarsa'deshae.

REDTHORN WARRIOR. Greenwalking warriors dedicated to the Old Ways and the vigorous defence of the Folk.

RIEKMERE SWAMP. A fetid marsh at the heart of the Pit Fields of Karkûr.

RIVEN SEA. The stormier of two freshwater seas intersecting the Reach of Men.

ROSEWOOD HILL. The gated and gardened district of the First Families of Chalimor.

S

SAAZJA THE DREAMER. In Tetawi tradition, the Anomalous flying Stag-Rabbit and companion to Guraadja.

SANCTIFIED. Those Folk who have been transformed by the Dreyd Creeds. See also EDIFIED.

SARVANNADAD. A wide territory to the north of the Reach; though largely friendly in matters of trade, Sarvannadad is as yet independent of the Republic's political authority, and it zealously guards its sovereignty. People of Sarvannadad are known as shrewd political adversaries, but they are also widely feared, as their imperial ambitions are no less expansive than those of the Reach, and they have had much longer trade with the Ubbetuk Swarm for war technologies.

SEEKER. The lower rank of the Dreydcaste. Seekers wander through the Reach in search of Folk Wielders and Human witches, whom they bring to Dreydholds for the use of Binders and Reavers.

SENSORY STALKS. Fleshy head-tendrils that give the Kyn a deeper sensitivity to the elemental and emotional world around them. He-Kyn have one on each temple; she-Kyn have two on each side; zhe-Kyn generally have three, with two on one side, one on the other.

SETTLEMENTS. Tetawi community sites.

SEVEN SISTER NATIONS. The Kyn, Tetawi, Gvaergs, Ubbetuk, Wyrnach, Ferals, and Beast-tribes, representing most of the Everland Folk.

SEVENFOLD COUNCIL. A political assembly of Folk leaders, called only at times of great importance to all the Folk. Succeeded in Folkhome by the permanent Free Folk Alliance.

SEVENFOLD ROSE. A red and white flower with seven petals, previously unknown, that began to bloom after the Folk arrived in their new homeland.

SHAKAR. "Traitor" in the old Kyn tongue, and a name given to Neranda Ak'Shaar after she signed the Oath of Western Sanctuary.

SHEMSHÉHA. "The Place of the Good Red Earth." The proper name for Folkhome, the new homeland of the majority of the removed Folk. From the Tetawi tongue.

SHEYNADWIIN. The ancient peace-city and capital of the Kyn Nation in the Old Everland, destroyed in the Expulsion.

SHIELD. The spiritual, political, and economic leaders of the Celestial Path.

SHOBBOK. The Winter Witch of the Ice-Pierced Heart; a spirit-being of the Eld Green.

SINOVIAN AL'DAAR. He-Kyn Redthorn warrior and resistance fighter; brother of Jitani Al'Daar.

SISTER SUNS. The two celestial spirits of the daytime: Goldmantle, the bronze elder sister, is calmer and larger than Bright-Eyes, who burns white-hot with the fires of youth.

SISTERS OF WANDERING VIRTUE. The name chosen by Denarra Syrene, Jitani Al'Daar, and their friend Essiana on their youthful adventures through the Reach.

SKEEGER. Cannibalistic Tetawi changeling.

SKRIKER. A predatory spirit-hound under Shobbok's thrall. Those killed by a skriker become one after death, and the face of each hound resembles that of its mortal self.

SMUDGE. Ill-tempered mule deer mount of Tobhi Burrows killed in the siege of Sheynadwiin.

SOVEREIGN REPUBLIC COURT. The foremost legal authority in the Reach Republic.

SPINDLETOP. A small Tetawi settlement in the Terrapin Hills of the southern Everland and hone of Quill Meadowgood.

SPIRIT WORLD. The hidden realm of elemental beings, the dead, and spirits of the Green world.

STONESKIN. A fierce carnivorous creature with an unquenchable appetite. Named for the layer of protective stones embedded in its flesh.

STORM DRAKE. A massive winged and lightning-spitting serpent that inhabits the upper sky.

STORM-BORN TWINS (SKYFIRE AND THUNDER). In shared Folk tradition, descendants of great Guraadja; two powerful and much-respected transformer spirits of the ancient times.

STORMBRINGER. The preferred Ubbetuk term for their airships, named for the storms that surround each airship when in flight.

STORY LEAVES. See LORE-LEAVES.

STRANGELING. A descendant of a he-Kyn/female Human union. If born into a Branch, the descendant is understood as a Kyn; if born out of a Branch (that is, if the youngling's father is non-Kyn), the descendant is generally defined as a Strangeling. The Jaagas are a distinct people born of Strangeling unions and now known by their own name for themselves.

STRIVIX. "The Unseen." The great and fearsome Owl of Tetawi teachings.

SUPREMACY CREED. See CREEDS.

SWARM. The collective Ubbetuk Nation.

T

TARSA'DESHAE. "The Spear, She Breaks It," or "She-Breaks-the-Spear." She-Kyn of Cedar Branch. Redthorn Warrior and Wielder; adopted sister of Tobhi Burrows. Later Tarsa'meshkwé: "The Spear, She Plants It," or "She-Roots-the-Spear," in honour of her duties as keeper of the Forevergreen Tree.

TEMPEST SPARKS. Self-taught Tetawi historian and author of the great genealogical and documentary tome, *History of the Everland Folk and their Legends and Hearth-Tales.*

TETAWI NATION. One of the Seven Sister nations, the Tetawi are an honest and forthright people, short and brown-skinned. Their social and political lives are centered in their matrilineal Clans, each of which is descended from a spirit animal of the Eld Green. They make their homes in squat moundhouses, generally in rough hill country or in forested areas. Their connection to the *wyr* is through empathy with the beast-folk; due to this, Tetawi are the greatest healers amongst the Folk.

THANAEL TIBB-WOOSTER. A devoted Dreyd Proselytor to the Folk before and during the Expulsion. When his settling house was confiscated by the Eromar militia, Tibb-Wooster walked the Darkening Road with his charges and continued his work after the establishment of Folkhome. His vocal opposition to the Old Ways of the Folk and active political manoeu-vring against the elected governments made him widely unpopular. His departure from Folkhome back to Chalimor—it is unknown whether the move was voluntary—was, in the end, mourned by few.

THEEDEET THE WHISPERER. In Tetawi tradition, the dreamy Moth spirit.

THRESHOLD. A pocket of the Eld Green that survived the Melding. The Everland is the largest 'Hold in the Reach.

TOBHI (ETOBHI) BURROWS. Tetawa of Badger Clan. Leafspeaker, scribe, and lore-keeper. Adopted brother of Tarsa'deshae.

TOWNS. Kyn community sites.

TRADE-TONGUE. The shared economic, cultural, and political language of the Folk.

TREE-BORN. See KYN NATION.

TURTLETOWN. A Tetawi settlement in Folkhome, named in memory of a settlement of the same name in the Old Everland.

U

UNAHI SAM'SHEYDA. Cedar Branch elder she-Kyn Wielder of Thistlewood. Aunt of Tarsa'deshae. Killed by Neranda/Shakar in the assault on the Eternity Tree.

UNHUMANS. The pejorative term used by Humans for the Folk.

UNSANCTIFIED. In Dreyd teachings, the name for those Folk who have not yet submitted to the authority of the Creeds.

UPPER PLACE. One of the three primary worlds of existence in the Eld Green and, to a lesser extent, the Melded world. It is a realm of order and light, though not necessarily good.

V

VANSAAYA. Cedar Branch she-Kyn of Red Cedar Town and eldest aunt of Tarsa'deshae. Sickened on the Darkening Road and died in Dweshamaagamig.

VEIL BETWEEN WORLDS. See CANOPY VEIL.

VERDANT GRANGE. A large trading post in the Certainty Hills of Dûrûk.

VERGIS THANE. Unassuming one-eyed Seeker of the Dreydcaste and patient vengeance-taker.

VORGHA. Trusted attendant of Lojar Vald.

W

WAKING WORLD (also WAKING TIME). The world of awareness in the waking hours of life.

WARRIOR'S LOCK. A symbolic gesture of endurance and disregard for physical harm among Redthorn Kyn, the lock is a braided strip of hair down the centre of the head; the rest of the hair is painfully shaved away. In an exercise of strength, the warrior is forbidden from binding her, his, or hir sensory stalks against the pain.

WAY OF DEEP GREEN. See DEEP GREEN.

WEARS-STONES-FOR-SKIN. Stoneskin that ravaged the Kyn towns of Downbriar, High Marching, and Nine Oaks.

WHITE CHAMBER. The Reachwarden's private offices in the Hall of Kings.

WHITECAP COUNCIL. Members of the Ruling Council of the Ubbetuk Swarm.

WIELDER. Greenwalkers and *wyr*-workers of the Kyn.

WITCHERY. The use of *wyr* or other medicine skills toward selfish and generally destructive aims.

WYR. The life source of the Everland, formed from the living voices and embodied memories of the ancestors, the spirits of the Eld Green, and the life-spark of the Folk themselves. It is the elemental life-song of creation, drawing on and giving sustenance to all remnants of the Eld Green, strengthened by attentive care and weakened by neglect. Its embodied manifestation is the Eternity (now Forevergreen) Tree. According to the Tetawi historian Tempest Sparks, the word *wyr* is actually a much-corrupted form of the original Wyrnach term *dweidwiir*, roughly translated as "all that is, which, when spoken, becomes."

WYRNACH. The eldest of the Seven Sister Nations, the Wyrnach are also known as the "Spider-Folk" for their eight limbs and multiple eyes. They are a rare and reclusive people, standing well over eight feet high, and are well known among the Folk for their *wyr*-fed powers of divination.

WYR-WARD. A device of Human Crafting that addles the mind and blocks the access of Wielders to the *wyr*, thus leaving them vulnerable and confused.

WYRWEAVE. Fabric made of the inner fibres of the wyrwood tree.

WYRWOOD. A type of tree that grows only in 'Holds, the wyrwood is a vital resource to the Folk. Its leaves and naturally-shed outer bark, when stripped and pounded into flexible fibres, can be used for durable wyrweave fabric, clothing, and armour; its red roots and fallen branches can be shaped by Wielders into both armour and weapons, as can its rarely-accessed heartwood; and its golden sap is both nourishing and medicinal. The tree roots of living wyrwood draw poisons out of the surrounding soil, thus purifying both earth and water. Its lofty canopy provides housing for many Folk, as do the massive trunks of the more ancient trees. In many ways, the wyrwood tree provides the daily link between the Folk and the *wyr*-currents of their homeland.

WYR-WORKER. Those Folk gifted with the strength and talent to draw upon and guide the *wyr* toward particular aims or goals.

Y

YELSETH KATHEK. Boorish but wealthy husband of Mardisha Kathek.

Z

ZHAIA. Tree-Mother. The ancient spirit of the green world from whom the seven Kyn Branches are descended.

ZHE-KYN. A third gender among the Kyn that shares some of the qualities of both the she-Kyn and he-Kyn. Zhe-Kyn are border crossers between genders, and they often excel at healing, which requires sensitivity to the different challenges of the often distinct male and female social worlds. See BETWEEN-WORLDERS.

Daniel Heath Justice is a citizen of the Cherokee Nation and a permanent resident of Canada. Raised in the Colorado Rockies, he now lives with his partner and their three dogs in a cabin on the shores of Georgian Bay, in the territory of Wendake (Huronia), the traditional lands of the Huron-Wendat Nation. He is associate professor of Aboriginal literatures in the Department of English at the University of Toronto, where he also teaches in the Aboriginal Studies program. His previous books include *Our Fire Survives the Storm: A Cherokee Literary History* (University of Minnesota Press) and the first two volumes of the Way of Thorn and Thunder trilogy, *Kynship* and *Wyrwood*, both published by Kegedonce Press.

The Folk continue, as do their stories. For more information on Daniel's scholarly and creative work, and for news of forthcoming tales and projects, please go to his website at www.danielheathjustice.com.